# Tilly's
# Tuscan Teashop

## by

## Daisy James

# Copyright

To Kate & Gino, for their kind guidance

To everyone who loves to indulge in a sumptuous
afternoon tea

# Contents

# Chapter One

'Well, I think that has to be *the* best midsummer festival we've ever had at Blossomwood Bay,' said Tilly, dropping down onto her white leather sofa and lacing her fingers around a mug of her favourite Jamaican Blue Mountain coffee. 'I loved the old-fashioned carousel Dexter hired for the end of the boardwalk, although I did worry that someone might end up taking an unscheduled dip in the sea after one too many of Chloe's famous gin cocktails.'

'I agree, although I'm disappointed Dexter didn't stick around after playing the opening gig on Friday night. I mean, he *does* own the marina and rent out the boathouse and the beach hut studios to all of us,' said Freya, joining Tilly on the sofa and sending a waft of jasmine perfume into the air between them. 'I thought he'd have relished the opportunity to hang loose for a

1

few days at that gorgeous Edwardian manor house of his, and bask in the sweet glow of his fans' adulation this weekend. His band *has* just finished a *very* successful tour of the UK and Ireland.'

'And that's probably why he couldn't wait to get away!' Holly laughed, fondling the silky ears of her beloved golden-brown springer spaniel, Ariel, who was staring up at her with wide-eyed devotion. 'Remind me where he's gone this time?'

'California,' said Tilly. 'He's doing the Pacific Crest Trail.'

'Oh my God, the guy is totally obsessed,' said Freya, rolling her eyes. 'He must have done every single epic hike and pilgrimage route in the world by now. Hasn't he just completed his third Camino de Santiago across northern Spain?'

'Yes, but this is the biggie, and he'll have started it already; taken his first steps on the two-thousand-six-hundred-mile walk. Now *that's* an adventure, but I suppose it's also a chance to have some total alone time – no one can contact him no matter how hard they try, which I think is part of the attraction. It's six whole months with no suffocating entourage, no screaming fans, and no paparazzi jostling him everywhere he goes; just Dexter, his thoughts, and the great Californian outdoors.'

'That sounds like my idea of hell,' said Holly, tucking the sides of her blonde bob behind her ears so she could drop a kiss onto Ariel's head, receiving a lick of gratitude in return.

'Mine too.' Freya laughed, taking a quick sip of her coffee before changing the subject. 'Hey, did Suzie tell you that she sold more of her hand-made jewellery this weekend than she has during the whole of the last two months?'

'She did,' said Holly, fingering the intricate silver bracelet around her wrist. 'And there was a permanent queue outside Chloe's beach hut too, but then she does make the most amazing flavoured gins – have you tried her cucumber gin yet? – *and* you couldn't get a table in the Boathouse Bistro for love nor money. Beckie's over the moon. She said she's got bookings right the way through July and August now. I have to say, the boathouse does look particularly pretty, sitting there at the end of the boardwalk, especially on warm summer nights with the fairy lights and lanterns and the seaside-themed bunting flapping in the breeze.'

'Your beach hut looks pretty amazing, too, Holls,' said Tilly loyally, reaching out to refill her mug from the cafetière before curling her feet underneath her bottom, exhaustion dragging at her bones despite the infusion of caffeine. It had been a long and tiring weekend, but a successful one and that was worth celebrating with her two best friends who rented the beach hut studios on either side of her own.

'Thanks, Tilly. I did get lots of enquiries about the dog-walking and boarding side of the business, and people seemed to enjoy the grooming demonstrations I did on Saturday afternoon, especially the children. Did I tell you that Chloe's sister Martha wants me to transform her Bichon Frise's fluffy white tail into a rainbow for a Crufts-type competition she's taking part in next month?'

'Sounds like fun,' said Freya, gathering up her long wavy hair, the colour of burnished copper, and tying it away from her face with an emerald silk scarf. Tilly could see the dark smudges around her friend's eyes and was surprised when she glanced at her wall clock to see that it was after two a.m. She was about to suggest they called it a night when Freya met her eyes with a determined look. 'Maybe you could do a doggy photoshoot and Holly could use the images in her promo material?'

Tilly sighed. She knew what Freya was getting at, but she was too tired to argue with her.

'Sure, just let me know when you need me, Holly.'

'Really?' said Holly, looking across at Freya in surprise. 'But I thought you only photograph things in black and white. I mean, the whole point of creative canine grooming is that we use a kaleidoscope of colourful dyes to portray...'

Holly stopped, clearly unsure how to go on without offending Tilly, but Freya had no such qualms. Tilly realised that her best friend had been waiting for the opportunity to raise the subject for a while, especially after they'd both heard more than a few visitors to her beach hut gallery that weekend commenting that whilst they loved her images of the gorgeous Devonshire countryside, they wished she had photographed it in colour, too.

She hadn't felt the need to justify her artistic choices to the anonymous tourists who were just passing through the village to enjoy the festival, but that didn't apply to Freya – although Freya knew exactly why she preferred to work with a more restricted palette and she really didn't want to go there at two o'clock in the morning after one of the busiest weekends of the year so far.

'Can I get anyone a refill?' she asked, abruptly changing the topic.

'Do you have any chamomile tea?' asked Holly, blowing her over-long fringe from her eyes. 'I'll never get to sleep if I have any more of this coffee.'

'You're joking, right?' Freya laughed. 'Tilly hates tea; loathes it, in fact. You'd never believe that her sister is a trained tea sommelier and is the proud owner of a café in Tuscany that just serves tea! And don't ask her for a biscuit either, she doesn't do biscuits, or cake, or sweet treats of any kind.'

'I just prefer savoury things, that's all.'

But Freya wasn't listening; she swept her hand around the monochrome décor of Tilly's attic flat, which Tilly liked to call Scandinavian minimalist chic and Freya called dull, dowdy and drab because it housed none of the ornaments, lamps or trinkets that might be expected to adorn a seaside holiday home overlooking the English Riviera, and certainly no throws or cushions or curtains even, just sleek white Venetian blinds to block the glare of the sun.

'Look at this place; it's like a showhouse. Don't get me wrong, the artwork is spectacular – you're a truly talented photographer, Tilly – but Holly's right; you need to get a little more colour in your life! What's

5

wrong with the occasional shot of a scarlet Ferrari or a pyramid of colourful cocktails or cupcakes?'

Tilly glanced at the framed photographs of stormy seascapes, drizzle-soaked rooftops, bleak wind-swept moors, boats bobbing in the marina – all scenes that she had purposely washed the colour from.

'You know I only do landscapes…'

'Scenes from horror movies, more like! Take that one over there, for instance – the one of the disused factory with all the broken windows and the coven of crows, it's—'

'Murder.'

'Exactly!'

'No, it's a "murder of crows".'

Freya rolled her eyes. 'Where are all those wonderful photographs you took when you were jetting off around the world as high-flying cabin crew? They were gorgeous! Stunning sunsets in Hawaii, palm-fringed beaches in Miami, the vineyards of Napa Valley, Hong Kong harbour after dark… I could almost *feel* the energy thrumming from every image. Oh, and talking of jetting off around the world, where's Josh this weekend? I thought he'd be here supporting his girlfriend, quaffing Dexter's Champagne, and joining in with the partying?'

'He couldn't make it. He's at a pilots' conference in Singapore and then he's heading over to Bali to fly the new Boeing 787 back to Heathrow.'

# Tilly's Tuscan Teashop

Tilly cringed when she heard the defensive tone that had crept into her voice and she knew Freya had a point. She had asked Josh months ago to try to plan his flight schedule so that he had the last weekend in June free to come down to Devon for the festival. After all, it had been his idea to buy a seaside bolthole they could escape to during the busy summer months of back-to-back long-haul flying. However, she could count on one hand the times he'd been down here this year, preferring to stay at their apartment in London while she, on the other hand, lived here permanently now that she'd opened her gallery.

'You look tired, Tilly,' said Freya, finally taking pity on her and reaching out to thread her fingers through hers. 'Why don't you drop by my salon tomorrow and I'll treat you to one of my special aromatherapy massages? I'm thinking lemongrass, chamomile, grapefruit … maybe a touch of ylang-ylang?'

'Thanks, Freya, that's really kind of you but I can't. I've got the charity show at Jonti's gallery in Sidmouth at the end of the month and I still have lots to do to get ready for that. I need at least five more photographs to add to my portfolio and I'll be working flat out to get them done in time.' Tilly's spirits edged up a notch when she remembered what Jonti had said the last time they spoke. 'If it goes well, there's a possibility that Jonti will recommend my work to his brother, Rory Farrington-Smythe, who owns a gallery in Belgravia. You know how much I'd love to have my work seen by a wider audience, and oh my God, if I can get an exhibition at the Farrington-Smythe gallery that would be a dream come true!'

'Oh, Tilly, I really hope so. I'll keep my fingers crossed for you!'

Holly held up her crossed fingers and smiled, clearly relieved that the conversation had moved into a different direction, but sadly her relief was short-lived. Freya was obviously determined to say what was on her mind and she hadn't finished yet.

'You work too hard, Tilly. You know what they say, all work and no play…'

'Freya, I love what I do. I—'

'Ever since you came down to Devon you've spent every minute dashing from one photoshoot to another, before spending hours and hours alone in your darkroom or staring at your computer screen. It's like you're still in London, volunteering to take on everyone else's holiday shift, jetting from one exotic location to the next, never stopping anywhere for more than a few hours, barely sleeping, barely eating, fuelled by coffee, toast and adrenalin.'

'I know, but—'

'You bought this flat so that you and Josh could spend some quality time together away from the high drama of the skies, so you could take time out to smell that gorgeous Colombian coffee you love so much, maybe get a dog or a cat, but you seem to have brought your workaholic tendencies along with you.'

Tilly met Freya's eyes and her stomach performed an uncomfortable lurch.

'Frey, can we not do this now please?'

'Yes, Freya,' began Holly, her face pale, her blue eyes wary. 'I really think we should—'

'All I'm saying is that you need to work less and have more fun. When your exhibition at Jonti's gallery is finished, why don't you go over to visit your sister in Florence? She'd love to see you, you know that. Take Josh with you, have a break, get a bit of sunshine, eat lots of Italian food, drink their delicious Chianti, dance to the music, sing at the opera, live your best life, just like your parents used to do.'

'Yes, and look what happened to them!'

Tilly regretted her words as soon as they were out of her mouth. A spasm of scorching pain sliced through her chest and radiated out to her fingertips, but it was the expression on Holly's face that upset her more; the colour had drained from her habitually rosy cheeks and she was twisting her silver necklace round and round her finger, a sure sign that she was distressed. Holly didn't do confrontation and when Tilly saw Freya take a deep breath to continue with her uninvited pep talk, she decided the best solution was to turn the tables.

'By the way, I meant to ask you, Frey, any news on the sale of your uncle's chateau?'

Freya wrinkled her nose in irritation, just as she always did when someone mentioned the estate that her late uncle Toby had left to her parents the previous year. As they were too busy working for Médecins Sans Frontières in one of the world's many war-zones, it had fallen to Freya as their only child, and in their words "living locally" – as though the south of France was a hop, skip and a jump away from Devon – to deal with its sale.

'It's not a chateau, it's a farmhouse; a ramshackle, over-grown, paint-blistered old farmhouse; home only to a family of mice who don't mind that it has half a roof, plaster falling from the walls, no kitchen or bathroom to speak of, and an all-pervading aroma of damp dog, not to mention the fact that you need a scythe to clear a path through the garden.'

'I thought the estate agent described it as a "charming Provençal chateau, crammed with period features, handsome fireplaces, parquet flooring, and intricate ceiling mouldings with mature south-facing gardens and a quaint glasshouse, just perfect for a discerning buyer to put their own stamp on it"?'

'Oh my God, don't get me started on Xavier!'

'Who's Xavier?' asked Holly, the colour returning to her cheeks.

'The French real estate agent. He's totally useless; would you believe he's... Hey, Tilly, is that your phone ringing? It's almost three a.m.! Who could possibly be calling you at this time of the morning?'

'I have no idea.'

Tilly pulled her phone from the pocket of her jeans and squinted at the screen.

'It's Beckie... Hi, Beckie. What—' Tilly's heart bounced painfully against her ribcage as she listened to what Beckie was trying to say between huge gulping sobs. 'Slow down, Becks, slow down, I can't...'

'What's going on?' said Freya, scooting closer to Tilly. 'Put her on speakerphone.'

Tilly tapped the screen and the three girls leaned forward to listen to what Beckie was still struggling to articulate, her voice an octave higher than normal.

'It's the boardwalk! Oh my God, I can't believe it, I just can't believe it!'

'Beckie, please, just tell us what's happened!'

'There's been a fire! You'd better get down here right away.'

# Chapter Two

Tilly's heart cracked when she saw the charred wreckage of what had once been a handsome wooden boardwalk bordering the Blossomwood Bay marina, lined with a row of jaunty super-sized beach huts decorated in pale pastel colours and sporting seaside-themed bunting. Only the Boathouse Bistro remained intact; every single one of the beach hut studios had been destroyed in the fire, leaving nothing but stubby support posts poking out of the sea like arthritic fingers.

A sudden surge of nausea took her by surprise. She inhaled a deep breath in an effort to steady her rampaging emotions, but the acrid stench of the thick, dank smoke caught the back of her throat, causing her to cough repeatedly and her eyes to smart.

Everywhere she looked there was frantic activity. The fire had been extinguished but the various personnel from the Devon and Somerset Fire and Rescue Service were still there in force, their hoses weaving along the length of the marina walkway like elongated snakes as they continued to dampen down the smouldering slats. To her right, a coterie of police officers was gathered around what had previously been the pretty antique carousel but which was now nothing but a blackened steel skeleton.

The contrast was stark.

Yesterday the boardwalk had been teeming with tourists and visitors perusing and sampling the many artisanal products on offer – from Chloe's flavoured gins and Freya's perfumed soaps and candles, to Suzie's hand-crafted rings and bracelets and Poppy's hand-made chocolates – and today it was like a scene from a post-apocalyptic horror movie. And yet, amidst the devastation, she could see Beckie, standing at a table outside her bistro, pouring tea from a huge brown teapot, adding milk and heaped spoons of sugar, and handing the mugs round to everyone who wanted one.

'Oh, Tilly, there you are, I really can't...' But Chloe couldn't continue and burst into a fit of noisy tears, her shoulders shaking as Tilly wrapped her arms around her, holding her close until her distress subsided. 'I'm sorry, I don't seem to be able to stop crying, it's all just so... just so...'

'It's okay to be upset, Chloe,' said Freya, pulling a bunch of tissues from the floral rucksack that went everywhere with her and which contained an assortment of essential oils for every eventuality –

although Tilly suspected she didn't have anything remotely suitable for what had happened that morning.

'Was… was anyone hurt?' asked Holly, her eyes wide with anguish.

'No, thank God, but as you can see, all eight of our beautiful beach huts have been completely destroyed, along with the boardwalk and the carousel.'

'Do the police know what happened yet?'

'They think the fire was started by a faulty generator linked to the carousel that Dexter hired, and then spread; first to Freya's salon, then to your studio and gallery, Tilly, then Holly's pet grooming boutique, and when it reached my gin emporium… well, there was a mini-explosion and the ethanol I use in the distilling process acted as an accelerant and that's why there's absolutely nothing left of the remaining beach huts,' Chloe explained.

Tilly looked across to where her gallery used to be, her stomach performing a somersault of devastation. All her equipment had been in her studio; her cameras, her lenses, her lights, her tripods, her reflectors and filters – everything. However, what upset her the most was that she had lost all her artwork, some of which she'd spent months perfecting, as well as designing or sourcing the frames that would enhance the features of each individual image. There was no way she could reproduce the pictures in time for Jonti's show at the end of the month, which meant that not only had she lost her gallery and her equipment, her chance of fulfilling her long-held dream of exhibiting in London was in tatters, too.

But she wasn't the only one who had lost her livelihood.

She linked her arm through Holly's and was shocked to discover that her friend was trembling, her jaw loose, her pale blue eyes filled with disbelief as she stared at the spot where her peppermint-coloured beach hut had been. It was now just an expanse of turquoise water where a string of shiny white yachts bobbed jauntily, oblivious to the misery in their midst.

'Holly, are you okay?'

'I… Oh, Tilly, what if Ariel had been in there? She would have… she would have…'

Holly crouched down and wrapped her arms around her beloved spaniel's neck, sobbing into her glossy coat as the dog licked away her salty tears.

'The fire happened in the middle of the night, Holls. You *never* leave any of your furry friends in the grooming parlour overnight.'

'I know, but…'

Thankfully they were interrupted by the arrival of Beckie carrying a tray with four mugs of steaming hot tea so thick you could stand the spoon up in it. Freya, Holly and Chloe took one each, sighing with gratitude as they sipped the sweetened beverage. Tilly, however, politely declined, earning herself an eye-roll from Freya.

'I'm so sorry about the beach huts,' said Beckie, combing her fingers through her short ginger bob and leaving three parallel streaks of soot across her left cheek, à la Adam Ant. 'It's just awful, so awful.'

'What about the boathouse?' asked Holly, her trembling subsiding as the hot tea did its job. 'Is it damaged too?'

'There's no fire damage, so that's good, but there's been extensive smoke damage. All the perishables are ruined, and everything is coated in a fine layer of soot so it will have to be either deep-cleaned or thrown out and replaced before I can re-open to paying customers – which I can't do until I know what's happening with the insurance.'

'What do you mean?' asked Tilly, her previously befuddled mind clearing sharply. 'Surely there's no problem with the insurance? This was obviously an accident; the carousel was over seventy years old, and the police have already identified the cause of the fire.'

'No, no, there should be no problem with our insurance claims, at least as far as the *contents* of your studios and the boathouse are concerned; it was a term of our respective leases to ensure we took out our own insurance tailored to our individual business needs. But as far as the actual structures are concerned…'

Beckie paused and Tilly was surprised to see her cheeks redden slightly.

'What?'

'Well, apparently the boardwalk and the beach huts are covered by Dexter Hawkins' insurance.'

'So?'

'The police, and several of Dexter's friends, have spent the last two hours trying to contact him and there's no reply. As you know, he's on one of his epic hikes in the wilderness so it might be a while before anyone can get hold of him to let him know what's happened and to ask him to start the ball rolling with his insurance company.'

Beckie had the grace to squirm slightly under their intense scrutiny, clearly aware that unlike the rest of the group, her bistro was still intact and once the place had been fumigated and commercially cleaned – and her insurance money came through – she could start serving the discerning diners of Blossomwood Bay again.

Tilly glanced around at her friends, each one as astonished as she was.

'You mean we can't even *start* the process of rebuilding the boardwalk and replacing our beach huts until Dexter's insurance company says so? It could take weeks to contact him, especially as he actually doesn't *want* to be contacted, and will probably be actively *avoiding* the possibility of reconnecting with the outside world until it suits him. He's not even carrying a mobile phone!'

Tilly sat down onto one of the wooden benches outside the Boathouse Bistro, which had miraculously escaped the ravages of the fire, and dropped her head in her hands, struggling to douse the rising tsunami of panic that threatened to overwhelm her. Then another much more worrying thought burst into her head.

'Oh my God, what if Dexter didn't *have* insurance?'

'I'm sure he did,' said Freya, joining her on the bench and patting Tilly's hand gently.

'What makes you so sure?'

Everyone swung round to see their friend and fellow beach hut entrepreneur Suzie Sandringham standing in front of them, her tufted white-blonde-with-pink-streaks hair even more spiky than usual. She looked like she'd forgotten to change out of her sleepwear, sporting a pair of loose sunflower-yellow trousers with a turquoise vest top, and yet she'd taken time to accessorize with a chunky aquamarine necklace with matching bracelet and earrings, and every finger showcased the most stunningly beautiful ring that glinted in the early morning summer sunshine.

'What do you mean, Suzie?'

'Well, correct me if I'm wrong, but to date, Dexter Hawkins has never shown even the slightest interest in the boathouse or the beach huts, and the marina is just a place to moor his yacht when it's not sailing around the Caribbean hosting celebrity parties. I mean, has he ever visited any of your studios, or eaten at your bistro, Beckie, even *once*?'

Everyone shook their heads.

'Thought not. The Blossomwood Bay boardwalk is not a project to support the local economy and promote hand-made artisan products, like his press release insists. If you ask me, it's just a convenient tax write-off.'

Tilly's heart went out to Suzie – whom she noticed with alarm had also forgotten to wear shoes, although that wasn't an infrequent occurrence – and she understood her pessimistic words came from a place of desolation. Like all of them, apart from Beckie, Suzie had lost everything, but – as the designer and creator of high-end jewellery that involved the use of precious metals and gemstones – the value of what she had lost was likely to be ten, if not twenty times more than Tilly herself had lost.

However, the fire wasn't Dexter's fault *and* he had every right to take time out of his hectic life to recharge his batteries. Whilst Suzie was right that the Blossomwood Bay project *was* probably a tax-efficient scheme dreamed up by Dexter's accountants, at the same time, the rent he charged on the beach huts was minimal, generous even. She noticed that Holly's face had blanched as she contemplated the effects of Suzie's assertion that their beach huts might not be insured and she was about to divert their conversation onto safer ground when Beckie did it for her.

'Look! Aunt Kath has arrived with bacon sandwiches. Come on, let's go and grab one; it's going to be a long and stressful day and we all need to keep our energy levels up.'

Beckie gathered the empty mugs and, along with Holly, Chloe and Suzie, made her way back to where her aunt had pulled up in her ancient blue Volvo estate, already surrounded by a crowd of hungry emergency responders keen to sample the bacon rolls and the hot soup she was dispensing from a huge commercial Thermos flask.

'Are you coming, Tilly?' asked Freya, her eyebrows raised.

'I'll catch you up. I'm going to give Josh a call first.'

'Okay, I'll save you a roll.'

'Thanks, Frey.'

Tilly selected Josh's number and waited for him to answer, but the call went straight to voicemail, which she thought was strange; he rarely had his phone switched off unless he was in the cockpit. She checked her watch and calculated that it must be just after four p.m. in Bali, so she called again and left a message, telling him in as few words as possible what had happened and asking him to give her a call as soon as he could.

She had loved her life as a flight attendant. Eight years of jetting around the globe for a well-known airline, visiting every corner of the world, photographing the awe-inspiring scenery, learning about the wide variety of cultures, sampling the amazing food, enjoying the sparkling nightlife. It had been a wonderful experience, made even better when she met Josh on a layover in Barbados. They had clicked instantly over a couple of Mai Tais and spent two amazing years together making sure their schedules aligned as frequently as possible so they could enjoy long weekends together in cities like New York, San Francisco, Hong Kong and Singapore.

Josh Clarke was charismatic and undeniably handsome in his white-starched pilot's uniform, a thought that caused a smile to tug at her lips amidst all that morning's devastation. She wondered briefly whether she should go home, pack a bag, and head to their apartment in Pimlico so she would be there when he got back from Bali. She had missed him since she'd stopped flying the previous year. In fact, over the last six months they had been like ships that pass in the night, with Josh's busy schedule and her growing business at the art gallery.

While she wouldn't admit this to anyone, after her parents' accident she had become more and more anxious every time she stepped onto an aircraft, and although she wasn't exactly *frightened* of flying, it had lost its glamour and attraction. Josh had tried to dissuade her from handing in her notice, but had quickly grown tired, and then irritated, with her inability to "move on" after the funeral. When her sister, Olivia, and her husband, Enzo, decided to leave London for a new life in Tuscany, he suggested she should spend some time away, too, at their bolthole in Devon, and it had quickly become her permanent base.

She tried to call Josh again, leaving another message, and also sending him a text, then tucked her smoke-infused hair behind her ears and made her way towards the marina's car park to claim her bacon sandwich – and hopefully find a cup of coffee – but was instead met by a white-faced Freya and a very jittery Holly.

'What's the matter? What's happened now?'

'Let's go and sit down over there, shall we?'

Freya pointed to a row of painted wooden benches perfectly placed to enjoy the view of the bay, fringed by a crescent of golden sand that on any normal day at the end of June would be dotted with dog-walkers, joggers and parents with young children. It was an idyllic scene, one which she had photographed on many occasions. She dropped onto the seat and turned towards Freya, shocked to see that the distress on her friend's freckled face was even worse than when she first saw the burnt-out wreckage of her beach hut salon.

'Freya, what's going on?'

Freya glanced at Holly who nodded, tears glistening along her lower lashes as she stroked Ariel's head, for some reason unable to meet Tilly's eyes.

'Frey?'

'I'm so sorry, Tilly.'

'What for?'

Her heartrate increased and her stomach churned with a cauldron of dread as she watched Freya remove her phone from her flowery rucksack, swipe her finger across the screen, then bring up her Instagram feed. She selected an image and, with a shaking hand, turned the phone round towards Tilly.

Tilly stared at the reel, unable to believe her eyes.

There was Josh, on a tropical, palm-fringed beach, wearing a pair of smart navy-blue swimming shorts, his blonde hair uncharacteristically ruffled, his naked chest bronzed and shimmering in the sunshine... with his arm slung round a dark-haired woman in the tiniest of bikinis. The woman giggled, whispered something in her ear, then dashed off into the waves. Laughing, Josh chased after her, caught her arm, paused for an infinitesimal second to hold her gaze, then dropped a long, lingering kiss onto her waiting lips.

Tilly gasped as a shard of pain sliced through her heart. 'What the…'

Against her better judgement she played the reel again, and then again, before going on to read the accompanying comments, from which she discerned that the girl was Melissa, a member of the cabin crew that plied the Heathrow to Singapore route. She opened her mouth to express her disbelief, but no words ensued; her throat was tight, and she felt as though a block of concrete was pressing the air from her lungs. She could barely breathe.

'Are you okay?' asked Freya, her voice soft.

'I'm… I'm not sure. I—'

Suddenly, she could no longer hang on to her emotions and hot tears trickled down her cheeks. The world she had so carefully constructed over the last year – a quiet, low-key life in a small seaside town – came crashing down, and her thoughts scattered in every direction causing her to feel disorientated and nauseous.

'I'm sorry, I need to go.'

Before Freya and Holly could stop her, she leapt from the bench and sprinted along the main street towards her flat, not stopping until she was ensconced on her sofa, wrapped in a blanket with a cup of her favourite coffee in her hands.

# Chapter Three

Tilly had no idea how long she sat there, staring unblinkingly at the white walls, focusing solely on calming the maelstrom of emotions swirling through her veins, but when her heartbeat had finally slowed from canter to trot and she could breathe again, her coffee was cold and there was only one person she wanted to talk to.

'Hi, Liv, it's Tilly.'

'Hey Tilly. How was the festival this weekend? Did you sell all your beautiful photographs?'

'No, I—'

To her dismay, Tilly was ambushed by an overwhelming barrage of distress. She swallowed down hard, inhaled several lungfuls of air, but it didn't help.

'Tilly? What's wrong?'

'Oh, Liv, I really don't know where to start.'

'Then start at the beginning and don't stop until you get to the end.'

# Daisy James

Tilly recognised the mantra her mum had been fond of using whenever her daughters came home from school with stories to tell, good or bad, happy or sad, and another layer of anguish wrapped itself around her heart. Olivia had coped with their parents' loss much better than Tilly had, and was able to sprinkle references of their childhood into her conversations without experiencing the same crushing feelings of grief that she did.

'Tilly? Talk to me. Is everything okay?'

The anxiety in her sister's voice broke the dam and the whole sorry saga came tumbling out of her mouth; the shocking news of the fire, the loss of her precious photography equipment, the destruction of the artwork she had worked so hard to create over the last few months, before she went on to relay every excruciating detail of the Instagram reel starring Josh and Melissa in their own personal version of a Hollywood romcom.

'Oh, darling, I'm so sorry you had to see that. Have you spoken to Josh? What did he say?'

'I've tried to call him several times. I've sent texts and left messages, but so far, he hasn't called me back. But what *can* he say, Liv? He can hardly deny it, can he? There's photographic evidence of him jumping the waves and kissing another woman.'

A sharp spasm of pain sliced through her like an electric shock as she replayed the image in her mind's eye with her professional photographer's hat on; the cinematography was accomplished, showcasing the stunning Balinese scenery to its best advantage, the subjects were perfectly placed mid-screen, their chemistry clear for all to see. She wondered who had shot the video and who had uploaded it to Josh's Instagram account.

Clearly it couldn't have been Josh, or Melissa for that matter, but that wasn't the point.

'Do you know who the woman is?'

'Yes, it's Melissa Stonehouse, one of the cabin crew. Now I come to think about it, Josh has mentioned her a few times in passing.'

'And do you think it's a one-off; a slip-up after a drunken night out, maybe?'

She thought of the way Josh had looked at Melissa before kissing her and certainty replaced disbelief. She knew in her heart of hearts that it was more than just an innocent kiss after a few drinks – after all, the video had been taken during the day and neither of them looked under the influence of alcohol – and she realised for the first time that their four-year relationship was over. Tears trickled down her cheeks as yet another wave of desolation rolled over her.

'Oh Liv, what am I going to do?'

There was a brief pause. 'Actually…'

'What?'

'Why don't you come over to Tuscany?'

'Liv, I'm not sure I—'

'Hang on, hear me out first. As you know, Enzo and I were due to fly over to Boston for a few days on Friday to see his mum and his sister, Daniella. Remember? His mum's had a fall and broken her hip and Enzo wants to make sure she's okay.'

'Yes, I—'

'I'd arranged for Enzo's cousin Eleanora to come over from Bologna to run the teashop while we were away, but she called me this morning to say that her boyfriend has booked them a surprise, all-expenses-paid trip to Paris – staying at The Ritz, no less – and she can't come anymore, which means I'll have to stay here and Enzo will have to fly over to Boston on his own. But if you could come over and help out, it means I can still go. Tills, it will be the first real holiday we've had since we moved here, and I've been looking forward to it for weeks – getting to spend some quality time together after Enzo's been working so hard at building his architect's practice. This is the perfect solution!'

Guilt joined the unpleasant swirl of emotions rotating through Tilly's chest, an all-too familiar feeling that was so strong that it almost-but-not-quite obliterated her sorrow over discovering Josh's betrayal. She was ashamed to admit that despite her sister's many invitations, she had never taken her up on her offer to stay with them at their villa in a quaint yet thriving village in the hills above Florence.

It wasn't that she didn't want to see her sister, or spend time with her, it was just that she was used to her quiet life in Devon, living below what Freya called the "adventure radar", especially after everything that had happened over the last two years. And yet her plan hadn't worked; her grief remained ever-present, smouldering like a glowing ember of agony that she was woefully ill-equipped to eradicate.

Unlike Tilly, Olivia had handled the untimely passing of their parents by engaging a strong determination to follow her dreams without delay. Within weeks of the funeral, she had agreed to Enzo's suggestion to relocate to his hometown of Florence. She had invested her share of their inheritance in their villa in San Vincente, as well as a previously mothballed café in the village, utilising her skills as a tea sommelier to launch her own teashop that served a kaleidoscope of teas from Earl Grey to lapsang souchong, from gyokuro to shou mei, along with a myriad of English cakes, biscuits, scones, and fruit tarts.

'Liv, I can't run your teashop! You *know* I hate tea! And I don't eat cake!'

'Don't worry about that. Remember Helen?'

'Your best friend from high school?'

'Yes. Well, her younger sister, Jess, is here. She's waitressing at the teashop and helping me out in the kitchen over the summer before she goes off to med school in September. She's amazing; she speaks fluent Italian and she knows everything you'll need to know about making tea. Anyway, what do you mean you can't run a teashop? We were always helping Mum out at her café after school and at the weekends; running a café is in our DNA!'

Tilly experienced another sharp stab of pain at the casual mention of her mum's beloved Orange Blossom Café – a place her mum had adored and where she had experimented with all the new recipes she brought back from her travels around the world with Tilly's father, the village vet. The way Olivia spoke about their parents all the time, it was as though they were still around, still part of their lives, just away chasing their next adventure or striking the next experience from their never-ending bucket list. Tilly, on the other hand, preferred not to think about what had happened, and certainly not to talk about it; avoidance was the only way she could function.

'I don't know, Liv. I think I need to be here to deal with the insurance claim and—'

'I thought you said it could be weeks before anyone manages to contact Dexter?'

'I did, but—'

'So what are you planning to do until then?'

'I'm not sure yet.'

Olivia softened her tone. 'Why sit around, drinking coffee, staring at the walls while you wait for Dexter to interrupt his radio-silence when you could be roaming the streets of Florence, Siena and Lucca, replenishing your inspiration coffers, ready for your next exhibition? You'll love it here, Tilly – it's a photographer's paradise. Everywhere you look there's a jaw-dropping vista to feast your eyes on, and I know I don't have to tell you that the museums and galleries are world-class. Come and enjoy a little slice of the real Italian *dolce vita*. How can you resist?'

'I just think I need to be around in case—'

'In case of what? Tilly…'

Olivia paused and Tilly's stomach performed an uncomfortable plunge. She had endured similar conversations with her sister many times before, so she knew exactly what was coming and a zip of panic reared its head. However, past experience had also taught her that when her sister was on a roll, nothing could stop her, so she steeled herself to hear a few difficult truths – with the kindest of intentions – for the umpteenth time.

'You know, Mum and Dad would hate to see you like this, Tills. What happened was a tragic accident whilst they were living their lives to the full, squeezing out every moment of joy from the time they had left, not hiding away in a tiny attic flat, nursing their grief and never doing anything that isn't work – even though you do it so well. At least they died doing something they loved and if they could say anything to you now, it would be to get out there and live your best life, just like they did.'

'I *am* living my best life, Liv.'

But as soon as she'd said it, Tilly knew her words didn't ring true.

# Tilly's Tuscan Teashop

'Please come, Tilly, even if it's just for a few days until they locate Dexter. You'll love the villa; Enzo has just this week finished work on the pool and we've started to clear the old tennis court, too. You used to love playing tennis, remember when Mum—'

Tilly groaned inwardly; she couldn't take any more.

'Okay, okay, I'll think about it.'

'Promise?'

'I promise.'

'*Fantastica!* Okay, I have to go, Jess needs me in the kitchen; a coach trip has just arrived to partake in an authentic English afternoon tea. We have ham, cucumber, and cheese and home-made pickle sandwiches, a selection of fresh-from-the-oven scones with clotted cream and strawberry jam, and a cornucopia of cakes and tarts, all served with lashings and lashing of Earl Grey tea. I love you, Tills, and don't worry, everything is going to work out fine. I'll call you later.'

Tilly sighed, dropped her phone onto the coffee table and went to make herself a fresh cafetière of coffee, this time a Columbian coffee, and a round of buttered toast – her staple diet – before returning to her nest on the sofa.

How could she say no to Olivia?

How could she be the one to stand in the way of her sister enjoying her first holiday in two years?

Ever since the worst had happened, her sister had been there for her, flying back to London to spend time with her every month without fail, despite launching and then running her new teashop business and helping Enzo to renovate the rather run-down villa they had bought with the rest of Olivia's inheritance, which had turned out to need a great deal more than a lick of paint.

She knew she should have done more to support her sister after the accident, and there was a hard nugget of shame lodged in her chest at her neglectful behaviour, and yet she just couldn't face making the trip. She had only left Blossomwood Bay a few times since relocating there, mainly to meet Olivia when she came over to London, and once to travel over the border to Cornwall to finalise the sale of her mum's Orange Blossom Café and sign the probate paperwork at the solicitors' office.

If she was honest, it was her turn to step up now, her turn to support Olivia so that she could, in turn, support her husband while he visited his mother who had emigrated to Boston to be with Enzo's sister, and her two grandchildren, after his father's death the previous year. Maybe if she agreed to her sister's not unreasonable request, she could assuage a little of the guilt that had built up over the last two years.

But Tuscany?

She didn't know anyone there.

And managing a café that involved the daily act of brewing artisan teas and baking cupcakes in the land of espressos, cappuccinos, macchiatos, and ristrettos, not to mention the cream-laden cannoli or the sugary almond biscotti?

That part was almost laughable.

However, before she could dissolve into a bout of denial and self-pity, there was a knock on the door and she tumbled down the three flights of stairs to let Freya in.

'Coffee?'

'Love one.' Freya held up a white confectionery box tied with peppermint-coloured ribbon. 'I brought macarons; raspberry with prosecco-flavoured buttercream, pistachio with vanilla buttercream, and lavender with lemon buttercream.' Tilly scrunched up her nose and Freya laughed. 'Don't worry, they're for me.'

Freya plonked herself down on the sofa, sending a waft of gardenias mingled with burnt wood into the air. Tilly suspected that the fragrance wouldn't be featuring on the shelves of her aromatherapy salon any time soon. She placed a mug of rich, dark coffee on the table in front of Freya and joined her on the sofa. Unsurprisingly, her friend cut straight to the chase.

'Did you speak to Josh yet?'

'No, but I've spoken to Liv.'

'What did she say?'

'She asked me to go over to Italy.'

'Great idea. It will do you good to spend some time with her and Enzo.'

'Ah, but that's just it.'

'What do you mean?'

'They won't be there. Enzo's mum has had a fall and they're going to visit her in Boston.'

'Then do it for you, Tilly. Go to Tuscany, channel your inner Sophia Loren, sample the delectable wine, devour the delicious food, listen to the charming operatic arias, kiss a few frogs…'

'Frey, I really don't think that's—'

'What I mean is, that it's time for you to discard that mantle of mourning you insist on draping around your shoulders, time for you to step out into the light again and bring a little vibrancy into your life *and* your artwork, and Tuscany is the perfect place to do that! The place is positively *brimming* with a kaleidoscope of colour and fragrance, history and culture, not to mention sunshine and gorgeous Italian men! It's the perfect opportunity for you to start filling your portfolio with a different kind of image, as well as gaining a new perspective on life. Look how happy Liv is over there. Don't you want a slice of that, too? Oh, and if that isn't enough to persuade you, I hear the Italians make an amazing *caffè corretto!*'

Tilly smiled. 'That's what Liv said.'

'Go on, then. Call your sister back, right now, and tell her you accept her very generous offer to spend the next few weeks in Tuscany so she can enjoy a decent break from her very busy life and spend some quality time with that handsome husband of hers and his family!'

A tickle of nerves rippled through Tilly's chest, but when she saw Freya give her an encouraging nod, a surprise whoosh of optimism infiltrated her natural tendency to stick within the boundaries of her comfort zone.

'Okay,' she whispered, and before she could change her mind, she reached for her phone.

'Hi, Liv, I—'

'Oh, Tilly, does this mean it's a yes?' Olivia cried before Tilly could say anything and when she heard the excitement in her sister's voice, she knew she was doing the right thing despite the reservations and anxiety that were already starting to creep into her brain.

'It's a yes!'

'Oh my God, thank you so much. I can't tell you how grateful I am, and Enzo is going to be so relieved that he doesn't have to make the trip by himself; it's going to be like a second honeymoon for us. Are you sure, really sure?'

'Yes, I'm sure.'

'And you can stay for the full three weeks?'

'Three weeks?! I thought you said a few days?'

# Tilly's Tuscan Teashop

'Boston's a long way away so we might as well make the most of the trip, don't you think? Especially as I know the teashop is going to be in such safe hands. I'll hire you one of those cute little Fiat Cinquecentos to tootle about in while you're here. Oh, and don't worry, I'll withdraw my entry into the annual San Vincente food fiesta competition.'

'Hang on, competition? What competition?'

But Olivia had already rushed off to start on her packing.

# Chapter Four

As soon as Tilly handed over the fare to the taxi driver and scooted out of the back seat, the Alpha Romeo shot off as though on the starting grid of the Italian Grand Prix, dust flying into the air as he greeted an oncoming tour bus with a sharp toot of the horn even though the bus had right of way.

She sighed, grabbed the handle of her suitcase, and walked through an impressive stone archway into a wide sun filled piazza complete with marble fountain – where Olivia had told her she could collect the hire car that would take her the final two kilometres from Florence to the village of San Vincente. A tickle of excitement wove its way through her chest as she imagined herself navigating the serpentine Tuscan roads in a cute Fiat 500 with the windows rolled down, instead of the serviceable black Renault estate she was used to driving back in Devon.

She spotted a huge plate glass window with the legend *Antonio's Autos* emblazoned across the front in gold letters, and trundled her suitcase across the cobbled square, pausing briefly to appreciate the beauty of the buildings that surrounded her on all four sides. To her right was a picturesque church, its façade reflecting the golden glow of the mid-morning sun. Next to the church was a flower shop, in front of which was a tiny, rust-blistered Ape that had been pressed into service as a display stand for the sunflowers, white roses, and tiger lilies that were being snapped up by the many passers-by.

To her left was a neat row of shiny new Vespas, lined up like cadets on parade and providing a convenient vehicular barrier between the car hire company and a busy pavement café where a handful of patrons were indulging in a late breakfast espresso, watched over by an attentive, and rather attractive, Italian waiter. The air was filled with the buzz of daily life and the aroma of freshly ground coffee – a fragrance Tilly preferred to any perfume, although she would never say that to Freya.

A woman in a wide-brimmed sunhat, huge Gucci sunglasses and chic black trouser suit dropped a few coins onto a saucer, collected her over-sized shoulder bag and left the café. Tilly smiled as the elegant woman strolled past her, enveloped in a cloud of Chanel N°5, then grinned even more widely when she caught sight of a pair of furry ears and a tiny pale pink nose peeking from the top of the woman's bag. She scrambled for her phone and took a quick snap of the cute Pekinese to send to Holly.

'*Buongiorno*,' came a deep voice from the doorway behind her, followed by a long stream of unintelligible Italian that Tilly had no hope of understanding.

'Oh, yes, sorry, *buongiorno*, I… My sister, Olivia Molinari, she has reserved a hire car for me… Natalie Nicholson?' Tilly smiled, hoping the man with the shoulder-length brown curls who looked like he had just stepped from a Milanese catwalk understood some English.

'Ah, *sì*.' He nodded. '*Seguimi*.'

The man, whom she assumed was the "Antonio" of *Antonio's Autos* fame, led her into the car hire shop and gestured towards a surprisingly stylish glass-topped desk in front of which was a lipstick-red leather chair worthy of a high-end fashion boutique. She sank into its welcoming embrace and took a moment to glance around the beautifully appointed room, which, with its white marble floor and duck-egg blue walls, was more like an upmarket art gallery than a place to rent a car.

After another barrage of Italian, Antonio pushed a sheet of pink paper in front of Tilly, handed her a gold fountain pen, and pointed to the dotted line at the bottom of the page. Wondering whether she would regret it later, she scribbled her name and was immediately handed a set of keys.

'*Numero cinque.*'

'I'm sorry, I don't understand.'

Antonio pointed out of the window and repeated 'Numero cinque.'

Tilly looked over her shoulder and scoured the piazza, but for the life of her couldn't spot any cute Fiat 500s waiting to be temporarily adopted by a string of discerning foreign tourists keen to embrace everything Italy had to offer, including its most popular transport choices. In fact, the only vehicles she *could* see were the row of Vespas belonging to the patrons of the café next door.

Confused, she met Antonio's gaze and shook her head.

Antonio rolled his eyes, muttered something under his breath in high-speed Italian, pushed back his chair, and with not a little irritation, strode out of the office, clearly expecting her to follow him. To her surprise, instead of leading her to a parking garage, he stopped in front of one of the Vespas, and said in heavily accented English 'This is your vehicle, *signorina.*'

'What?'

Tilly stared at the bright scarlet scooter basking in the Tuscan sunshine like a sleek stallion waiting to be tamed, and her stomach started to churn with panic.

'Oh, no, I think there's been some kind of misunderstanding. My sister booked a Fiat Cinquecento for me.'

'I don't rent Fiats, only Vespas.'

'But… I can't ride that!'

Antonio simply raised his palms in the air, shrugged his shoulders, and returned to his marble-floored, air-conditioned office, oblivious, or unconcerned, to her plight. Tilly glanced around the piazza where everyone was going about their business, unaware of the flustered visitor in their midst. Thankfully, the café had quietened and only two of the ten or so tables were occupied by people reading the daily newspaper instead of scrolling through their emails or social media accounts as they would have been in London or Devon. She had no idea what to do. The only thing she could think of was to grab her phone and call Olivia.

'Hey, Liv, I thought you said you'd hired a cute little Fiat 500 for me?'

'I did. Enzo's sorted it out with a friend of his. What colour is it? I asked him to try and get you a yellow one.'

'Well, it's not yellow, and it's definitely *not* a Cinquecento!'

'What do you mean?'

'It's a Vespa, Liv; a bright red Vespa.' She heard her sister giggle. 'Are you laughing?'

'No.'

'It's not funny! I can't ride a Vespa!'

'Sorry, darling, I'll talk to Enzo; he probably misunderstood me when I asked him to hire you something quintessentially Italian. Although you *have* ridden a scooter before; I remember you telling me a couple of years ago that you and Josh hired them for a few days when you were in Vietnam and wanted to travel up the east coast.'

'Yes, but—'

'Look, I'm sure you'll be fine. You could say that it's just like riding a bike!'

And with that, to Tilly's utter amazement, the line went dead. She shook her head, slotted her phone back into the pocket of her black jeans, and spun on her heels to return to the hire shop to ask Antonio to talk her through the controls, but was flabbergasted to see that the door now sported a sign with the word "*Chiuso*" – Closed.

'What the…!'

Seeing no other way forward, she decided to take her courage in both hands and just go for it. She slung her leg over the seat of the Vespa, took a moment to gain her balance, and forced herself to recall the time she and Josh had travelled north from Hoi An to Da Nang – without the benefit of helmets – sampling *cao lầu*, *bánh xèo*, and *bún chả* along the way. If she could do that, she was sure she could ride a Vespa through the narrow streets of Florence, although the controls did look a little more complicated.

She turned the key, twisted the throttle, and to her horror, shot forward at speed, ploughing into several of the – thankfully vacant – café tables, knocking down chairs and scattering menus, cutlery and napkins in every direction.

'Oh my God!'

Terrified, she clung onto the handlebars for dear life as the handsome waiter she had seen earlier dashed forward to stop her from doing any more damage or tumbling head first into one of the many ceramic flower pots that were stationed around the fringe of the café.

'*Stai okay?*'

Tilly nodded; at least she understood the word "okay".

The waiter indicated for her to dismount, and wheeled the Vespa away from the chaotic scene. He then quickly reinstated the fallen tables and chairs before returning to her side, his dark, chocolate-brown eyes crinkling at the corners in amusement.

'English?' he asked in a very sexy Italian accent.

'Yes.'

'I thought so.'

'Why?'

'Because Italians are born with the innate ability to ride a Vespa!'

An intoxicating waft of fresh minty cologne tickled at Tilly's nostrils as she took in her rescuer's carefully tousled curls, his white-shirt-and-black-trousers waiter's uniform, and what looked like a very expensive pair of hand-stitched Italian loafers. His shirt cuffs had been rolled back to reveal a ripple of dark hairs on his tanned forearms and when she finally met his gaze, she saw there was an unmistakable glint of mischief dancing in his eyes, along with something else she couldn't quite put her finger on.

'Would you like me to give you a quick lesson?'

'Yes please, but would you mind if I had a coffee first?'

Again, the waiter smiled, cute dimples bracketing his lips.

'I thought the British only drank tea?'

'Not me. I don't like tea,' Tilly said, before adding, 'But don't tell anyone I said that.'

'No problem. What about one of our pistachio cannoli?'

'Thanks, but I'm not a cake eater, either, I'm afraid.'

'Okay, one espresso coming right up. I'm Matteo, by the way.'

'And I'm Natalie, but my friends call me Tilly.'

'Please to meet you, Tilly.'

Matteo disappeared into the café and moments later reappeared with a *caffè doppio*, which she drank in two quick gulps, the caffeine helping to deflate the balloon of anxiety that the inadvertent café rampage incident had caused. She inhaled a deep breath, squared her shoulders, and remounted the Vespa.

'Ready?' Matteo asked.

Tilly nodded. 'Yes.'

'Okay, so this is the throttle, this is the brake, and this is the gearshift. Oh, and this is the horn, which you'll definitely need to use with exuberance while travelling in Florence.'

As Matteo leaned forward to demonstrate the braking mechanism, another waft of his delicious eucalyptus-infused aftershave floated through the air between them and a surprise frisson of attraction swept through Tilly's veins.

Annoyed at her reaction, she pushed the emotion firmly away. While she'd had a short, unsatisfactory conversation with Josh about the fire on the boardwalk and the loss of her studio and gallery, as well as her intended trip to Italy, when she'd raised the issue of the Instagram reel of him frolicking on the Balinese beach with Melissa, he'd told her that it was something better discussed face-to-face and had promptly terminated their conversation.

They had been a couple for almost four years, and for the majority of that time – at least during the two years before her parents' accident – they had been happy together. Her head told her that their relationship was over, but her heart had different ideas and she'd decided that she owed it to Josh to hear his explanation, which she agreed should be done in person and not over the phone where misunderstandings could occur.

However, she couldn't think about any of that now. She had to concentrate on getting through the next few weeks – settling into Olivia and Enzo's villa and focusing on running Olivia's teashop to the best of her ability – but first she had to actually *get* to San Vincente. She realised Matteo had paused in his impromptu Vespa-training session and was looking at her expectantly.

'Sorry?'

'Now it's time for you to give it a go.'

Tilly nodded. She gritted her teeth, took hold of the handlebars, and wobbled forward a few metres, her feet hovering just a few inches from the piazza's cobbles as she gained her balance and familiarised herself with the controls. She increased her speed a little, made it to the far side of the square without falling off or causing any more mayhem, then spun round and returned to where

Matteo was standing with his hands on his hips, delight written across his face. When she came to a stop in front of him, a welcome feeling of accomplishment whipped through to her chest.

'*Congratulazioni,* you're a natural!'

'I don't know about that, but I think I might at least be able to make it to my sister's villa in San Vincente,' she said with a laugh. Then she spotted her discarded suitcase outside the car hire shop and a splash of panic doused her celebrations. 'Oh my God, I forgot about my luggage!'

'That's no problem.'

Before she could protest, Matteo had grabbed her suitcase and tied it to the back of the Vespa.

'I don't think I can…'

But as Tilly travelled a few metres across the cobbles without incident, a sudden whoosh of confidence flooded her veins. Gaining momentum, she tried to turn round to wave her thanks to Matteo, which caused her to wobble and swerve dramatically so she settled for calling '*Grazie mille*' over her shoulder and smiled when she heard him shout back '*Prego!*'

Within minutes she was heading out of the city, across the *Ponte alle Grazie* bridge and up the hill, leaving the dense traffic of Florence behind. As she became more and more accustomed to the Vespa's quirks, navigating the twists and turns felt like second nature and an intense sense of freedom washed over her.

Perhaps she was going to enjoy her brief sojourn in Tuscany after all.

# Chapter Five

A mere twenty minutes later, Tilly paused next to the wooden sign informing her that she had arrived at the Tuscan hillside village of San Vincente, the place that had been her sister's home for the last two years. When Enzo had suggested they made a fresh start and relocate to Italy, Olivia hadn't hesitated and Tilly was in awe of her courage to forge a new life in a country she had only previously visited a handful of times.

She removed her phone from her pocket and checked Olivia's text for directions and realised she had a decision to make; turn right if she wanted to head to the villa, take a much-needed shower, or maybe a dip in the pool, unpack the few things she had brought with her, and familiarize herself with her new accommodation; turn left and she would arrive at the village and be able to take a first look at her sister's teashop and find out exactly what she had in store over the next few weeks, as well as introduce herself to Jess whom she knew would be keen to meet her.

After a moment's consideration, she turned her handlebars to the left and rode the final three hundred metres to the village. As she squeezed her Vespa into the tiniest of parking spaces, it finally occurred to her why Enzo had chosen the transport he had; it wasn't a joke, as she had initially thought, it was about practicalities and she was grateful for his considerate selection.

She hitched her canvas satchel – black to match the rest of her outfit and her suitcase – onto her shoulder and paused under the shade of the red, white and green canopy of *Gelateria Gabriella* to survey the village piazza. Like the piazza in Florence where she'd had coffee, it too was cobbled and surrounded by an impressive collection of buildings, including a very glamorous ristorante sporting dark green and gold parasols and playing host to a clientele who looked like they had dressed for an evening at the opera instead of a leisurely lunch.

Instinctively, she reached for her phone again and spent the next ten minutes taking a myriad of photographs, hesitating before engaging the black and white filter. The terracotta of the roof tiles, the turmeric-coloured facades, the bottle-green window frames and shutters, the occasional flash of crimson from the hanging baskets and ceramic pots, and the ginger cat sunbathing languidly on a windowsill, all melded together to create the perfect depiction of an

Italian hilltop village, and for the first time in a long time she couldn't bring herself to remove the colour.

San Vincente was clearly popular with visitors; everywhere she looked there were groups of people exploring its nooks and crannies, taking selfies, partaking in a coffee at *Ristorante Rocco* or enjoying one of Gabriella's artisan gelatos. Multiple languages swirled through the warm afternoon air, along with the exquisite aromas of freshly baked focaccia and expensive French perfume.

However, amongst the various businesses catering for the tourists, Tilly couldn't see her sister's teashop. She checked the hand-drawn map Olivia had emailed to her the previous day and – after further exploration of the village piazza that housed a jewellery shop, a hairdressers and a dental surgery amongst other things – identified the narrow alleyway between the *farmacia* and the local estate agency.

She made her way towards it, coming to an abrupt standstill outside a golden sandstone building with a pretty powder-blue door and shutters, its window shaded from the glare of the sunshine by a matching powder-blue canopy with scalloped edges. A sign hanging from an ornate silver bracket announced she had arrived at *Té e Torta* and to Tilly's surprise a lump formed in her throat as she was ambushed by a rush of painful memories.

Olivia's Tuscan Teashop was almost identical to their mum's Orange Blossom Café.

Okay, so Olivia had chosen to paint the woodwork in a soft baby-blue colour instead of the pastel pink, and had switched the orange blossom trees that stood sentry at the front door for a duo of bay trees in terracotta pots, but apart from that Tilly could have been standing in front of the Cornish café, fighting to get a grip on her emotions. If this was what the teashop looked like on the outside, she dreaded what she would find inside.

Nevertheless, she inhaled a breath, swallowed down hard, and pushed open the door, unsurprised to be greeted by the jolly tinkle of a brass bell as well as the murmur of conversation and soft music playing in the background. A tickle of regret agitated at her chest; she missed her sister and wished she could have been there to greet her. Needing a moment to collect her thoughts before going in search of Jess, she slid into a seat at a vacant table by the window.

To Tilly's astonishment, no sooner had she sat down than a woman wearing a bright orange baseball cap pushed back her chair, stood up, glanced briefly in her direction, then made an announcement to the whole of the teashop in a rapid-fire language Tilly knew wasn't Italian. Immediately, every single customer took a last sip of their chosen tea and followed the woman outside where she raised an unopened orange umbrella into the air and, like the Tuscan version of the Pied Piper, led her followers towards the piazza, leaving the teashop empty, apart from Tilly who stared after them, her jaw loose, horrified that her arrival had cleared the room of customers.

However, their mass departure had given her the opportunity to survey the teashop's interior without obstruction. Like the exterior, the walls had been decorated in a soft powder-blue, the tables dressed in pale-blue-with-white-polka-dots tablecloths and napkins, each one sporting a multi-tiered cake stand that had clearly offered a selection of sandwiches, scones with cream and jam, and bite-size cupcakes and pastries.

It was as though she had been beamed back to Devon or Cornwall.

Quirky polka dot teapots, milk jugs and sugar bowls also dotted the tables, but the thing that drew her eye was the huge, powder-blue framed chalkboard listing the menu of teas available. There were those that most tea-drinkers would recognise like English Breakfast, Earl Grey, Chamomile, Jasmine and Oolong, along with a much wider selection of more unusual and exotic teas – Hibiscus, Artichoke, Chrysanthemum, even one called Butterfly Pea Flower tea – as well as Olivia's personal favourite, dandelion tea.

Despite her anguish at being reminded of her beloved mum's far-too-early passing, Tilly couldn't prevent a wry smile from stretching her lips; there wasn't a cappuccino, latte, Americano, macchiato or cortado in sight.

As she continued her scrutiny of her sister's new enterprise, her gaze snagged on the wooden dresser – also painted in the teashop's signature powder-blue – on which stood a trio of large china plates edged in forget-me-nots. Each plate was piled high with a pyramid of freshly baked scones, in front of which were miniature flags advising the hungry visitor of its variety – cherry and almond, rhubarb and custard, lemon and white chocolate – or for those with a more savoury tooth; tomato and basil, parmesan and sage, gruyère and fennel.

Tilly's thoughts scooted back to her childhood when she and Olivia would stand on tiny wooden stools in matching pink aprons embroidered with the Orange Blossom Café logo, their hands thrust into a bowl of flour, making scones, biscuits and cakes from their mum's precious hand-written and hand-illustrated recipe book, some of which were so "out there" that even their father refused to taste-test them.

'Oh, I'm so sorry, but we're finished with the afternoon tea service for the day, although I could do you a pot of Earl Grey and your choice of scone, if you like?'

With a concerted effort, Tilly managed to wrestle her heart-scorching reminiscences back into their proverbial box, and smiled at the twenty-something woman with white-blonde pigtails woven with pale-blue ribbons, her long fringe tickling her lashes. She wore a floaty chiffon blouse with huge puffed sleeves in a pale aquamarine colour, and over a dozen silver bangles jangled at her wrists, but what caught Tilly's attention was her manicure – each nail depicted a different coloured cupcake, topped with a shiny gemstone instead of a cherry or chocolate button.

Was this Jess? The girl who was due to start med school in September?

# Tilly's Tuscan Teashop

'Actually, I'm not here for the tea. I'm Tilly, Olivia's sister?'

'Oh my God, Tilly! I'm so pleased to meet you at last! I'm Jess, Jess Jones.'

And to Tilly's surprise, Jess flung her arms around her neck and hugged her tightly for several long seconds, sending a cascade of pretty floral perfume into the air between them, before dropping into the chair next to Tilly with a huge sigh of relief.

'Carlotta and I have been run off our feet today. We've had *two* coach parties in; the first was a group of women from Kent on a tour of Italy organised by their local Women's Institute, and the other one, the one that's just left, came all the way from Holland for one of our amazing afternoon teas.'

'Really?'

'Well, it was actually part of their tour of a few other tourist attractions, like the Duomo, the Ponte Vecchio, and Michelangelo's David at the Accademia,' Jess conceded. 'We don't get much passing trade at the teashop, so Livvie had to take the difficult decision to only cater for pre-booked tour parties now, and holidaymakers from the UK, of course. Unfortunately, for some reason, the locals don't seem to like Livvie's afternoon teas.'

'Why not?'

'I have no idea, because they're wonderful!' said Jess, her green eyes wide with excitement. 'For instance, today we've served thirty-two people with a selection of crustless finger sandwiches, home-made sultan or cranberry scones, and the most delicious mini cakes and pastries. Livvie always blends a special tea to complement the food, too, which in this case was peppermint and spearmint. I couldn't eat any of it, of course.'

'Why not?'

'Because I'm on the Paleo diet.'

'What's the Paleo diet?'

'It's based on the food that would have been available in Palaeolithic times; lean meat, fish, fruit, vegetables, nuts and seeds, which means definitely no sugar, bread or dairy products.'

'Okay…'

'But I'm actually thinking of switching to the Blue Glasses diet tomorrow.'

Tilly wasn't sure she should ask, but she couldn't help it.

'What's the Blue Glasses diet?'

'Japanese research suggests that by wearing blue-tinted sunglasses we can block out rays of red light that stimulate the appetite, but I'm not convinced – although I prefer their thesis to that of Lord Byron who advocated several cups of vinegar every day. Yuk!'

Tilly stared at Jess; she didn't know what to say. Jess was the same height as she was – around five foot six or seven – and if anything, she was on the slender side. Why on earth was she talking about dieting? However, she knew it was none of her business, so she decided it was time to steer the conversation back to the teashop. Unfortunately, she wasn't quick enough.

# Tilly's Tuscan Teashop

'Oh, Tilly, I'm so relieved that you agreed to come over to help us out. I just know you're going to *absolutely* love it here! Livvie said that it's your first time in Tuscany. Is that true?'

Warmth seeped into Tilly's cheeks and the familiar wriggle of guilt invaded her chest.

'Yes, it is. I've been really busy building up my new photography business in Devon.'

'Gosh, yes, your beach hut! I'm so sorry about the fire; you must be devastated. Is there any news on when they'll be able to start the rebuilding?'

'No, not yet. They're still trying to contact the owner of the marina.'

'So does that mean you can stay here until Livvie gets back at the end of July?'

'Yes, that's the plan.'

'*Fantastica!*' Jess's eyes sparkled and she clapped her hands in excitement. 'I can't wait to start practising.'

'Practising? Practising what?'

'Livvie's recipes.'

'What recipes?'

Jess stared at Tilly as though she was speaking Greek.

'The recipes for the San Vincente fiesta's foodie competition next week.'

'Ah, right, no, Liv told me she'd withdrawn her entry.'

Now it was Jess's turn to look uncomfortable.

'I… well, I thought we could do it together, so… I didn't send the e-mail.'

'What?'

'Oh Tilly, the whole village takes part in the fiesta in one way or another. We can't be the only ones that don't. What message would that send to the community? I promise you that it'll be lots of fun; and you'll get to experience a little slice of the famous Italian *dolce vita* first hand. This year was supposed to be Livvie's chance! Rocco Bianchi – he owns the upmarket restaurant in the piazza – has won the competition every single year for the last twenty years. He's always spouting on about Italian cuisine being the best in the world and sneers at anything to do with British food in general, but especially what we create here at *Té e Torta*. You should hear him, Tilly! It's like he's the Gordon Ramsey of Tuscany! Livvie worked so hard to finalise her recipes before she left for Boston, it would be such a shame not to take part in this year's contest.'

'But Jess, I'm not Liv.' Tilly was about to go on to explain that she loathed tea and hadn't indulged in any kind of cake or dessert for years, but decided that as she was about to spend the next month serving those very things to the public, it was probably better to keep those things to herself. 'I'm a photographer, and before that I was cabin crew, *not* a pastry chef or a tea sommelier. I'm sorry, we can't enter the contest, you have to send off that e-mail.'

There was a pause while Jess studied her wonderful manicure, then, without meeting Tilly's gaze she said softly, 'I thought we could do it for Livvie. It's her *dream* to snag the San Vincenzo trophy for best food in village. Do you have a dream, Tilly?'

'Yes, but I—'

'What is it?'

'Well, until the fire destroyed every photograph in my portfolio, I would have really loved to showcase my artwork to a wider audience, starting with a charity show at a local gallery in Devon, then, maybe, if that was successful, move on to an exhibition in a London gallery.'

'And don't you think Livvie would do *everything* she could to help you achieve that dream?'

This time Jess looked directly into Tilly's eyes, clearly knowing the answer to her own question, and Tilly groaned inwardly when she realised that her outward appearance disguised a steely inner resolve. If Jess changed her mind about going to med school in September, she would certainly make a formidable lawyer.

'Yes, she would.'

'Then it's settled!' Jess beamed, the cheery smile back on her face as she stood from her chair. 'Have you been over to the villa yet?'

'No, not yet, I thought I'd—'

'Then why don't you head over there now? Carlotta and I will tidy up here. I'll see you tomorrow around midday. We have a party of twelve from Oxford, over here on a yoga retreat, booked in for afternoon tea at two o'clock'

'Are you sure?'

'Absolutely. Shoo!'

Feeling slightly steamrollered, Tilly smiled at Jess, collected her bag and left the teashop, her disorientation causing her to stumble over one of the bay trees guarding the front door and go over on her ankle. To her horror, in her attempt to right herself, she lost her footing and catapulted into the arms of an astonished stranger for the second time that day, a stranger who also, weirdly, favoured eucalyptus-infused aftershave.

'Sorry, sorry, I mean…'

'Tilly? What are you doing here?'

Tilly stared at Matteo in a surprise. But before she could respond to his enquiry, his chocolate-brown gaze – framed with the longest lashes she'd seen on a guy – floated over her shoulder and landed on the sign above the teashop she had just tumbled from.

'I thought you said you *hated* tea? And *cake*!'

To Tilly's mortification, Jess had rushed out of the door to see what the commotion was about and had heard Matteo's question.

'What does he mean, Tilly?'

'I…'

Seeing her new friend's eyes widen in bewilderment, and then distress, a mixture of embarrassment and shame curdled in Tilly's stomach, made even worse when she saw Matteo's lips twitch in amusement as he waited to hear her response.

'Is it true? *Do* you hate tea?' asked Jess.

'No, it's just that I prefer coffee, that's all.'

'And cake?'

# Tilly's Tuscan Teashop

'I...'

Tilly paused, not wanting to be untruthful in her response, but equally not wanting to upset Jess by informing her that no biscuit, scone or cake had passed her lips for almost two years and the only reason she was there in Tuscany, offering her mediocre services at her sister's beloved teashop, was because her conscience had forced her to come to Olivia's aid, just as her sister had done for her so many times before.

Unfortunately, before she could formulate a suitable reply, Jess had shaken her head in dismay and disappeared back into the teashop. Feeling dreadful, Tilly spun round to speak to Matteo, to remind him that she had specifically asked him to keep her inadvertent confession to himself, but he, too, had walked away and was strolling across the piazza towards Gabriella's ice cream shop.

Tilly sighed; it hadn't been the best start to her stay in Tuscany.

# Chapter Six

When Tilly skidded to a halt outside Villa Avanti, she couldn't help but gape at its beauty. Not only had she been guided to its front door by a welcoming committee of ruler-straight cypress trees, but the property in front of her was *the* quintessential Tuscan villa with terracotta roof, ochre façade and dark green shutters, currently sealed against the rapidly descending sun that bathed the whole scene in a soft amber light.

To her left was a white marble statue in the shape of a cherub, frolicking in a cascade of water that sprinkled down into a wide lotus-leaf-shaped pond, which she knew Olivia and Enzo had bought when they were on their honeymoon in Venice. Ceramic pots dotted the steps, filled with geraniums and poppies, and a pair of miniature lemon trees stood guard at the front door.

The place was picture-postcard perfect.

That was until she looked over her shoulder and saw the garden. She had expected to see neat pathways edged with carefully considered planting, perhaps a bed of roses or a vine-covered gazebo offering a splash of much-needed shade in which to enjoy an evening sundowner, but what she actually saw was a tangle of overgrown bushes, parched plants and an ancient stone table covered in ivy.

It was a mess.

Clearly Olivia and Enzo had spent all their time and energy, and probably their money, on renovating the villa; a task that she knew had taken two years so far, although when she thought about it, she did recall her sister telling her that they'd employed a gardener who would also look after the pool whilst they were away. Maybe he had handed in his notice and they'd been unable to replace him.

She was about to drag her suitcase across the gravel driveway to the front door when she spotted a paint-blistered gate that she assumed led to the rear of the house, and decided to investigate. She left her luggage on the doorstep, made her way to the side of the villa, and pushed open the gate.

A smile stretched her lips when her gaze fell on the villa's newly completed swimming pool, its surface sparkling like a sheet of diamonds in the sunshine, the surrounding terrace playing host to a collection of green and white striped sun loungers and matching parasols. The turquoise water looked so inviting she had to fight a sudden urge to strip off, right there, and take a refreshing dip.

But she would have to wait.

Tilly retraced her steps to the front door and started to search for the terracotta pot beneath which Olivia had told her she'd hidden the key. She found it, retrieved the key, and let herself inside the house, pausing in the hallway to allow her eyes a few moments to adjust to the reduction in sunlight. The air was infused with the fragrance of furniture polish and the star lilies Olivia had arranged in the glass vase on the chic white console, above which hung a huge, gilt-framed mirror. The floor tiles were impressive, too, featuring an attractive pattern that directed the eye from the front door to the kitchen – the hub of every house her sister had resided in.

She checked her reflection in the mirror, shocked at the state of her hair, which seemed to have doubled in size since she had left Heathrow that morning. She groaned; was this the first impression she'd presented to Jess? And what about Matteo? No wonder he looked at her with such undisguised amusement; she looked like she'd stuck her fingers in an electric socket!

Stooping to appreciate the wonderful fragrance of the lilies, Tilly's eyes fell on a collection of family photographs next to the flower arrangement. She picked up one of the engraved silver frames, smiling when she recognised the image straight away because she had exactly the same photograph – in a less ornate frame – on her bedside table back in Devon.

The picture had been captured by their father – a keen amateur photographer, but predominantly of the animals he cared for – in the garden of their childhood home in Cornwall. Olivia must have been eight or nine and Tilly was five or six, their dark brown hair neatly plaited, and wearing the matching summer dresses their mother had made for them. They were both grinning broadly into the camera, arms around each other's shoulders, happy in each other's company. Some sisters bickered, some simply forged a life separate from their sibling, but Tilly had always felt a deep connection with Olivia, and as far as she could recall, whilst they spoke frankly to each other on occasion, they had never exchanged a cross word.

With care, she replaced the photograph on the console, but her sight snagged the picture behind it and a slice of pain cut through her heart. The image was of her mum and dad, posing against the backdrop of Niagara Falls, a trip they had taken to celebrate their silver wedding anniversary only a year before their accident. A fresh wave of grief flooded her body, and for a moment she was frozen to the spot while she waited for the pain to subside. When it did, she picked up the photograph and slid it into the drawer of the console.

Tilly inhaled a breath and continued on down the hallway towards the kitchen, heaving a sigh of relief when she entered the sun-filled room. Her sister had engaged her not insubstantial interior design skills here, too, but thankfully there were no polka dot teapots or forget-me-not plates on display. Instead, Olivia had chosen colours from a more Tuscanesque end of the colour spectrum, and had created a room thrumming with rustic charm, just like the building's exterior.

Unlike Tilly, who preferred to keep the culinary clutter to a minimum, hiding necessary appliances – apart from the coffee machine – in the cupboards and drawers, her sister chose to display hers proudly on every available surface… and looking around the room, she had *a lot* of kitchen appliances. Tilly knew all about Olivia's obsession with collecting a wide range of implements that could be used in her burgeoning culinary empire, not just those that could be useful, but also those which she thought were aesthetically pleasing.

Looking around, she saw the expected kettle, toaster, blender and coffee grinder, as well as several terracotta pots crammed with utensils such as whisks, spatulas, ladles, graters and corkscrews; there was even a set of old-fashioned scales with brass weights and a well-used pestle and mortar. But there was also a collection of more unusual gadgets, like egg-peelers and adjustable rolling pins, and, of course, a pasta machine with attachments in a see-through plastic box to create a myriad of different shapes.

Over to her right was a set of French doors, which lead out to the terrace that overlooked the swimming pool she had visited earlier, and to her left was a stripped oak door that piqued Tilly's curiosity. She turned the handle and found a well-ordered pantry, its floor-to-ceiling shelves sporting a myriad of brass canisters, each one labelled in her sister's neat handwriting; Assam, Ceylon, Oolong, as well as numerous pots containing dried herbs and spices. She had clearly found Olivia's tea apothecary, the place where her sister experimented with the wild and funky blends she would serve at her teashop.

Tilly scoured the shelves for coffee – withdrawal symptoms were setting in big time – but unsurprisingly she couldn't find any. Just as she was about to start panicking, she found one solitary sachet of instant coffee granules, which Olivia must have picked up from a hotel, and returned to the kitchen to boil the kettle, relief spreading through her veins as she sipped the dark, fragrant liquid like it was the elixir of life. She carried her mug to the upholstered window seat that was also home to a pile of her sister's favourite cosy mystery novels, and glanced out of the window.

If someone had asked her to describe what she thought Tuscany would look like, then this was it. Rolling hills clad in every shade of green imaginable, crowned by the village of San Vincente with its red higgledy-piggledy roofs and church tower with crenelated top, watched over by an infinite cerulean sky, now displaying wide bands of apricot, pink, and mauve as the sun finally merged with the horizon.

She reached for her phone, but before she could select the camera icon, it started to buzz.

'Hey Freya.'

'Hi, Tilly, how was the journey?'

Tilly laughed, tucking her feet under her bottom and settling in for a chat with her best friend. 'Well, the *flight* was okay.'

'But?'

'I had to do the final leg on a Vespa!'

Freya giggled. 'Really? I can't see you riding a Vespa! What happened to the hire car?'

'It's a long story, but I actually think Liv has done me a favour; the parking here is a nightmare. I don't suppose there's any news from Dexter?'

'Not yet. His business manager has contacted a couple of hotels and campsites along the trail and left messages for Dexter to ring him urgently, so hopefully we'll hear something soon, although there's no guarantee of that. Apparently, it a tradition for through-hikers to adopt a trail name, like "Braveheart" or "Stardust" or "Jazz" so who knows what Dexter has chosen. "Guitar Man" maybe? Oh, God, it could be weeks before he contacts anyone.'

'Have you thought any more about what you're going to do until you can reopen your aromatherapy salon?'

'I was hoping to focus on building up my stock of soaps and candles, but I don't know what I'm going to do when the raw materials run out, which will probably be long before the insurance money comes through. I lost three quarters of my stock in the fire, but I could handle that. It's the essential oils I lost that's the most devastating part; they cost a fortune, especially the agarwood, frangipani and rose oils.'

'Have you spoken to your parents?'

'Yes, but only briefly. They're in rural Ethiopia at the moment, so it's difficult to have a lengthy or in-depth conversation when the connection keeps getting cut.'

'What do they think you should do?'

There was a brief pause after Tilly's question.

'Frey?'

'They want me to go over to the south of France to sort out Uncle Toby's estate. They think if someone talks to the estate agent face-to-face, it might give him some impetus to start marketing the house more aggressively. If you ask me, I don't think meeting him will have any effect whatsoever; the guy's either lazy or incompetent. He hasn't shown anyone round the place for over three months now, and when I try to talk to him about it on the phone, he insists that he doesn't speak any English and asks me to speak in French. Last month I was so desperate to see some progress that I resorted to Google Translate and the next time we spoke I read out a speech I'd prepared and then translated – which was very embarrassing – asking him what the problem is, but he simply won't tell me. I mean, is it the price? Is it the location? Does the place have a woodworm infestation? Rats? Mice? A ghost?'

Freya sighed; the mounting frustration clear in her voice.

'I don't want to go to France. I need to be here in Devon to figure out how I'm going to earn a living so I can pay the rent until the beach huts are back up and running again.'

'I'm so sorry, Freya,' said Tilly, then a thought meandered into her head. 'I don't suppose...' She stopped. She knew Freya didn't like talking about her ex-fiancé, but it was a way she could keep her business afloat until her insurance money came through. 'I don't suppose you've spoken to Hugo, have you?'

'No, I haven't, and I don't intend to.'

'But he might be able to—'

'Hugo is ancient history, Tilly. I don't want anything to do with him, or his money. I'd rather go and stay with my parents in Ethiopia than contact Hugo after what he did.'

'Sorry, I just thought—'

'It's fine.' Freya paused. 'Talking of snakes, have you heard anything else from Josh?'

'Nothing since I told him I was coming to Italy. Oh Frey, you should see the villa. I'll send you some photographs; it's absolutely gorgeous, small, but perfectly formed, although the garden needs some attention.'

'Want a little piece of advice?'

Tilly wasn't sure she did, but she murmured her ascent.

'I think you should use the time while you're over there in fabulous Tuscany to resist the urge to fill every minute with some kind of high-octane activity, and carve out a few hours to contemplate everything that's happened in your life over the last two years. Find a place where you can relax, soak up the sunshine, and start to heal. It's time to move on, Tilly. Will you do that for me?'

'I'll try,' Tilly whispered, before saying goodbye.

As she climbed the stairs in search of the guest room, Tilly made a decision. She would do as her best friend had suggested; she would take the opportunity to work through the grief that held her in its clutches for far too long, and hopefully, when she returned home, she would be ready to make a fresh start.

# Chapter Seven

The next morning, Tilly woke to the first notes of the dawn chorus feeling more refreshed than she had done in months. She leapt out of bed, padded across the floor and flung back the shutters, her hand flying to her mouth in shock as one of the shutters came away from its moorings and tumbled onto the driveway below.

'Oh my God!'

She leaned out of the window, praying that Villa Avanti did not have an early morning visitor who was currently lying injured, or worse, squashed beneath the flying wooden plank. Satisfied that she wasn't going to spend the rest of the day sitting at some unfortunate person's hospital bedside, she hopped into the shower, rinsed away the final cobwebs of sleep and ran a dollop of coconut oil through her hair in the hope that she wouldn't look like she was experimenting with a new

candy-floss-esque hairstyle. She pulled on her black
jeans and a fresh black tee-shirt, then rushed down
the stairs to deal with the shutter incident.

\*\*\*

Thirty minutes, and several choice words later, she had
dragged the shutter round to the back of the house,
breaking two fingernails and sustaining a cut to her
ankle in the process. With perspiration bubbling at her
temples, she went in search of a much-needed caffeine
fix, only to realise that she had drank the last of the
coffee the night before. Sighing, she filled a glass with
tap water, spiced it up with a couple of ice cubes and a
handful of mint from the pot on the windowsill, and
took it out to the terrace; it certainly wasn't the delicious
Italian espresso she'd been hoping to enjoy on her first
morning in Tuscany.

It had been a surprisingly stressful start to the day,
but even though the sun had barely poked its nose
above the horizon, the air was warm, the sky was a
cloudless blue, and the bees and other insects had
already started to pursue their daily tasks
accompanied by the last strains of the birds'
symphonic overture.

Everywhere she looked, flowers, shrubs and
plants bobbed and bounced in the light breeze,
sending puffs of floral scent into the air as she
brushed past on her way to explore what was beyond
the overgrown pathways along the edge of the newly
installed swimming pool. Despite the horticultural

chaos, the garden held an undeniable beauty, a place of tranquillity and calm; the perfect environment to sit and relax, and maybe do a little of the contemplation Freya had spoken about.

She wanted to let her best friend know that she had taken on board what she had said, so she paused in her expedition to take a few photographs of the vibrant purple lavender that had trespassed across the cracked footpath, the random clumps of white geraniums that seemed to be growing wild, and the magnificent lemon tree, its branches heavy with fruit that made her tastebuds tingle.

Perhaps she could use some of the images she took in Tuscany to re-build her portfolio?

She had spoken to Jonti Farrington-Smythe before leaving Devon. He had been shocked to hear about the fire, and sympathetic about the necessary cancellation of her exhibition at his gallery in Sidmouth, promising to reschedule it for the end of August. Of course, fewer people would visit the seaside town at that time of year, but she was still grateful for the opportunity to showcase her work to a wider audience than those who visited Blossomwood Bay.

Tilly continued her meanderings until her progress was barred by a seriously overgrown rhododendron bush. She forced her way through its glossy leaves, receiving a few scratches on her forearms for her trouble, and arrived at a small, shady clearing where at least some of the foliage had been trimmed back to create an oasis amongst the botanical bedlam.

She was about to spin on her heels and return to the villa when she heard a rustle in one of the bushes to her right. Her heart gave a nip of concern, but she had to laugh when she saw a magpie launch from a branch above her head. However, a few moments later there was another, more determined rustle, the branches parted and a man emerged from within the leaves.

'Arrr…gh!' Tilly screamed.

'Arrr…gh!' screamed the stranger, echoing her shrieking rendition.

Tilly took a quick step backwards, her heart flaying her chest, but she noticed that the man – who was probably the same age as she was – looked even more terrified of her than she was of him, and she was the first of them to stop screaming.

'*Scusi! Scusi! Mi chiamo Eduardo, io lavoro qui.*'

'Sorry, I don't—'

'Ah, you are Natalia? You are Olivia's sister?'

'Yes, I am. I'm Tilly, and you are?'

'My name is Eduardo Armotti. I look after the garden and I've been helping Enzo with the villa's restoration work. Olivia told me you were coming to stay. It's good to meet you.'

Eduardo seized Tilly's hand and pumped it up and down enthusiastically – so enthusiastically, in fact, that he only released it when she started to whimper.

'*Scusi! Scusi!*'

'You're Liv's gardener?'

Tilly's Tuscan Teashop

She could hardly believe it; he looked like he was on his way to a wedding, or at least an important interview or business meeting. His jawline was clean-shaven, his short brown hair neatly barbered, and he was a member of the same "more-is-more" Cologne Club Matteo belonged to, although he favoured a more woody bouquet.

However, even more incongruously, he was wearing a beautifully pressed, and clearly expensive, pink linen shirt, cracked open at the neck to reveal a hint of chest hair, a pair of designer trousers that enhanced his physique to perfection, and pristine leather loafers – not the footwear she expected someone who worked as a gardener or in the construction industry to wear. In fact, Eduardo was catwalk-ready, with a comb poking from his pocket instead of a trowel or a screwdriver.

'*Si.*'

Tilly glanced at the woven bamboo basket hooked over Eduardo's arm, filled to the brim with a jumble of foliage and colourful flowers, and smiled.

'Are these for the villa?'

'No, these are the weeds I removed yesterday. I'm taking them to the compost heap that Olivia insisted I created to make organic fertiliser for the garden next year.'

Tilly looked more carefully at the bamboo basket. She was no expert as far as horticulture was concerned but her mum *had* been, and she knew that the "weeds" in Eduardo's basket were definitely not what he thought they were. In fact, she recognised at least one of the stems of delicate pink and white flowers that now sported browning petals after being denied water for the last twenty-four hours or more. She couldn't believe that orchids were so abundant in Tuscany that they were classed as weeds, but she could be wrong.

'Did you say that you helped Enzo with the renovations?'

'Yes, my father owns a building and landscape company.' Tilly saw a twist of something flit across Eduardo's face. 'My brother and I both work in the family business.'

'Do you know anything about shutters?'

'Shutters?'

Tilly pointed over her shoulder to the window above the Villa Avanti's front door that was now missing one of its green shutters.

'Ah, *persiane.* Yes, I hung those!'

She had no idea why there was a discernible hint of pride in Eduardo's voice when he could clearly see there was a problem; a problem that could have had very serious consequences.

'Do you think you could re-hang the shutter that fell off this morning?'

'*Sì, nessun problema.* I'll fetch my drill and do it straightaway.'

And before she could respond that there was no real urgency, Eduardo had marched from the clearing, his basket of "weeds" tucked under his arm, heading towards a small wooden shed at the other side of the swimming pool that she hadn't previously noticed. She followed in his wake, until he stopped abruptly in his tracks and she slammed into the back of him, exhaling a loud *humph!*

'What's the matter?'

'*Ape.*'

'A what?'

'A bee.'

'Okay…?'

'I don't like bees, or beetles, or butterflies, or any kind of insect, actually.'

Eduardo gave an involuntary shudder as he continued to stare at the lone bee who was nonchalantly going about her business of collecting her daily quota of nectar, totally oblivious to their presence in her domain, let alone preparing to launch a stinging attack.

Tilly's lips twitched. She couldn't believe what Eduardo was saying.

'But you're a gardener! You must come into contact with all kinds of insects, reptiles, and animals every single day. If you hate them so much, why didn't you train to do something else?'

She knew immediately that she had hit a nerve and she regretted the words she had spoken in jest. Eduardo's previously cheery demeanour changed, and his eyes took on a guarded expression, but he didn't offer an explanation or say anything further. When the bee flew onto another flower, Eduardo took his chance to make a swift getaway and all-but sprinted towards the little wooden shed where he kept his tools.

Tilly rushed to catch up with him. 'I'm sorry, Eduardo, I didn't mean to—'

'It's no problem. Please show me where you stored the shutter and I'll get to work.'

Tilly pointed to where she had hidden the green shutter and said, 'Can I get you a drink?'

Back was the cheerful smile. 'Yes, please, an espresso would be fantastic.'

Tilly cringed. She couldn't believe what she was about to say to an Italian.

'I'm afraid we don't have any coffee.'

'No coffee?' Eduardo gaped at her in astonishment.

'I can offer you a cup of tea?'

'A cup of tea?'

Tilly saw his astonishment morph into horror at her crazy suggestion, and, thankfully, she was saved from any further embarrassment by the sound of her phone ringing. 'Sorry, Eduardo, do you mind if I get this? It's Olivia.'

'Of course not.'

She left Eduardo to his carpentry and sauntered around to the other side of the swimming pool.

'Hi, Liv. Before you say anything, please tell me you have some coffee stashed away somewhere. Eduardo is here and he looked at me as though I had sprouted horns when I informed him that we didn't have any coffee in the house.'

'There's some Blue Mountain in the cupboard under the sink. Sorry, I should have told you before. I bought it for you when you said you were coming over; I know how much you love your coffee. By the way, I need to warn you about Eduardo.'

Tilly laughed. 'It's a bit late for that.'

'Oh God, what's he done now?'

'I take it you didn't want those gorgeous orchids with the pink and white petals?'

Olivia groaned. 'Of course I did; I adore them! I've told Roberto – Eduardo's father – lots of times that I don't want him "helping" with the gardening after he completely desecrated an orange blossom tree that Enzo and I planted the first spring we arrived. He's fine with the pool maintenance, though, and his plumbing and joinery skills are okay.'

'Does that include hanging shutters?'

'Why?'

But before Tilly could reply, there was a loud crash from the front of the house.

'What was that?' asked Olivia, a hint of panic in her voice.

'I'm not sure. I'd better go and investigate. I'll call you later, Liv. Love you.'

'To the moon and back, Tills,' said Olivia.

# Chapter Eight

After asking Eduardo to leave the shutter repair until Enzo returned from Boston, she left him to continue vandalising the garden, jumped onto her Vespa, and headed for the teashop. As she navigated the twists and turns of the road to San Vincente, the sun on her face, the breeze in her hair, the aroma of warm Tuscan soil caressing her nostrils, she felt all the stress of her early morning encounter with Eduardo seep from her body.

She couldn't deny it; the place her sister had decided to make her home was truly spectacular and no matter which direction she looked, her passion for the visual arts was reaffirmed. The light in Tuscany seemed to possess a sepia-like quality that washed everything in a soft golden glow, and she realised that there was no way she could insult such beauty by photographing the architecture and landscape in the medium of black-and-white.

'Hey Tilly, you're early; the tour group isn't due until two.'

'Well, I thought I'd come over to help with the sandwiches.'

'Oh, Carlotta and I have already made them.' Jess smiled as she tucked her pigtails – that day's ribbons a deep sapphire colour to match her puff-sleeved tee-shirt – behind her ears. '*And* the chocolate and chilli scones, *and* the mini chocolate roulades, mini chocolate tarts and mini white chocolate cheesecakes. Livvie also created a special tea made with hand-roasted cocoa shells to go with it, so everything is sorted. Why don't you grab a seat at the table in the window and I'll bring you a pot of Earl Grey over.'

Tilly groaned inwardly; she really didn't want to have to consume a whole teapot of tea under the close scrutiny of Jess – especially after she'd overheard Matteo's comments about her dislike of the beverage – so she cast around for a diversion. Thankfully, her gaze landed on the ice cream shop she'd passed the previous day, and whilst she wasn't a lover of anything cake-related, she didn't mind indulging in the occasional artisan ice cream.

'Actually, why don't I treat us both to an ice cream?'

'Gosh, you'd better not let Gabriella hear you describing her gelato as ice cream.'

'Why not?'

'Because gelato is not the same thing as ice cream.'

'It isn't?'

'No, it's made with less cream and has a softer, silker texture than ice cream. Actually, one of Gabriella's gelatos would be perfect for brunch because I'm on the Desserts Diet today.'

'What's the Desserts Diet?'

'It's where I get to eat desserts all day; cakes, puddings, tarts, flans, cantuccini, ricciarelli, and gelato! Come on, I'll introduce you to Gabriella. I think you two are going to get on like a house on fire.'

Jess called something in fluent Italian to Carlotta, removed her pale-blue apron with *Té e Torta* embroidered in curly white letters on the front, along with a teapot and a cupcake, and steered Tilly from the teashop. It was only ten o'clock, but already the piazza was teeming with residents and tourists alike, many of whom had snagged a table outside *Ristorante Rocco* and were enjoying a cup of rich, fragrant espresso or frothy cappuccino.

Tilly closed her eyes for a moment to better appreciate the aroma of freshly ground coffee that floated in the air, and she briefly contemplated suggesting to Jess that they amend their destination, but thought better of it. She'd already offended Jess once, she didn't want to do it again by frequenting the establishment where the locals probably preferred to take their early morning constitutional beverage rather than the teashop.

'*Buongiorno*, Jess!'

'*Buongiorno*, Gabriella.'

A woman with chin-length mahogany curls and soft brown eyes filled with kindness stepped from behind a huge, refrigerated counter to drop kisses on Jess's proffered cheeks. A diamond ring dangled from a gold chain around her neck, which spoke of a story Tilly hoped to hear one day. She felt drawn to Gabriella, as though they'd been friends in a former life, a feeling that was magnified when a white Bichon Frise emerged from the room at the rear of the shop to see what all the fuss was about.

'Gabriella, this is Tilly, Livvie's sister. She's helping us out at the teashop while Livvie's away visiting Enzo's family in Boston. Tilly, this is Gabriella Fontana, and this cute little chap is Sandro.'

Jess knelt down on the spotless marble floor, her silver bangles jangling as she greeted Sandro with enthusiasm and a stream of unintelligible doggie chatter, receiving a lick of appreciation for her efforts.

'Hi, Tilly, it's good to meet you,' said Gabriella, in a lilting Italian accent that caused Tilly to smile and decide that while she was in Tuscany, she would make a concerted effort to learn at least some Italian phrases beyond "please", "thank you" and "I'm sorry, I don't understand". 'Would you like to try one of my hand-crafted gelatos?'

'I'd love to.'

'What flavour would you like?'

Tilly peered into the huge glass cabinet where there were over twenty different flavours of gelato; from the standard vanilla, strawberry and chocolate, to the more unusual – to Tilly, at least – tiramisu, nocciola and castagna.

'I'm not sure, what do you recommend?'

Gabriella took a small wooden spatula from a box, scooped a sample of pale-yellow gelato from one of the tubs, and handed it over to Tilly.

'I think you might like this; it's limoncello flavour.'

As soon as Tilly wrapped her tongue around the tiny wooden spoon, a sharp, citrusy flavour swept through her mouth causing her tastebuds to zing with pleasure.

'Wow! The lemon is so fresh and intense.'

'That's because gelato is served at a slightly warmer temperature than ice cream, which means you taste the flavours more intensely. It's partly due to the fact that our tongues aren't as numb from the cold, but also because our tastebuds are more sensitive to warmer foods, especially sweet things. Now try this one.'

Gabriella took a scoop of a caramel-coloured gelato and handed it to Tilly.

'Mmm, that's delicious. Can I taste ginger?'

'You can; it's ginger and melon. And this is one I've been experimenting with for the last few weeks, but I'm not sure I've got the balance of the ingredients right yet.'

Gabriella selected two new spoons, handed one each to Tilly and Jess, then strode to a separate refrigerator that was crammed with a myriad of colourful, transparent plastic boxes and removed a smaller tub of gelato, this one a bright red colour dotted with speckles of green.

'What flavour is this?' asked Jess, a little wary of digging in her spoon.

'Tomato and basil.'

Jess wrinkled her nose – obviously it violated that day's Desserts Diet regime – but Tilly had no such qualms; tomato and basil gelato sounded right up her street. She scrapped her spoon across the surface of the gelato and popped it into her mouth, surprised at the rich, sweet, tomatoey taste that was definitely enhanced by the addition of finely chopped basil leaves.

'I love it, it's my favourite so far!'

'Thank you, Tilly.' Gabriella beamed, her cheeks colouring slightly. 'Okay, enough of the sampling, what can I get you?'

'I'd love a *noce*,' said Tilly, pointing to the gelato with a picture of a walnut.

'And you, Jess?'

'Pistachio for me, please.'

Gabriella filled two cups with the requested gelato and suggested they enjoy them on the patio outside, overlooking the piazza and the village's clock tower. Tilly thanked her and followed Jess from the gelateria where they found a vacant table in the shade and dug in.

'Oh my God, not again!' cried Jess, grimacing.

'What's the matter?'

'This isn't pistachio, it's kiwi. I hate kiwi, it's gross!'

Tilly couldn't help smiling at her reaction. Jess had the grace to grin too, and any remaining tension between them from Matteo's uninvited revelation of Tilly's views on tea and cake evaporated.

# Tilly's Tuscan Teashop

'Gabriella's eyesight is dreadful; she's always serving people with the wrong flavours, but she refuses to wear glasses. She says they made her look like her ninety-year-old *nonna*, and she's adamant she's not "putting those awful plastic discs" in her eyes. Sometimes, she makes mistakes when she's experimenting with new flavours, which is why I thought you were particularly brave for trying her ginger and melon gelato – brown gelato is never a good idea!' Jess giggled. 'Once she added white pepper to a mix instead of cinnamon – she got lots of complaints about that one – but usually her mix-ups are happy accidents, like her beetroot and toffee flavour.'

'Beetroot and toffee?'

'I know, it sounds disgusting, doesn't it? But it's one of my favourites, especially when I'm on my Red Diet.'

'Want to swap? I love kiwi fruit.'

'Are you sure?'

Tilly pushed her walnut-flavoured gelato towards Jess and, as her new friend scooped up a generous mouthful, she noticed that day's manicure for the first time; one featuring a whole orchestra of musical instruments – drums, guitars, tambourines, there was even a tiny trumpet on her little finger.

'I love your manicure, Jess. Did you do it yourself?'

'Yes, I did. I ran out of money when I was travelling in Thailand at the end of last year, so I took a job in a nail bar in Koh Samui and I've done my own nails ever since.' To Tilly's mortification, Jess glanced across at her own fingernails, chewed down to the quick after everything that had happened over the last week. 'Would you like me to do yours?'

'Erm, no thanks, I'm fine.'

'Okay, I'd better get back to the teashop. There's no rush, stay and enjoy your gelato.'

Tilly watched Jess saunter from the piazza, then relaxed into her chair and turned her face towards the sunshine. She inhaled a slow breath, her caffeine-loving demons immediately poking their heads above the parapet like rapacious meerkats when they realised the air was infused with the intoxicating aroma of freshly ground coffee emanating *Ristorante Rocco*. She checked to make sure that Jess was safely inside the teashop, and all-but sprinted across the piazza, slid into the first seat she came to, and ordered a double espresso from the waitress whose badge informed her was called Stefania.

When her coffee arrived, she took a tentative sip and had never tasted such sweet elixir in her life. Unlike the espresso she made for herself at home, this was the real deal, made with single-origin arabica beans, which, as a coffee afficionado, she knew were from the slopes of Mount Kilamcé in Nicaragua. She could immediately feel the extra-strength caffeine kickstart her energy levels, and she exhaled a long sigh of satisfaction.

She took another sip, then glanced over to the table next to her and had to do a double-take when she saw the glamorous couple were busy taking photographs of their meal from every angle possible. However, when she saw the exquisite presentation of the food on their wide-rimmed china plates, she understood completely; the meal was a miniature work of art, almost too good to eat, and the couple who had ordered it clearly agreed.

'Would you like another espresso?' asked Stefania, appearing at her table as if by magic.

'No, thank you, but could I ask, what exactly is that dish?'

She indicated the table next to her where the couple were now, almost reverently, eating their lunch, uttering superlatives with every mouthful they consumed.

'That is foie gras parfait in a vessel of baked lemon peel, with a pea shoot salad dressed with carrot caviar and balsamic pearls, served with charcoal crackers.'

'What are balsamic pearls?'

'They're small spheres of balsamic vinegar mixed with agar-agar and very cold olive oil to form pearls, which are then used to garnish our *amuse bouche* or hors d'oeuvres,' said Stefania, with more than a hint of pride in her voice. 'Senor Bianchi believes that these pearls provide an elevated aesthetic, as well as allowing the diner to experience a more concentrated burst of flavour.'

'And the carrot caviar?'

'It's made with pureed carrot, smoked paprika, cumin, garlic and a twist of lemon. My recommendation today is the arugula spaghetti; it's pure poetry on the tongue. Senor Bianchi is not a chef, he's a culinary alchemist, renowned for his innovative techniques using chemistry and physics to experiment with texture and taste. His gastronomy attracts diners from all over Tuscany, if not the whole of Italy, and I can assure you that every plate that leaves the *Ristorante Rocco* kitchen is a masterpiece in its own right. Would you like to see the menu?'

Tilly thought of how much it would cost her to enjoy a piece of such culinary artistry and panicked.

'Not at the moment, thank you, I...'

To her relief, an elderly diner in an Armani dinner jacket chose that moment to call for his check and Stefania abandoned Tilly to ensure that his meal had met, and hopefully surpassed, his expectations. How could it not? The experience was akin to a visit to one of the world-famous art galleries in Florence except better because here at *Ristorante Rocco* you got to *eat* the exquisite artwork in front of you!

As she didn't want to bother Stefania with the task of sorting out her bill for a single espresso, she wandered into the restaurant, unsurprised to see that every table inside was also occupied by people who were dressed for the occasion – a few of the women were even wearing hats. An image of Freya floated across her mind and she smiled when she recalled her often-quoted assertion that you could really judge the calibre of an establishment by the quality of their restrooms so she headed to the rear of the ristorante to investigate.

She didn't know what she had expected, but she found herself in a room that wouldn't have looked out of place in an Italian palazzo. From the gold-embossed wallpaper to the gilt-framed mirrors and watercolours of local landscapes, from the fluffy cotton hand towels embroidered with the *RR* emblem to the myriad of designer toiletries; it was like a mini-spa experience.

While she would have loved to have stayed there to enjoy the gardenia-perfumed ambiance, she knew that was a ridiculous notion, so she left quickly, pausing when she heard raised voices from the room at the end of the hallway.

'You idiot, I said poached nectarine with *rainbow* foam! What is this miserable grey drizzle? It looks like a wet weekend in the Dolomites!'

'Sorry, Chef.'

'I'm surrounded by incompetents! Total imbeciles who can't follow the simplest of instructions, let alone have any discernible talent. I want perfection, not lacklustre offerings. Do you think *this* is perfection? Do you think this dessert is good enough to be served to our esteemed customers, some of whom have travelled from Milan to be here today?'

Tilly gaped at the man in the white chef's jacket whom she assumed was Rocco Bianchi. Unexpectedly handsome, with bouffant salt-and-pepper hair and muscular upper arms, he certainly looked every inch the celebrity chef, and now it seemed he had the fiery personality to match. When she had seen that sort of behaviour on TV shows, she had thought it was exaggerated for the benefit of the cameras and viewer entertainment, but it seemed not.

Rocco's dark eyes flashed with anger at the hapless English sous chef who had presented him with the substandard dish, and he was now waving his arms in the air, sending scatter-gun invectives in Italian towards the rest of his staff, too. To Tilly's surprise, none of them seemed particularly upset by his outburst, and she realised with relief that they had seen it many times before and had learned to take it in their stride. She was about to creep away when, to her horror, she heard Rocco's voice boom down the hallway.

'Who are you?'

She froze like a deer caught in the headlights. Surely he couldn't mean her? But who else was there loitering outside the kitchen door, enjoying a ringside seat at Rocco Bianchi's culinary soap opera?

'I'm Tilly.'

She groaned inwardly. Why hadn't she left when she had the chance?

'Tilly who?'

Rocco strode from the kitchen, and if she hadn't been so terrified, she would have smiled at the palpable sigh of relief that emanating from his team when he exited his lair and they could get on with creating "perfection".

'Tilly Nicholson. My sister's Olivia Molinari.'

Why on earth had she said that? Oh God!

'Olivia Molinari?'

She could almost see the cogs working in Rocco's brain, his eyes narrowed, and then a smirk appeared on his lips. She caught a whiff of his heavy cologne and despite his rather turbulent personality, she had to accept that he gave off a very charismatic vibe.

'You mean the woman who runs the English teashop?'

# Tilly's Tuscan Teashop

The word "English" was enunciated with a derisory sneer, and Rocco Bianchi wrinkled his nose with distaste, as though someone had presented him with a fast-food burger instead of a one of the famous Bistecca Fiorentina. She really wanted to run away, but something kept her there, rooted to the spot.

'Yes, I'm helping out at *Té e Torta* for a few weeks.'

There was a pause.

'Are you a chef?'

'No, I'm a photographer.'

Rocco rolled his eyes. 'So I take it you'll be continuing to serve up a variety of soggy pastries and stodgy puddings with names like jam roly-poly and spotted Dick?'

'No, I don't think we serve—'

'That teashop makes a mockery of San Vincente's hopes of becoming the food capital of Tuscany. I've spoken with your sister on a number of occasions. I've asked her to reconsider her choice of cuisine for the sake of the village, but she refuses. I would have thought her failure to be recognised in the fiesta contests for two years in a row would have proved to her that she needs to think again about "bringing a taste of British baking to Italy".' Rocco flung his hands in the air. 'Here, food is art; it's drama, it's entertainment. *Ristorante Rocco* is an operatic aria, *Té e Torta* is an end-of-term kindergarten concert. I mean, who drinks tea in Italy?'

To Tilly's surprise, a wave of indignation reared into her chest.

How dare he say these things to her about her sister's teashop?

'Well, we'll have to see who wins the contest this year, won't we?'

'You're entering? I thought you said you were a photographer?'

'I am, but baking is in my DNA.'

'I have a Cordon Bleu-trained pastry chef! You're delusional if you think that you can compete with my team, but you don't have to take my word for it. I have it on good authority that the celebrated food critic Victor Vitali will be gracing our village with his presence sometime during the next two weeks. He is a man of *exquisite* taste, the epitome of gastronomic discernment, who has enjoyed the creations of some of the best chefs in Italy, and his visit will put our village firmly on the foodie trail. I doubt he'll want to frequent your sister's establishment if he wants to avoid clogging up his arteries! *Buongiorno, signorina.*'

Before Tilly could respond, Rocco strode back to the epicentre of his empire where she heard him shoot off a barrage of new instructions to his minions who scattered in every direction to do his bidding. She had only been in his presence for a couple of minutes, but she felt exhausted, and she had no idea how Stefania and her colleagues must feel at the end of a busy shift.

As she made her way out of the restaurant and towards the teashop in time for the arrival of the yoga retreat guests, she sighed. It seemed she had inadvertently confirmed their entry into the village's annual food competition.

# Tilly's Tuscan Teashop

Curiously, she didn't feel regretful. She felt energised and up for the challenge.

Perhaps this was a way she could repay her sister for all the support she'd given her over the last two years. She knew they wouldn't win, but that wasn't the point. It was the taking part that mattered, the showcasing of the teashop's artisan teas and delectable scones and cakes to a wider audience, although the irony of Rocco's question about the Italian's not drinking tea wasn't lost on her.

Hadn't she said exactly the same thing?

# Chapter Nine

'What can I do to help?' asked Tilly, securing the strings of her *Té e Torta* apron around her waist, keen to keep busy to prevent memories of working at the Orange Blossom Café from crowding into her brain and overwhelming her.

'Could you arrange these sandwiches on the cake stands, please?' said Jess, who had just removed a tray of scones from the oven, the aroma of sweet, warm pastry infiltrating the air as she placed them on the wire rack to cool. 'Then we need to fill these little pots with cream and Livvie's home-made strawberry jam.'

Tilly set to work, taking care to follow exactly what Jess and Carlotta were doing so that her cake stands looked just like theirs. First, a selection of crustless sandwiches cut into neat triangles were placed on the bottom tier – egg and cress, local cheese, smoked salmon, cucumber – then, the freshly baked scones went on the next tier with the pots of clotted cream and jam, and finally, the top tier was crowned with a medley of miniature chocolate cakes. They then placed two cake stands on each of the polka-dot-bedecked tables.

'They do look pretty,' said Tilly, standing back to survey the teashop now that it was ready to welcome its guests. 'I think I'll take a few photographs to send to Liv, just to reassure her that we've got everything in hand.'

'Oh, we're not finished yet,' said Jess, reaching up to remove several spotty teapots from the top shelf of the dresser. 'Every table gets a milk jug and sugar basin, and we offer each of our customers their own choice of tea, which we make fresh every time, with as many refills as they want.'

Tilly glanced at the chalkboard; there were three columns and over twenty different teas listed there, most of which she recognised from hearing her sister talk about them during their regular telephone and video calls over the years. However, there were some teas in the third column that she hadn't heard of, like honeybush tea, moringa tea and ashwagandha tea, and she realised that Olivia had been busy expanding her product range to appeal to as many customers as possible.

Her sister was proud of her occupation, often explaining to people who asked that being a tea sommelier was akin to being a wine sommelier in that both are experts in their respective fields, and both understand the importance of colour, taste, aroma and appearance. However, unlike a wine sommelier who curates a wine list and advises a diner on an appropriate pairing with the food on a menu, a tea sommelier's job is much more diverse and includes not only sourcing, but blending and then actually *creating* the particular tea.

Having trained in and visited many of the most fervent tea-drinking countries in the world, Olivia was *very* particular about the tea-making process, following the same strictly observed steps with every pot of tea she made, no matter how ordinary. Making tea, she said, was a serious business; the water had to be just the right temperature, the leaves steeped for the correct period of time – white and green required less brewing time than the darker black and oolong teas – even the shape and composition of the cup was important.

'Okay, are we ready, girls?' said Jess, when she'd placed the last of the teapots on the kitchen bench, ready to be pressed into service.

Tilly and Carlotta nodded in unison and within moments the bell above the door jangled and the teashop was invaded by a group of women – every one of them sporting beautiful summer dresses, from floor-length to buttock-skimming, and a pair of sparkly sandals – their hair beautifully coiffed, their make-up perfectly applied, and smelling like they'd spent the morning at a perfumery.

\*\*\*

For the next two hours, Tilly dashed around the room refilling the cake stands with sandwiches, replenishing the teapots, and talking about the various teas that were available. A low hum of conversation swirled around the room, interspersed with the occasional staccato of laughter, and accompanied on percussion by the clink of teaspoons in china saucers and the tinkle of Jess's silver bangles.

Tilly learned from Sophie, the person who had organised the trip that day, that they were all members of their local gym in Oxford who had signed up for a week-long yoga retreat at a stunningly beautiful farmhouse on the outskirts of Lucca where they were expected to adhere to a raw vegan diet and drink only water or vegetable smoothies. Apparently, they'd managed only two days before deciding to "play hooky" on the pretext of visiting the Uffizi Gallery.

'I enjoyed my Lady Grey tea, but I'd really like to try something a little different,' said Sophie, popping a miniature Victoria sponge cake topped with edible flowers into her mouth. 'What do you recommend?'

'Well, there's lavender tea, which is said to be good for relaxation,' said Jess, pointing to the list of teas in the right-hand column of the chalkboard. 'We have osmanthus tea, which has a delicate peach flavour and is said to help fight allergies, and we often recommend yerba mate tea to aid digestion after a meal.'

'What's ashwagandha tea?' asked the woman wearing the skimpiest of playsuits in a pretty rosebud-patterned fabric. She was the youngest of the group and looked like she visited their yoga studio every day.

'Oh yes, that's one of our most popular blends.'

'Really? Why?'

Jess smiled. 'Because it's said to have aphrodisiac qualities.'

'I'm having that!' exclaimed a dark-haired woman, before realising how loud she'd responded. She giggled and then wriggled her eyebrows. 'I'll let you know tomorrow if it works. Hey, you should do a themed afternoon tea where you pair that tea with avocado sandwiches, soft gooey fig scones and chocolate-smothered strawberries; all those things are supposed to be aphrodisiacs, too.'

'That sounds like fun!' Sophie laughed, her eyes sparkling. 'You'll have queues out the door and around the block for that!'

The atmosphere in the teashop ratcheted up a notch as the group of friends excitedly ordered their choice of tea from the third column on the chalkboard – mostly the ashwagandha blend – and waited impatiently for the time it took to brew, then taste-test it, with lots of laughter, merriment and cheeky comments about ordering an industrial supply when they returned home.

***

Another hour later, all of the sandwiches, scones and cakes had vanished and the teapots had been drained of their contents. With a profusion of thank yous and promises to leave five-star reviews, the yoga group left the teashop to head to the next venue on their itinerary – a local vineyard for a wine-tasting tour, alcohol being another illicit item on the menu at the yoga retreat.

With a sigh of relief, Jess turned the sign on the door to "*Chiuso*" and dropped down into one of the chairs, her chin cupped in her hand, her cheeks glowing, and the ribbons in her previously neat pigtails hanging loose around her shoulders.

'You look exhausted, Jess, and you, too, Carlotta. Why don't you leave the clearing up to me? It's the least I can do after you've been here since first thing this morning preparing the food.'

'Are you sure?'

'Absolutely. Off you go, I'll see you tomorrow. Oh, and I forgot to tell you, I… I bumped into Rocco Bianchi earlier and… well, I told him we were definitely taking part in the San Vincente foodie competition this year, so maybe you can think about what we're going to enter. I'll talk to Liv, too.'

'Really? Are you serious?' Jess's green eyes shined.

'Yes, I'm serious.'

'Oh, Tilly, that's fabulous, absolutely fabulous!' Jess flung her arm around Tilly and hugged her tightly, then, in case Tilly had an immediate change of heart, she whipped off her apron, grabbed Carlotta's arm, and headed for the door where she paused to call over her shoulder, 'And we don't have any more groups booked in for afternoon teas until a group of gardening enthusiasts from York on Saturday, so I'll see you then. *Ciao.*'

# Tilly's Tuscan Teashop

'*Ciao.*'

Tilly exhaled a long breath and surveyed the room. It looked like a herd of wildebeest had been let loose and gone on the rampage, and she was already questioning the wisdom of her offer to sort it out by herself. She pushed herself from her chair and made her way to the kitchen to collect a tray to start clearing the crockery from the tables, surprised to see a rose-rimmed cake stand that for some reason hadn't been taken out to the teashop and still sported a collection of sandwiches, scones, and tiny cakes.

She had an idea.

She carried the tiered cake stand back into the teashop, placed it on the pretty powder-blue dresser, surrounded it with a polka dot teapot and lots of cups and saucers, and stood back to take a few photographs to send to Olivia when she reported that the first of the *Té e Torta* afternoon teas she had helped with had gone swimmingly.

As she wasn't accustomed to photographing food, she spent a minute or two arranging the tableau, taking a few shots, checking them, tweaking the cups, and taking the shots again until she was satisfied, then, out of habit, she selected the black-and-white filter on her phone.

She was just about to compose her text to Olivia when she heard the tumble of the teashop's brass bell. She spun round to see Matteo standing in the doorway, a brown paper parcel tucked under his arm, looking extraordinarily handsome in a pair of buttock-hugging black jeans and a pale lemon shirt, his long curls flopping into his eyes. When he spoke in his very sexy Italian accent, a surprise ripple of attraction rotated through her veins.

'Is Carlotta around?'

'No, I'm sorry, she's left for the day. I said I'd do the clearing up.'

'Why would you do that?'

Tilly cringed, but she knew she had to come clean. 'Because I work here.'

The cute dimples appeared around Matteo's mouth as he smirked. 'You work in a teashop?'

'Actually, this is my sister's teashop.'

'Olivia Molinari is your sister?'

'Yes, I'm helping out while she's visiting family in America.' Tilly cast around for a change of subject before Matteo could remind her about her declaration within minutes of meeting him that she loathed both tea and cake, and her gaze fell on his parcel. 'Is that for Carlotta?'

'Oh, erm, yes, I'll just...'

Matteo disappeared into the kitchen and Tilly heard the door of the fridge being opened then slammed shut before he returned to the teashop, looking relieved, which Tilly thought was a little strange.

'What was in the parcel?' she asked, worried that it was some kind of contraband.

'It's just some local cheese,' he said, rather dismissively, then indicated the dresser where she'd arranged the crockery for the photographic montage she was intending to send to Olivia. 'What are you doing here? Some kind of ad campaign?'

'Oh, no, I'm just taking a few photographs to send to Olivia.'

'Mind if I take a look?'

She stared at him for a beat, then handed over her phone.

'Mmm,' Matteo murmured as he scrolled through the images.

'What's wrong with them?'

'Well, they're black and white for a start!'

'So?'

'Have you done any food photography before?'

'No, I haven't. I tend to stick to landscapes, and the occasional pet portrait for the owners of my friend Holly's canine clients. She's a dog groomer,' she added unnecessarily.

'I could give you a few tips, if you like.'

'Okay…' said Tilly.

Matteo scooted in close to point to one of the black and white images she'd taken, gifting her with a waft of his delicious mint-scented cologne.

'When it comes to photographing food, styling is key. There's too much going on here, the eye doesn't know where to look first, so we need to remove these spotty teapots, and these flowery tea cups, and concentrate only on the cake stand and the gorgeous food on it. Lighting is next; if we're not careful, shadows can look like mould, especially when photographed in black and white, which is a no-no when we're dealing with food, so we need to use natural light where possible to bring out the colours and textures.'

To Tilly's surprise, Matteo jumped onto a chair and began taking photographs of the cake stand from several angles, crouching down low, leaning to his left and right, then standing on his tiptoes to photograph it from above. The chair wobbled precariously and Matteo performed a comedic balancing dance with his arms outstretched, his hips swinging from side to side like some kind of perilous disco move.

'Oh my God, be careful,' Tilly cried, rushing to steady the chair but instead, in her haste, grabbing hold of Matteo's surprisingly firm calf causing him to tumble forward and crash into her arms.

For a moment, it seemed to Tilly as though time stood still while they stared into each other's eyes, lips mere inches apart, trying to understand what had just happened, then they both shot backwards simultaneously. To her surprise she was unusually flustered, her heart hammering a concerto of confusion against her ribcage, her breath coming in spurts and she could feel heat spreading into her cheeks. There was something about Matteo, something beyond the sexy Italian vibe he projected and his nostril-tingling cologne, something smouldering deep in his soul that drew her to him like an invisible thread.

Fortunately, Matteo managed to collect his thoughts first and continued with his lesson in the visual arts as though nothing had happened, although she could detect a slight waver in his voice, evidence that he was just as surprised about what had passed between them as she was.

'Food photography is different to other types of photography in that the subject matter can change a great deal during the shoot. Take gelato, for instance, it melts quickly, so instead, food photographers use mashed potato.'

'Mashed potato? Really?'

'It works surprisingly well, with a little food dye added for the different flavours. And tooth picks are used to hold sandwiches together, and hairspray is used to give certain foods a shine, and believe it or not, white glue is used on cereal instead of milk.'

'You know a lot about this,' said Tilly, her suspicion radar suddenly twanging. 'Are you a photographer, too?'

'No, I'm not a photographer,' Matteo said as he returned her phone so she could look at the images he'd taken which, as she suspected, were so much better than hers, although in her defence, this was her first attempt. 'I simply appreciate good food in all its guises, and I know how important it is to present it in the best way possible. In Italy, we enjoy our food, it's our passion, and it's about more than just sating the appetite; it's about friendship, it's about family, it's about love.'

Matteo averted his eyes, and turned his back on Tilly, but not before she'd seen a surprise streak of pain flash across his face. She wanted to ask him about it, to offer a listening ear, but when he turned back round, his smile had returned and she wondered whether she might have imagined it.

'So, are you going to send these photographs to your sister?'

'Of course.' She smiled, composing a quick text. 'In fact, I'd like to upload a few to my Instagram account, if you don't mind.'

'No problem.' Matteo grinned. 'As long as they're not in black and white.'

# Chapter Ten

When Tilly arrived back at the villa, every single muscle in her body ached and she had to accept that it was time to do something about her fitness levels. Since moving from London to Devon, she had let her gym membership lapse and whilst she had repeatedly promised Freya she would join her on her regular early morning beach jogs, she hadn't got round to it yet and now she was paying the price.

She wheeled the Vespa into the shade of an umbrella tree and glanced up at the missing shutter, a part of her surprised that the rest of the house was still standing. Thankfully, there was no sign of Eduardo, whom she assumed had finished his tasks for the day, and when she walked through the side gate and caught sight of the glistening aquamarine of the pool, she decided that after the day she'd had, she deserved to enjoy her first swim;

the fact that she hadn't brought a bikini with her wasn't going to stop her.

She kicked off her shoes, peeled off her tee-shirt and jeans, and before she could change her mind, dived into the deep end, relishing the feel of the cool water sliding over her skin. After completing a few lengths, she paused to catch her breath, resting her arms on the side of the pool as she took in the panoramic view spread out before her; the gently undulating hills cloaked in a tapestry of greenery and embroidered with cypress trees, olive groves and vineyards, the fields filled with vibrant poppies bobbing about in the early evening breeze, and the terracotta-roofed village of San Vincente crouched beneath an arched cerulean sky.

For the first time, she truly understood why her sister had agreed to pack up her life in the UK and relocate to this picturesque corner of the world. Thinking of Olivia reminded Tilly that she had promised to call her, so she pulled herself from the pool, collected her clothes, and padded barefoot into the villa. She changed quickly into dry clothes, grabbed a glass of iced lemonade, and found a shady spot on the terrace.

'Hi, Liv, how's Boston?'

'Oh, Tilly, it's a beautiful city, with lots of museums and art galleries and parks; there's even a zoo! Yesterday we did the Freedom Trail, which starts on the famous Boston Common and meanders past wonderful shops, houses and churches that we spent hours exploring before stopping off for dinner. But the best part of being here is spending quality time with Enzo's family.'

'How's his mum?'

'She's doing great. Her hip's healing well, and she's managing to get around a little more every day. She's obviously delighted to see Enzo, and so is his sister, and her husband, Giovanni. In fact, Giovanni has roped Enzo into helping him to finish off the summerhouse he started last summer, and they're both loving getting their hands dirty, and then partaking in a few beers as a reward for all their hard work.'

'And what about you?'

'I'm having a ball! I've been having fun in Daniella's *huge* kitchen, learning lots of traditional Italian recipes from Enzo's mum – along with quite a few New England ones, too, like the classic Boston Cream pie, but also the blueberry buckle, apple cider donuts, and Daniella has a great recipe for pumpkin-walnut bread, which is delicious. And guess what?'

Tilly smiled. 'What?'

'We're planning a trip to New York next weekend! How exciting is that? We're going to do all the tourist things like visit Ellis Island and the Statue of Liberty, and we've got tickets for a Broadway show. Remember when Mum and Dad went for their twentieth wedding anniversary? How much Mum enjoyed seeing the view from the top of the Empire State Building, but Dad said he was terrified the whole time?'

Tilly experienced the sharp flash of pain that always happened when Olivia mentioned their parents, but it didn't last as long as it usually did because her sister was forging ahead with her excited chatter.

'And Enzo has promised to take me for a meal at Serafina and then a romantic carriage ride through Central Park. I can't wait! Anyway, enough about me, how's the teashop? Did the yoga ladies enjoy themselves this afternoon?'

'They loved it.' Tilly laughed. 'But they especially enjoyed sampling the teas from the more exotic end of the selection; the ashwagandha tea in particular went down well.'

Now it was Olivia's turn to laugh. 'I thought it would; I blended it with them in mind. Oh, and I have to say, the photographs you sent through earlier were amazing. Since when did you switch from everything being in black and white to full-blown technicolour?'

'Actually, I had a little help with the photos.'

'What sort of help?'

'It was a bit weird to be honest. I take it you know Matteo?'

'Matteo Ferretti? The guy who supplies the cheese to the teashop?'

'Yes, that's right, but did you know he's also a waiter at a café in Florence?'

'I didn't, but I don't think he makes the cheese himself. If I remember correctly, a family member owns a farm somewhere on the way to Siena. He's gorgeous, isn't he?'

Tilly knew her sister was fishing and she had no intention of taking the bait.

'Don't let Enzo hear you say that,' she joked. 'Anyway, it was Matteo who styled the shoot *and* took most of the photographs I sent over to you, and he refused to allow me to engage the black and white filter; something about food photography being different to other types of photography.'

'Well, he's *almost* as talented as you are behind a camera.'

'Thanks, Liv. I met someone else from the village, too.'

'Who?'

'Rocco Bianchi.'

'Oh yes, Rocco; he's quite a character, isn't he?'

'He's scary. I'd hate to work with him.'

'Me too, but his food is to die for. He deserves his reputation as one of the best chefs in Tuscany, and all of his success with his eponymous ristorante. You should try his lobster gnocchi; it's one of the most delicious things I've tasted since arriving in Italy. That being said, I'd still like him to acknowledge that British cuisine has a great deal to celebrate, too.' Olivia sighed. 'Although to be honest, he's not the only one who turns his nose up at our afternoon teas. It seems most of the locals agree with him.'

'What do you mean?'

'When we launched the teashop, a few of the San Vincente residents came in to check out the menu, and then left before even giving us a chance. Some, like Rocco, made some pretty disparaging comments, and I didn't tell you at the time, but the local news reporter wrote a rather hurtful review of the afternoon tea he sampled, which didn't help our quest to increase footfall. It's been a difficult couple of years – business-wise – which is why we now only cater for pre-booked parties. However, I still believe in what we're doing at *Té e Torta* and I love living in San Vincente. Apart from Rocco, most of the people are lovely. Have you met Gabriella yet?'

'Yes, Jess and I had gelato there this morning. I'm sorry about the teashop, Liv. I had no idea you were struggling with getting customers in.'

'It's fine. Enzo earns a decent salary so we manage. How's Jess getting on?'

'She's amazing. She could definitely run the teashop by herself. I think I'm more of a hindrance than a help to her.'

'I'm sure that's not true, but I *am* grateful to Eduardo.'

'Eduardo?'

Olivia laughed. 'Yes, Jess thinks he's adorable, although I had to ban him from coming into the teashop because every time he was there, he managed to break one of my precious Emma Bridgewater teapots; the guy's a total liability, but he's the reason she's still in Italy. She should have gone back to Cornwall to spend a couple of months with her parents before heading to university, but she stayed on so that she can drool over him from afar. Is there any more news?'

'Actually, there is; Jess and I have decided to enter the village food contest after all.'

'You have?'

'I just thought it would be interesting,' Tilly said quickly, hoping her sister wouldn't cross-examine her motives. 'So, if you could e-mail through the recipes you were going to use, we'll start practising them.'

'Sure, I'll do that, but don't spend too much time on it; it's just a bit of fun.'

'That isn't what Jess said.'

'What did Jess say?'

'That it was your dream to win it.'

'Not win it, but it would be nice to get one of the rosettes; bronze, maybe.' Olivia paused for beat before saying, 'Anyway, people can make new dreams.'

Tilly wondered what that meant, then remembered something else she had to tell Olivia.

'Rocco mentioned something about a food critic coming to San Vincente.'

'Victor Vitali?'

'Yes, that's right.'

'Just ignore him. Rocco says the same thing every couple of months and the great man has never graced our little corner of Tuscan paradise with his royal presence yet. When he's in Tuscany, Victor Vitali prefers to frequent the more upmarket establishments of Florence, Siena and Lucca, so there's nothing to worry about, although it would be nice if he *did* stop by one day. A good review of *Ristorante Rocco* would put San Vincente on the foodie map, and more visitors to the restaurant would mean more visitors to the village, which would mean more people might see the teashop and take a peek at what we offer too. The more the merrier! Now, before I go, promise me that you'll take some time away from the teashop to explore Florence; the museums, the galleries, il duomo, stroll through the gardens of the Palazzo Pitti, grab a ticket for the open-air opera, maybe head over to Siena and take in a wine tour. Being a workaholic in Tuscany is a no-no; the Italians work to live, not the other way round.'

Tilly smiled. 'I promise.'

'Great. Love you, Tills.'

'To the moon and back, Liv.'

As the sun had already dipped behind the horizon, sending ripples of pinks and mauves through the darkening sky, Tilly returned to the kitchen, her thoughts lingering on the fact that she hadn't realised her sister's beloved teashop was struggling. Every time she spoke to Olivia, whether on the phone, via Zoom, or face-to-face during one of her frequent trips to London, she had always been upbeat about her new business venture, chatting animatedly about her plans for its future.

Again, an uncomfortable swirl of guilt invaded her chest that her sister hadn't felt able to confide in her until now. She popped a slice of bread into the toaster for her evening meal and wondered if there was anything she could do to drum up business whilst she was there. She remembered something one of the yoga women had said that afternoon about queues forming around the block, and the kernel of an idea formed in her head, followed swiftly by a tickle of excitement.

What if she offered *themed* afternoon teas?

# Tilly's Tuscan Teashop

Not the aphrodisiac-themed one the woman had suggested – although why not? – but a chocolate-themed one, or a flower-themed one, or a strawberry-themed one, or maybe even a coffee-themed one. The ideas kept coming thick and fast, and not wanting to forget any of them, Tilly scoured the kitchen for a pen and paper to start making a list. She couldn't see anything, but recalled seeing a notebook in the drawer beneath the console in the hallway where she had hidden Olivia's photograph of their parents. With a little trepidation, she pulled open the drawer, found the notebook – and a collection of coloured pens – and carried them back to the kitchen.

She finished her buttered toast, filled her glass with Olivia's home-made lemonade from the fridge, then sat down at the huge oak table in the middle of the kitchen and turned to the first page, the shock reverberating through her whole body as she saw her mum's familiar handwriting.

This wasn't any old notebook; it was her mum's recipe book, the place she recorded all the recipes she had collected throughout her life, not just those she had inherited from her own mother and her grandmother, but those she had created herself or brought back from her travels. Several yellowing photographs had been slotted between the pages, and some of the recipes had been illustrated by her mum's own hand and were still as vibrant as they day they were sketched.

It was a beautiful record of her life-long passion for food in all its guises, sweet and savoury, plain and exotic, and Tilly was saddened that one of the items on her mum's famous bucket list had not been achieved – turning it into a book to give to family and friends. Memories of her childhood rushed at her, one after the other; the time when she and Olivia had made their first Princess cake with the iconic green marzipan, and the cute rainbow beignets that looked like they'd been left out in the rain, and the white chocolate soufflés that sank every time. They were happy days, filled with tea and cupcakes, joy and laughter, cut short far too soon.

The pain of her parents' loss caused her to catch her breath and she snapped the notebook shut, hoping the swift action would douse some of the agony that was flowing through her veins. Of course, it didn't, so she opened the recipe book at a different page and saw one of her mum's favourite recipes; the recipe that had launched her new business venture after she'd left teaching – the orange blossom tart – and an idea burst into her mind.

She tried to push it away, but it refused to release its grip.

As she sat there, staring at her mum's neatly written words, the scorch of pain seemed to diminish just a little, its sharp edges soften, and she remembered what Freya had said about starting to come to terms with her loss. Perhaps this was a way she could begin that process, to shed just a little of the grief that had clung to her like a tenacious limpet for the last two years.

She made a decision.

# Tilly's Tuscan Teashop

She would go to the teashop the next day and spend the morning making a batch of her mum's orange blossom tarts.

# Chapter Eleven

The next morning, Tilly woke not to her alarm clock or the dawn chorus, but to a loud, resounding crash from outside her bedroom window. She leapt out of bed to investigate, pulling on her shorts and a random tee-shirt as she dashed down the stairs, her heart pounding painfully against her ribcage. She pulled open the door to the terrace and her gaze fell on a large pool of blood and a fallen step-ladder.

'Oh my God! Oh my God!'

Tilly's hand flew to her lips, her throat tightened and the shock forced the air from her lungs, causing her to gasp for breath as multiple, increasingly horrific scenarios shot through her mind.

Had Eduardo…?

She glanced to her left, and to her immense relief she saw Eduardo standing there watching her, a paintbrush in one hand, a paint pot dangling from the other, but otherwise alive and well and sporting his usual Sunday Best attire, his hair immaculately coifed and his handstitched loafers encased in a pair of protective plastic bags that were splattered with red paint.

'I'm sorry, Tilly, did I wake you?'

'Yes, but it's fine.'

She looked again at the pool of what she now knew was paint. 'What happened?'

'I accidentally knocked the ladder and this paint pot was balanced on the top step and, well...' Eduardo shrugged, but he had the grace to look contrite as the pool of paint was now spreading across the terrace towards the edge of the swimming pool.

'I thought... never mind. Come on, I'll help you clean it up.'

She dashed back into the kitchen, the relief flooding her veins making her feel lightheaded. What she wouldn't give for a rich, dark, revitalising cup of espresso right now! She grabbed the jug of water from the fridge, poured two glasses and handed one to Eduardo. She then filled a couple of buckets with soapy water and they spent the next hour scrubbing red paint from the tiles before it dribbled into the swimming pool. The thought of having to drain and refill the pool made Tilly work as fast as she could, even when Eduardo temporarily abandoned the task because an inquisitive wasp had arrived to supervise their toil.

# Tilly's Tuscan Teashop

'*Una vespa! Una vespa!*'

Tilly stared at him. Why did he want to know where her Vespa was? Was he going to leave her to clean up the mess *he'd* made?

'I've parked it at the front of the villa, in the shade.'

Now it was Eduardo's turn to look confused. 'What are you talking about?'

'What are *you* talking about?'

Eduardo pointed to the wasp who had abandoned his ringside seat in favour of a clump of lavender growing in a huge terracotta urn. '*La vespa?* The wasp? I hate wasps!'

'Ah.' Tilly grinned at her misunderstanding, as well as the fact that she was dealing with a gardener who panicked every time any kind of animal, insect or reptile crossed his path. 'Eduardo, do you mind if I ask you something?'

'Sure.'

'Why are you doing this?'

'Doing what?'

'Working as a gardener and pool maintenance guy?'

'It's the family business,' said Eduardo, as though that explained it. 'Family is important in Italy.'

'But is it what you really want to do?'

Eduardo considered her question. 'When I was in school, I wanted to be an actor.'

'Then why didn't you go to drama school?'

'Because we're not all as brave as Matteo.'

'You know Matteo Ferretti?'

Eduardo looked at her as though she had two heads.

'Of course! Everyone knows everyone in San Vincente.'

'Does Matteo live in San Vincente?'

'Yes, he rents a room above *Gelateria Gabriella*.'

'Okay.' She wondered why Matteo hadn't mentioned that snippet of information, but she stored it away for later dissection as she wanted to pursue another line of questioning. 'What makes you think you're not as brave as Matteo?'

'Because he *did* follow his dreams; he refused to join *his* family's business and went off to study in Rome instead.'

'What is his family business?'

'They owned a restaurant in Siena.'

Tilly was confused. 'His family own a restaurant? Then why is he working as a waiter at a café in Florence?'

'They don't own it anymore,' Eduardo muttered, his cheeks turning pink, clearly having strayed into unintended territory. 'Anyway, if you'll excuse me, I've got lots to do this morning, and I'm sure you have, too. I'm grateful for your help. *Grazie mille,* Tilly.'

'*Prego*, Eduardo.' Tilly smiled, and before she could offer him another glass of water, he'd collected his wheelbarrow, filled it with his garden implements and the empty paint pot, and disappeared into the tangled jungle that was Villa Avanti's garden.

Tilly meandered back to the house, her thoughts lingering on what he had said about Matteo. She now understood why he knew so much about photographing food – obviously he must have been responsible for the marketing and promotions side of his family's restaurant business – but she wondered why he hadn't mentioned it.

She paused on the threshold to the kitchen, glanced down at her hands and groaned; she looked like that she'd been auditioning for the Tuscan Chainsaw Massacre with splashes of red across the back of hands, all the way up her forearms and down the front of her shins. She changed her mind about washing her hands in the sink and instead climbed the stairs to the bathroom where she took a shower, luxuriating in Olivia's jasmine and bergamot shower gel, and then left her hair to dry naturally in waves around her shoulders.

She dressed quickly, slotted her mum's recipe book into her satchel and threw her leg over the seat of her Vespa, surprised at how quickly she had grown accustomed to her new mode of transport. She started the engine then paused, realising for the first time that she had inadvertently grabbed one of Olivia's baby-blue tee shirts instead of her usual go-to black. The cheerful colour edged her spirits up a notch and she set off towards San Vincente, a sense of freedom rushing through her body as she navigated each bump and bounce in the road; it was a feeling she hadn't experienced for a long time.

She parked the Vespa in a convenient space right next to the teashop and opened the door, smiling when she heard the brass bell welcome her arrival, and made her way to the kitchen to start her baking marathon.

'What the—?!'

Tilly looked down at her feet, astonished to find herself standing in a puddle. On further investigation, she found there was a steady trickle of water coming from the hallway that led to the bathroom. To her horror, when she pushed open the door, she saw that the tap was running and the sink was overflowing onto the floor and out of the door.

Oh God! Had Eduardo paid a visit to the teashop, too?

She quickly turned off the tap, then spent the next hour mopping up instead of baking a batch of the orange blossom tarts as she had hoped. When the floor was dry and every towel and tablecloth in the teashop was hanging on the line in the tiny rear patio, she poured herself a glass of homemade lemonade from the fridge and had just sat down at one of the tables to catch her breath when the bell tinkled again.

'Oh, I'm sorry we're… Oh, hi, Gabriella, come in, come in.'

'I saw your Vespa outside so I thought I'd… Hey, what's going on?'

Gabriella pointed to a pile of wet tea towels that Tilly had forgotten to deal with.

'We had a bit of a flood.'

'A flood? How did that happen?'

'Someone must have left the tap on in the bathroom. I thought I'd checked it before I left last night, but obviously I hadn't done it properly.'

Gabriella tucked her short dark curls behind her ears and wrinkled her nose in puzzlement. 'How did it flood, though? Did someone also leave the plug in the basin?'

'I…' Tilly stared at Gabriella; she hadn't thought of that.

Gabriella clearly regretted her inquisition so she moved on quickly. 'What are you doing here today, anyway? Jess said the next booking wasn't until Saturday; a group of visitors over from the UK on an organised tour of the gardens and parks of Tuscany?'

'I was hoping to spend the day trying out a few recipes.'

'Oh, do you mind if I join you?'

Tilly smiled. 'No, of course not. In fact, I'd love that.'

She jumped from her seat and handed Gabriella one of the pale-blue aprons embroidered with the teashop's logo, collected her mum's recipe book and headed to the kitchen, knowing that Gabriella's presence would distract her from becoming too absorbed in painful memories and make the baking a much more pleasurable experience.

'When Liv and I were growing up, Mum used to make a batch of her special orange blossom tarts every time we had a celebration; it could be for birthdays, anniversaries, musical or sporting achievements, or sometimes just because it was Sunday. It was her favourite recipe, and seeing the smiles on everyone's faces when we devoured them and asked for more always made her happy.'

'Olivia told me that she named her café in Cornwall after them.'

'She did. So, I thought we could make a batch.'

'Sounds like fun. Where do we start?'

'First, we make a sweet shortcrust pastry.'

Tilly had no need to consult the recipe because she knew it off by heart. When her mum had opened the Orange Blossom Café, she had made the tart every single day the café opened its doors to the public, and over the years both Tilly and Olivia had made more tarts than they could count. Nevertheless, she still turned to the appropriate page in her mum's recipe book; seeing her hand-drawn illustration of a sprig of orange blossom, and how the final tart should look, was strangely reassuring.

She quickly collected the ingredients for the shortcrust pastry and they set to work. With Gabriella's help, the dough was wrapped in cling-film and placed in the freezer to chill within minutes and they could turn their attention to making the filling. Had this been any other café, restaurant or teashop, Tilly knew she would have struggled to find the ingredients she needed to make an orange blossom tart, but not at *Té e Torta*. Here, every item on the list of ingredients in her mum's precious recipe book was stored in a pretty polka-dot basket, ready to use.

Being a gelato maestro, Gabriella required minimal direction as they weighed out the sugar, butter and cornflour and sliced and grated dozens of oranges ready for the orange blossom custard. Tilly then removed the pastry from the freezer, they rolled it out as quickly as possible, lined six large, fluted tart tins, pricked the bottom and returned them to the freezer while they enjoyed a well-deserved iced lemonade.

'Gosh, I needed that,' said Gabriella, unconsciously twisting her gold chain around her fingers. Tilly glanced at the pretty diamond solitaire dangly from its length, then quickly looked away. She was curious about the reason why the ring wasn't on Gabriella's finger, but they had only just met and she didn't want to pry. However, she didn't have to because Gabriella had seen her interest and after a moment of hesitation, she spoke.

'I was engaged once.' She paused for a moment as her thoughts travelled down the memory super-highway to a time that clearly caused her distress. 'Dario lived in the next village and we grew up together; everyone knew we would get married one day, and there was a huge party when we announced our engagement.'

'What happened?'

'It's a story repeated all over the world; he went to visit his cousin in Naples and fell in love with someone else. Unfortunately, the trip was just two weeks before the wedding. Everything was arranged, the church booked, the reception organised, the dresses hand-stitched, the rings bought, the honeymoon in Sardinia paid for, and Dario didn't have the decency to face the repercussions of what he had done – or my family – so he simply didn't come back. He's lived in Naples ever since; he has a son and a daughter, now.'

'I'm so sorry, Gabriella.'

'I was inconsolable; I had loved him since I was twelve years old. There had never been anyone else, and I expected us to grow old together, with our families around us. It took me five years to even consider dating again, but no one came close to what I'd had, or thought I'd had, with Dario. He was my soulmate; it's not easy to find another one and it's possible I never will, but I have my gelateria, which keeps me busy, as well as Sandro, of course.'

A few moments of silence passed, and because Gabriella had shared her heart-wrenching story with Tilly, she decided to share a little of her own.

'Before I came over here, I… I stumbled on a video of my boyfriend, Josh, frolicking on a tropical beach with another woman. He's an airline pilot, with a very busy schedule, so we haven't yet been able to talk about what happened face-to-face, but it was one of the reasons I came to Tuscany – to decide what I want to do. As well as help Liv out while she's away in Boston, of course,' she added hastily.

'Do you still love him?'

'I… I don't know.'

It was a difficult question and Tilly wasn't sure how to answer, despite the fact that she had thought of little else when she wasn't busy with the teashop and cleaning up after Eduardo. She and Josh had been a couple for almost four years, through good times and difficult times, and she didn't want to throw that away without serious consideration.

But then the image of Josh dancing in the Balinese waves with Melissa would float across her mind's eye and her desire to repair their relationship waned. Not only that, after their first conversation about what had happened, Josh had made no attempt whatsoever to contact her, not even a courtesy call to make sure she'd arrived in Tuscany safely. That wasn't the behaviour of a loving partner, even if he was probably in a different time zone.

She realised with a sudden thud of regret that even though they hadn't yet had their face-to-face conversation, their relationship was actually already over.

She saw that Gabriella was watching her, her face wreathed in concern, so she sprang from her chair and headed back to the kitchen. She removed the pastry-lined tins from the freezer, filled them with a generous handful of dried beans each, then slotted them into the oven to bake.

'Okay, now for the custard filling.'

Tilly filled a saucepan with the sugar, eggs, cornflour, orange juice and orange zest, whisked it until smooth, then heated it gently, stirring all the time so it didn't scramble.

'Can you pass me the orange blossom water from the shelf over there, please?'

Tilly pointed to Olivia's extensive collection of essences and flavourings on the shelf above the sink. She saw Gabriella squinting at the bottles and remembering what Jess had told her, checked the label on the tiny, brown-tinted bottle her new friend handed to her before adding it to the smooth, silky custard mixture. She was relieved she'd had the foresight to do so, otherwise she would have ended up with a bubblegum-flavoured filling for her tarts instead of the delicate orange blossom flavour she was aiming for.

Once Tilly had swapped the bottles and added the correct flavouring, she grabbed the oven gloves and removed the pastry cases from the oven, enjoying the warm, buttery aroma that floated through the teashop, even though she probably wouldn't indulge in the final product. When the cases were cool, she and Gabriella filled them with the custard and slotted them into the fridge to set. The tarts looked almost as good as her mum's, and instead of the expected whoosh of pain, a surprise feeling of accomplishment wove its way through her chest.

'So, Tilly, what do you have planned for the rest of the day? Why don't you do a little sightseeing? Florence? Pisa? Lucca? Siena?'

'Actually, I was going to try out an idea I've had that might draw in a few more customers to the teashop, not just the pre-booked tour parties.'

'What do you have in mind?'

'Themed afternoon teas, such as chocolate-themed, or heart-themed, or Chianti-themed, or doggie-themed, or kitten-themed… Well, you get the idea.'

'Oh, that sounds wonderful! Maybe Sandro could model for a few promotional photographs!'

'I'd love that!' said Tilly, really getting into the flow. 'So, for the guests from the gardening club who are coming to the teashop on Saturday, I thought we could do a flower-themed afternoon tea; daisy-shaped sandwiches, rose-scented scones, cupcakes decorated with edible petals, hibiscus and chamomile tea, and I could bring some flowers from the villa's garden for the tables. If that's a success, then I'll create a few sample menus – like the chocolate one because I know Liv has a blend of chocolate tea in the store cupboard. Everyone likes chocolate, so hopefully we can get a few more bookings, and then maybe we can open the teashop to passing trade again.'

'*Grazie mille* for letting me help you today, Tilly. I had lots of fun. If it's okay with you, I think I might make a batch of orange blossom gelato.'

'Sounds delicious. I'll be the first in the queue to try that one.'

Tilly smiled, then realised that Gabriella was the perfect person to ask the question that had been niggling at her since her conversation with Eduardo at the villa that morning.

'Eduardo told me that Matteo rents a room above the gelateria,' said Tilly as casually as she could so as not to twang Gabriella's suspicion radar.

'Yes, that's right. Matteo has lived there since he came back from Rome.'

'Why doesn't he stay with his family in Siena?'

'Because his parents don't live there anymore,' said Gabriella, replenishing their glasses with iced lemonade. 'When their restaurant was sold, they moved to Sicily; it's where his mother's side of the family are from.'

'Why did they sell their restaurant?'

Just as Eduardo had done, Gabriella looked uncomfortable and evaded the question.

'Do you think the tarts will be set now? They're so pretty I think we should take a few photographs and put them on the teashop's social media pages to let people know what's on offer, don't you?'

'Great idea.'

Tilly removed the tarts from the fridge, decorated them with the sliced oranges she and Gabriella had prepared earlier, then grabbed her phone and took several photographs from different angles, trying to utilise the tips Matteo had taught her. She then uploaded them to Olivia's various *Té e Torta* accounts, and Gabriella announced on her Instagram page that a new flavour would be arriving at *Gelateria Gabriella* in the next week or so.

'Hey, what about a butterfly-themed afternoon tea?' said Gabriella as she tucked her phone into the back pocket of her pink capri trousers. 'You could serve the butterfly pea tea with that.'

'Great idea, or we could do a chess-themed afternoon tea, with chequerboard sandwiches and scones in the shape of the chess pieces.'

'Or a panda-themed afternoon tea. I adore pandas; it's my dream to see one in real life.'

'Did you know there's a panda dung tea?'

'Ergh! Really?'

Gabriella wrinkled her nose in disgust, which was exactly what Tilly had done when her sister had told her about it many years ago. 'Don't worry, it's not actually made from panda dung; the dung is just used to fertilise the soil in which the tea plant is grown. I don't think we'll be using it though; it's one of the most expensive teas in the world.'

# Tilly's Tuscan Teashop

When Tilly finally closed the door behind Gabriella with a profusion of thanks and a promise to pop over to sample her orange blossom gelato when it was ready, she was exhausted, and yet exhilarated. She felt as though she had achieved a great deal that day. Glancing at her phone, she saw that the photographs of the orange blossom tarts had already gained over two hundred likes, and she hoped that the renewed interest would translate into more customers for the teashop so that her sister's business would not just tick-over while she was there, but thrive.

She was also proud of the fact that instead of returning her mum's much-loved recipe book to the drawer beneath the console – along with the photograph she had also stashed there – she had been brave enough to bake one of the recipes that had shaped her childhood; something she hadn't done since losing her mum.

To her surprise, she had enjoyed making the orange blossom tarts, and spending time in the teashop kitchen had made her feel closer to her mum than she had for a long time. Having Gabriella by her side, talking about her own loss, had made hers easier to bear somehow, even though she hadn't spoken about it. She now realised that the only way to deal with her grief was to face it; pain was inevitable if you had lost someone you loved, and avoiding it at all costs was not the solution.

She still had a long way to go, she knew that, but she felt like she had, at last, taken the first step in the process, and that felt good.

# Chapter Twelve

On Saturday morning, Tilly was grateful to be woken by the sweet symphony of the birds welcoming in the new day instead of the cacophony of noise Eduardo seemed to prefer. As it was the weekend, she assumed he wouldn't be at the villa, so she took her time in the shower, rinsing away the last vestiges of sleep and styling her hair so that she looked presentable for the first of the teashop's themed afternoon teas.

A tickle of nerves agitated at her stomach but she ignored them. The previous day she had spoken at length to Jess, who was as excited about the new venture as she was and had assured Tilly that it would be a huge success.

As she had a limited wardrobe with her in Tuscany – mainly from the darker end of the colour palette and fashioned from thick, heavy fabric – she had been forced to raid her sister's closet. She chose a pair of loose-fitting palazzo trousers in a rich paprika, added a plain white tee-shirt, and finished off the outfit with one of Olivia's long gold necklaces.

When she looked in the mirror, she didn't recognise herself.

Her chestnut-coloured hair hung around her shoulders in casual waves, her nose sported a generous sprinkle of freckles from the many Vespa rides she'd undertaken between the villa and the teashop, but it was the colourful clothes that surprised her the most. Like Olivia, she had once loved experimenting with colour, pattern and texture but then she had lost interest in sartorial matters, and now she realised that her adherence to a black dress code – whilst making her daily outfit choice easier to make – did nothing to enhance her mood.

Seeing herself now, modelling the clothes that Olivia had bought in Italy, she couldn't help but smile.

She grabbed her satchel, popped in the jar of Blue Mountain coffee from the cupboard under the sink, placed the flowers she had collected from the garden that morning in the box on the back of the Vespa, and zipped off along the winding roads towards San Vincente. The gods of parking must have been on her side because she scooted straight into a vacant spot outside *Gelateria Gabriella*, her good fortune edging her spirits even higher. Humming a random tune, she headed towards the narrow street that housed the teashop, and when she rounded the corner, she come to an abrupt halt.

'Oh my God!'

Tilly could barely believe what her eyes were telling her.

It was only eleven o'clock; they weren't expecting the *Gardens of Tuscany* tour party to arrive until after one, but there was a queue of at least half a dozen people outside the teashop's front door. What was going?

'*Buongiorno*,' said the woman in a floppy red sunhat at the head of the queue.

'*Buongiorno*.' Tilly smiled at the fifty-something woman, her Italian not good enough to enquire why she was standing with five friends waiting for the teashop to open when they only catered for pre-booked guests.

'Are you the owner of the teashop?' the woman asked in almost accent-less English, clearly realising that Tilly didn't speak Italian.

'Yes, I mean, no, my sister's the owner.'

'Do you have a table for six available?' asked the woman who was second in the line and had favoured a straw trilby set at a jaunty angle.

'*Now?*'

Surely they didn't want afternoon tea at eleven o'clock in the morning?

But then Tilly chastised herself. What kind of businesswoman was she? Hadn't she said that she hoped to expand Olivia's tea and cake empire while she was away in Boston? If these people wanted afternoon tea at eleven o'clock in the morning, then they should be able to have afternoon tea at eleven o'clock in the morning.

'Sorry, yes, of course we have a table. Please, come in.'

Tilly opened the door and showed them to the table by the window, listening to their excited chatter that sounded so lyrical in high-speed Italian. Although she had no idea what they were saying, it was clear they were delighted by the interior decor as they pointed to the teapots on the powder-blue dresser, the china cake stands edged in blue forget-me-nots, and the hand-embroidered tablecloths and napkins.

She quickly tied an apron around her waist and handed round menus, then headed to the kitchen. She had hoped to get an early start on her flower-themed afternoon tea, and when she heard the bell tinkle again, she sighed with relief that Jess had had the same idea. However, when she went back into the teashop to explain to her why there was a party of six sitting at one of the tables, she saw that it wasn't Jess but another group of customers – this time two young couples.

'*Buongiorno.*' She smiled, a little bewildered at the teashop's sudden popularity. She seated the second group at a table for four and this time when she handed them the menus, she also pointed to the selection of teas available on the chalkboard, before hurrying back to the kitchen to call Jess.

'Jess, we've got ten customers!'

'I'm not surprised.'

# Tilly's Tuscan Teashop

'What? But it's only eleven o'clock and I—'

'I'm on my way, and so is Carlotta. We'll be with you in ten minutes. Oh, and you might like to take a look at the teashop's Instagram account.'

'Why?'

But Jess had rang off. Tilly took out her phone and quickly scrolled through *Té e Torta*'s Instagram feed, shocked to see that the photographs of the orange blossom tarts that she and Gabriella had uploaded the day before now had over five thousand likes – *five thousand!* – as well as lots of comments in Italian.

Before she could compute what that meant, Jess and Carlotta arrived and swung into action like a well-oiled machine, seating another four parties and serving everyone with their signature *Té e Torta* afternoon tea, along with their customers' choice of beverage from the chalkboard.

Tilly remained in the kitchen, focusing on creating her flower-themed afternoon tea for the Garden Tour party from Yorkshire who had pre-booked, taking extra-special care to make sure everything was perfect; from the daisy-shaped sandwiches filled with chicken, parmesan and fresh basil, sliced ham with rosemary, fennel and garlic, and halloumi, hummus and locally grown salad leaves, to the rosewater-infused scones served with Olivia's home-made raspberry jam, and the cupcakes topped with swirls of buttercream and edible flower petals. She also made sure the kettle was boiled and the teapots were ready for the hibiscus or chamomile tea, and when she finally stood back to admire the cake stands, she was delighted with what she had created.

'Wow, Tilly, they look amazing!' said Jess, that day's manicure on-theme with a different flower on each of her nails.

'*Grazie mille*, Jess.' Tilly smiled, more thrilled with her compliment than she wanted to let on. 'Do you think I should—'

'They're here!' Carlotta called through the kitchen door. 'The tour party is here!'

\*\*\*

For the next two hours, Tilly did not stop for breath. Not only was she in demand from the *Gardens of Tuscany* tour group wanting an explanation of what they were enjoying, but to her astonishment there was also a steady influx of on-spec customers asking for tables, and in the end, they had to turn the sign to '*Chiuso*'.

Conversation swirled around the teashop, with frequent expressions of delight and requests for teapot refills as Tilly, Jess and Carlotta continued to replenish the cake stands and chat to the horticulture enthusiasts about the various blends of available tea and their origins. When Tilly handed the check to one of the teashop's solo customers, she saw her slide her pen into the spine of her elegant initialled notebook and slip it into her hand-stitched leather shoulder bag.

'I hope you enjoyed your afternoon tea,' she said, smiling at the woman who was probably the same age as she was and with the same shoulder-length waves, but dressed like she was about to launch herself down a Milanese catwalk in a black designer dress and vertiginous heels. She also smelt divine.

'*Sì*, I thought it was delicious; a totally unique experience, and no snail's breath or deconstructed ravioli in sight.' She laughed, shaking her head at the thought. 'I'll definitely be back for one of those pretty floral afternoon teas. I love those cupcakes!'

'We hope to offer a few more themed afternoon teas, too.'

'What do you mean, "themed"?'

Tilly smiled, recognising an opportunity to hone her promotional skills on behalf of Olivia. 'Well, Jess and I have a chocolate-themed afternoon tea planned for next week, then a butterfly-themed afternoon tea after that, and we were thinking of doing a sailing theme, and a zoo theme, maybe a flag-themed one with a quiz to guess the countries and a prize for the winner.'

'Oh, please could you book me in for the chocolate-themed one? I'll try and bring my colleague with me; she's a complete chocoholic, and I'll have a chat to my editor when I get back to the office, and if she agrees, we might do a feature on *Té e Torta*.'

Tilly's heart bounced to her toes and back again.

'A feature?'

'Yes, I'm Elisa Orsini. I work for the *Gazzettino*. I'm heading back there now; I'd better dash if I want my review of this afternoon tea to make the deadline for the magazine section tomorrow. *Ciao*, Tilly. *Grazie mille*.'

Tilly gaped.

'*Ciao*, Elisa,' was all she could manage to say as she watched Elisa leave, unable to believe what had just happened.

'Who was that?' asked Jess. 'I *absolutely adore* her handbag!'

'Elisa Orsini.'

'Who's Elisa Orsini?'

'She works for the *Gazzettino*.'

Jess stared at her. 'What did she say?'

'That she wants to do a feature on the teashop.'

'Wow, that's awesome!'

\*\*\*

The rest of the afternoon was spent handing out checks, thanking the tour group's organiser for choosing the teashop, and wishing everyone the very best for the rest of their visit to the many beautiful gardens of Tuscany. When the last guest had left, Tilly flopped into a chair, flung back her arms, and exhaled a long breath.

'What a day!'

'I can't believe it; we served over fifty covers,' said Jess, closing the till with a flourish. 'It's the busiest day we've had all year. Olivia is going to be thrilled. Your themed afternoon teas are a great idea, Tilly. I think we should start advertising them properly. Maybe, after the chocolate-themed one on Monday, we can do a romance-themed afternoon tea?'

'What's a romance-themed afternoon tea?'

'You know, heart-shaped sandwiches, honey and fig scones, passionfruit cheesecakes, strawberries dipped in chocolate, red roses on the tables and napkins embroidered with Cupids, and maybe you could call Livvie and ask her to create a "love potion" tea.' Jess smirked. 'And I might invite Eduardo over to help me taste-test everything before we serve it up to our romance-loving customers.'

Tilly laughed. 'I thought Liv had banned Eduardo from the teashop?'

'She did, which means he'll have to come over to my studio!' Jess's green eyes glistened with mischief as she waggled her eyebrows suggestively.

'Why don't you just suggest meeting up for a coffee? It's a lot less pressure, and I'm not sure how he'll feel if he turns up at your apartment and sees hearts and flowers everywhere.'

'Maybe,' said Jess, considering what Tilly had said. 'Yes, actually, that's probably a sensible idea because I'm on the Banana Diet next week – he might get a little suspicious if I refused to eat any of the food that I make for him.'

Tilly knew she shouldn't, but she asked anyway. 'What's the Banana Diet?'

'It's where I can *only* eat bananas; banana smoothies, banana fritters, banana chips, banana kebabs, banana sushi, bananas drizzled with honey, bananas coated in chocolate—

'Okay, okay, I get the idea. It sounds—'

'Erm, Tilly, Jess?'

Tilly and Jess looked towards the kitchen door in unison.

'What's the matter, Carlotta?' asked Tilly.

Carlotta held up her palms; they were bright blue, as though she'd washed them in ink.

'How did you do that?'

'It took me a while to work it out, but I think it's the soap in the restrooms.'

'What do you mean?'

Carlotta disappeared into the hallway, then came back holding one of Olivia's favourite liquid soap dispensers. 'It's this.'

Tilly and Jess followed Carlotta into the kitchen and she squirted a generous dollop of soap onto their hands. They massaged it into their palms, then ran their hands under the tap. To Tilly's astonishment, her hands had been stained blue and so had Jess's.

'What's going on? We've had this soap for months, and this hasn't happened before,' said Jess, her forehead creased in consternation.

'I don't understand,' said Tilly, scrubbing her hands under the tap with a pan scrubber but the colour was strangely stubborn.

'It's dye,' said Carlotta. 'Not food dye, more like marker pen dye!'

Tilly stared at her, then she remembered the bathroom flood the previous day and filled Jess and Carlotta in on what had happened and what Gabriella had said about how strange it was that the plug had been in the sink.

'Do you think someone sabotaged the soap, too? Oh my God, what about the customers?' Jess exclaimed. 'Do you think their hands—'

'No one complained, did they?'

'No.'

'If someone did switch the dispenser, they did it towards the end of service.'

'But how?'

All three of them looked over their shoulders at the door that led to the patio at the rear of the teashop, which was standing wide open to let fresh air into the overheated kitchen, and their question was answered.

'But why would someone do that?'

'No idea.'

'Oh my God, do you think—'

But Jess didn't get any further because they were interrupted by the jolly tinkle of the doorbell, and they all rushed into the teashop to see who had arrived.

'Oh, *ciao*, Matteo,' said Jess, greeting him with the usual duo of cheek kisses. 'I didn't think we were scheduled for a cheese delivery today?'

'I'm not here on a delivery,' said Matteo, glancing in Tilly's direction.

Jess read the situation immediately, smirked, then hooked her arm through Carlotta's and guided her back to the kitchen to make a start on the mammoth task of washing, drying and storing the delicate china plates, cake stands, and teapots, humming the tune to *Love is in the Air*. Tilly was grateful when she saw the confusion on Matteo's expression; clearly he didn't recognise the John Paul Young song.

'I know how busy you've been today, and how you've been surrounded by nothing but tea, tea, and more tea – not to mention the cake!' Matteo smirked, the cute dimples bracketing his lips. 'As it's my night off from the café, I thought you might like to take a trip over to Florence and indulge in a decent cup of coffee or two?'

Tilly hesitated. Then she remembered what her sister always said; embrace the now, because that was all we have. And the offer of a decent cup of Italian coffee did sound like the perfect way to round off what had been a good day.

'I'd like that, thanks. I'll just go and grab my satchel.'

She pulled off her apron as quickly as she could and went to the kitchen to make sure Jess and Carlotta were okay about finishing the chores, smiling and rolling her eyes when she saw them rush away from the door where they had obviously been eavesdropping. She hooked her arm through her bag's strap and followed Matteo out of the teashop.

# Chapter Thirteen

'Is this your car?'

'Yes, why?' said Matteo, his voice surprisingly defensive as he paused before inserting the key in the door of his white Fiat Cinquecento that had clearly seen better days.

'Because this is exactly the sort of car I'd hoped my sister's husband Enzo would hire for me while I was in Tuscany. Although I have to admit that I do love the Vespa, now that I've got the hang of the controls, and the parking is *soo* much easier.'

She smiled at Matteo, relieved to see his stiffened demeanour relax as he dropped into the driver's seat and revved the engine, impatient to be on his way. Within minutes, they had left San Vincente behind and were heading along the winding hillside roads towards Florence, the windows down, soft music playing on the stereo, the breeze a welcome addition as apparently the air-con didn't work.

Tilly wanted to enjoy the journey, to feast her eyes on the picturesque countryside flashing by, but she was too busy gripping onto the sides of her seat because Matteo seemed to think he was auditioning for the next Italian Grand Prix, just like every other driver on the road that day. Everyone seemed to treat the necessity of engaging their brakes at a crossroads or a particularly tight bend as a personal affront, protested by the liberal use of the horn, and by the time they arrived at Piazzale Michelangelo, Tilly felt as though she'd been through several cycles of a tumble dryer. She had never been more grateful than when Matteo scooted into the tiniest of parking spots and she was able to clamber out of the passenger seat and catch her breath.

'Are you okay?' asked Matteo, slamming the car door shut with a flourish.

'Why do Italians drive so fast?'

'We love speed, except when it comes to cooking; in that arena we subscribe to the slow-food movement!' Matteo laughed, his dark eyes shining. 'Come on, I want to show you the view; it's one of the best in Tuscany, if not the whole of Italy.'

Matteo reached for her hand as though it was the most natural thing in the world. Ignoring the tingle of attraction she experienced when he laced his fingers through hers, she walked with him across the wide, paved terrace, past an impressive bronze replica of Michelangelo's David set on a raised marble pedestal, until they reached the stone balustrade that ran the whole way around the piazza.

'Wow!' Tilly gasped.

From their elevated position, the city of Florence was spread out below them; a mosaic of higgledy-piggledy terracotta roofs – punctuated by church spires and bell towers – beige, ochre, and mustard-coloured facades, multi-arched bridges, and presided over by the majestic red brick dome of the Santa Maria del Fiore cathedral. Framed by the emerald-clad hills to the north and the winding River Arno to the south, Tilly had to agree with Matteo that it was truly one of the most beautiful views she had ever seen.

She raised her phone and spent the next fifteen minutes photographing the scene from every conceivable angle while Matteo perched on the steps of the Michelangelo statue, scrolling through his emails, clearly accustomed to the beauty that was his home. She could have stayed there all night, just drinking in the spectacular panorama and soaking up the atmosphere, but Matteo had other ideas. He abandoned his seat, pointed to a flight of stone steps to the right-hand side of the piazza, and headed off towards them.

'Where are we going?'

'I remember you saying how much you enjoy photographing landscapes, so I thought you'd appreciate spending some time here.'

Matteo pushed open a small, almost hidden gate and they stepped into what Tilly thought looked like a quintessentially English garden set on a terraced slope. Everywhere she looked there were flowers from every colour of the rainbow, their soft petals rippling in the early evening breeze and sending delicious wafts of perfume into the air. However, as she strolled along the carefully designed pathways, pausing frequently to snap a particularly attractive bloom, she realised that the flowers were all the same – roses.

'This place is amazing!'

'This is the *Giardino delle Rose*, created by Attilio Pucci in 1895 when the garden was opened to the public; there are over three hundred and fifty varieties of rose here from all four corners of the world, as well as lemon trees and strawberry trees,' said Matteo, slipping into the role of tour guide. 'Come, I want to show you something.'

Once again, Matteo grabbed her hand and guided her to a bronze sculpture in the shape of a huge suitcase with a protruding handle, its centre cut out to create a frame through which was yet another panoramic view of the city of Florence.

'There are twelve sculptures like this one dotted around the garden – the Sleeping Cat, the Birdman, the Booklover – all designed by the Belgian artist Jean-Michel Folon, which were donated by his widow in 2011, an act that instigated the decision to open this stunning park to the public all year round, instead of just when the roses are in bloom. Come, there's something else.'

A few steps further and they came to standstill in front of a neatly manicured garden, fenced with bamboo poles and featuring a rocky stream, stone bridges, and oriental-inspired sculptures.

'This is the Japanese garden designed by Yasuo Kitayama, given to the people of Florence by our twin city of Kyoto. It's a real oasis, and it's where I come when I need to escape from the hustle and bustle of the city.'

Tilly left Matteo sitting on a wooden bench, gazing at the trickle of water making its way down the hillside, and resumed her photographic exploits, her heart filled with joy at being able to spend some time doing what she loved the most. When she was in the zone, her mind focused solely on the subject matter in front of her and getting the best shot possible, all other thoughts fell by the wayside. It was the only time she was at peace with herself. Her photography sessions were a kind of meditation, something she had returned to time and time again during the months that had followed her parents' passing, and now it had become a career that she loved; she just wished it hadn't come at such a cost.

'I've never seen someone take so many photographs.' Matteo laughed. 'Has it always been your dream to be a photographer?'

To Tilly's surprise, she experienced a sudden upswing of emotion, causing her to catch her breath and tears to threaten. She raised her phone on the pretext of taking another shot, but also so she could hide her feelings behind its screen, but she knew that Matteo had seen her reaction and the ever-present sadness in her eyes.

'Hey, are you okay?'

'Yes, yes, I'm fine,' she began, until she met his gaze and saw the genuine concern there. She glanced around her, noting that they were the only visitors lingering in that part of the rose garden, and decided to share a little of her current situation to prevent him from digging too deep into areas she didn't want to talk about. 'I'm taking so many photographs because I'm trying to rebuild my portfolio. I lost most of my artwork in a fire the week before I came over to Tuscany.'

'I'm sorry to hear that, Tilly. That must have been devastating.'

Tilly's stomach clenched uncomfortably as an image of the charred remains of her little beach hut studio on the boardwalk floated across her mind – it was an image she knew would stay with her for a long time – but she inhaled a breath and forced herself to continue.

'It was, but it wasn't just me; several of my friends lost their businesses, too.'

'How did it happen?'

'They think it was started by an electrical fault, and as our studios were wooden beach huts, the fire spread rapidly. I lost everything, not just my artwork but all my cameras and photographic equipment, too; that's the reason I'm using my phone to take pictures and not a professional camera. Until the insurance money comes through, I just can't afford to replace them. So that's why I'm here, stepping in for Liv at her teashop, serving tea and cake, and entering a village food contest that I have no chance of winning.'

Matteo's whole body stiffened. 'You're going up against Rocco Bianchi?'

'I know, it's crazy, but the guy just wound me up, and I suppose I rose to the bait.'

'Well,' said Matteo, his jaw tight, his eyes holding a steely glint. 'If you need anyone to help you bake up a storm in the kitchen, I'm at your service.'

Without preamble, Matteo rose from the bench and strode off towards the exit. His habitual smile had returned by the time Tilly caught up with him, and yet there was still something dark lingering in his eyes. Before she could press him on its cause, he pointed to a chic restaurant called La Loggia that looked more like a miniature palazzo than an eating establishment.

'Let's get that coffee I promised you.'

They were shown to an elegantly dressed table on an open-air terrace by a smiling waiter whose badge informed them was called Sergio, and who didn't bat an eye when they simply ordered two coffees instead of a sumptuous feast from the extensive menu. Tilly was relieved; the place was far more glamorous than she had expected or dressed for. With chequerboard flooring, stone columns, and impressive arched windows overlooking the iconic view of Florence, it was truly a magical place; one for romance, not a quick coffee between new friends.

As they waited for their drinks to arrive, they watched the sun head inexorably for the horizon, washing the whole spectacular scene in a swathe of rich golden light, and Tilly decided it was her turn to offer a listening ear.

'Matteo, is everything okay?'

For a moment, Matteo didn't say anything, clearly struggling with whether or not to confide in her, but then he sighed and, without meeting her eyes, he said, 'My family lost everything, too, but not in the same way as you.'

Tilly couldn't fail to see the anguish written across Matteo's handsome features and her heart gave a sharp nip of sympathy. All thoughts of her own troubles evaporated and she was keen for him to share his burden with her in the hope she could offer a little solace. Unfortunately, Sergio chose that moment to deliver their drinks, along with a trio of *stuzzichini*, chatting in high-speed Italian to Matteo for a few minutes before leaving to serve another table of diners. They both took a sip of their coffees, and when Matteo didn't continue with his explanation, Tilly gave him a gentle nudge.

'What do you mean, your family lost everything?'

'My parents used to own a trattoria in a small village on the outskirts of Siena, and when they had to leave, they too were devastated. The food they served there was nothing like that served at *Ristorante Rocco*; it was much more authentic. Real Tuscan cuisine made using recipes handed down from generation to generation, with none of the pretentiously labelled dishes that are created in a "lab" rather than a kitchen, like cantaloupe caviar or fish-eye fettuccini.'

'So what happened?'

# Tilly's Tuscan Teashop

But Matteo wasn't ready to jump to the end of the story.

'Growing up, my brother and I used to help out serving the customers, many of whom were, or became, friends, but I was never interested in a career as a waiter or running a restaurant. I wanted to make my own way in the world. For as long as I can remember, I wanted to be a filmmaker, so when I finished school, I left home and headed to Rome to study. When I qualified, I landed a job with a great film production company based in the city and I lived the high-life; fast cars, designer clothes, extensive travel in private jets, photoshoots on millionaires' yachts.'

'That sounds like fun,' said Tilly, sipping her coffee, relishing the infusion of caffeine.

'It was, at first. It took me a long time to realise that in life, not everything is as it seems; that images can be manipulated to reflect a false impression, that people can disguise their intentions for their own gain and because we rarely look beyond the superficial, we can be easily fooled into believing something is right when the opposite is true.'

Tilly stared at Matteo, taken aback at the bitterness in his voice, and she wondered what had happened to make him so cynical. Before she could frame a question that wouldn't cause offence or distress, Matteo was speaking again.

'Why are humans so contrary, Tilly? For years I dreamed of becoming a recognised filmmaker, resisting my father's pleas to join the family business at every turn, and yet now, ten years too late, all I want to do is own my own restaurant, not work as a waiter at my friend's café in Florence, which I love, by the way. There was no one more surprised than me when I came back to Tuscany and realised how much I enjoyed working in the hospitality business, and the irony of that discovery is not lost on me. I just wish I'd done it sooner, then I would have…'

'Would have what?'

But the bubble of memories Matteo had inhabited briefly had burst. When he met Tilly's gaze, he seemed shocked that he had spoken so frankly, and clearly regretted that he had revealed more than he'd intended. He forced a smile onto his lips as he reached into his pocket, dropped a few euros onto the table, and held out his hand to Tilly.

'Are you hungry?'

'What do you have in mind?'

'I know a place that makes a fabulous *pasta al ragù*. Don't worry, I won't make you eat dessert.' He smirked, his eyes twinkling. 'Although Gino does make an amazing *tiramisù*.'

Tilly followed Matteo back to the tiny white Fiat and, with music blaring from the stereo, they zipped down the hill to the city centre where they spent fifteen minutes searching for a parking space. She was happy that Matteo had opened up to her, but it was clear there was so much more to the story than he was telling her. Why had he abandoned what sounded like a glittering career in Rome to come back home to a position as a waiter, especially when his family were no longer here but in Sicily?

# Tilly's Tuscan Teashop

She had never expected, or wanted, to form a friendship with anyone while she was in Tuscany, but she couldn't help feeling drawn to Matteo. Clearly something terrible had happened to him, and his family, something that had caused the pain that festered deep in his soul that only others who had suffered similar trauma noticed. And yet, unlike her, he still lived life to the full; a life filled with vibrancy, with colour, with *speed*, as well as good wine and great food.

\*\*\*

Later, as she sipped on a pre-dinner Aperol Spritz in the Piazza Santa Croce, watching tourists and locals alike taking their evening *passeggiata* before dinner, listening to snippets of conversation in a variety of languages, and appreciating the many delicious aromas swirling through the humid night air, she realised that for the first time, the ever-present nugget of pain that had taken up residence in her chest two years ago had softened a little and she actually felt relaxed.

Maybe Italy's famous *dolce vita* was starting to rub off on her after all.

# Chapter Fourteen

Tilly pushed back the curtains, flung open the window, and breathed in the cool, early morning air perfumed with the lavender that grew in the pots on her bedroom window sill. The sun had only just poked its nose above the horizon and yet the resident bee alliance was already hard at work collecting that day's quota of nectar. She wondered where Eduardo was, then remembered that, thankfully, he wasn't due to visit the villa that day, and her mood lifted even further.

After rummaging in Olivia's wardrobe, she chose a satsuma-coloured tee shirt with ruffled sleeves and a pair of white Capri pants. She didn't know what it was about Villa Avanti, but every morning she woke up with a smile on her face, eager for the day to begin, her heart lighter, her mood brighter than it had been for years. And not only had she abandoned the all-black outfits in favour of more colourful sartorial choices, she was also eating more healthily, too – well, she'd at least ditched her reliance on buttered toast as the main staple of her daily meal.

She skipped down the stairs to make herself a coffee, happy that she didn't have to be at the teashop until midday to start the preparations for another of her themed afternoon teas – this time for the members of a book club from the Cotswolds who had recently read *Under the Tuscan Sun* and wanted to experience their own little slice of the Italian good life. Instead of the traditional afternoon tea they were expecting, they would be indulging in book-shaped sandwiches, and a selection of scones and cupcakes decorated with edible rice paper printed with miniature books that Tilly had sourced from a specialist website.

She switched on the radio, humming along to one of the tunes as the kettle boiled, then took her cup of coffee out to the swimming pool terrace where she could sit in the sunshine and enjoy a few minutes scrolling through her social media accounts, something she had also cut down on since arriving in Tuscany. However, when she turned on her phone, she saw she had a missed call from Freya and decided to call her back instead.

'Hey Freya, how are things? Any news about Dexter?'

Freya groaned. 'Nothing yet. The guy's like the Scarlet Pimpernel. I don't know about rock guitarist; he should get a job as an International Man of

Mystery. His manager has tried everything to contact him, short of flying over to California and searching the Pacific Crest Trail himself, but I can't see him doing that; apparently long-haul plays havoc with his skin.'

'How's everyone doing?'

'Not good, I'm afraid. Until the insurance money comes through, we're all in limbo. Without her equipment, Holly can't continue with her pet grooming services, so she's offering dog-walking instead, but it doesn't pay enough for her to meet her expenses. There's a job going at the local kennels, but they had over fifteen applicants, so she's not holding out much hope of getting that.'

'How is Poppy getting on?'

'Beckie's taken her on part-time at the Boathouse Bistro to help her with the clean-up, and then when they get the all-clear from the health and safety people, she's going to start making her hand-made chocolates again and sell them from the bistro, so that's something. She's a qualified pâtissière and she wouldn't have had any difficulty finding work in one of the five-star hotels around her, but she's adamant she wants to stay in Blossumwood Bay and rebuild her artisan chocolate business, especially after what happened last year.'

'What about Suzie?'

'She's the one I feel most sorry for; she lost the most out of all of us. Apparently, the value of the stock she lost runs into the tens of thousands of pounds, and it's heartbreaking to think of all those sparkling gemstones just washed out to sea for the fish to enjoy. She's devastated about letting her clients down, too, especially those who were waiting for their engagement and wedding rings. It's all just so upsetting.'

Tilly heard the crack in Freya's voice and her heart gave a nip of sympathy for everyone who was affected, although she was relieved that the bistro had survived the fire and that Poppy and Beckie's livelihoods at least could be salvaged.

'How are you holding up, Frey?'

'To be honest, I'm bored; it's my own fault, really. To keep my mind off everything, I spent the whole of last week in a frenzy of activity; I made candles, soaps, bath bombs… I even went back to my roots and made a signature perfume for Chloe's birthday to cheer her up. But now I have no stock left and I have nothing to do. I've looked into starting a mobile aromatherapy business, and a few of my salon clients have shown an interest in that, but until the insurance money comes through, I can't even think about buying new equipment.'

'You can't just sit at home and stare at the walls, Frey.'

'I know, I know.'

Tilly considered avoiding the issue that hung heavy in the air – after all, she was an expert at that – but as Freya's best friend, she couldn't bear to think of her sitting in her tiny cottage, without anyone around to make sure she was okay, so she inhaled a breath and delved in.

'You know, once your uncle Toby's chateau is sold, you'll have a decent lump sum to invest in your business, and not just your aromatherapy business –

you could also think about launching the perfume business you've always wanted to do. Your uncle was a famous "nose" for over twenty years and you've inherited his gift, and his flair, for fragrances. You'll be amazing! Maybe this is your opportunity to shoot for your dream.'

'I really don't—'

'It's the perfect time to take a trip to the south of France, to pay a visit to that useless estate agent – perhaps fire him and instruct another one – and tie up the loose ends over there, if not for you, then for your parents. And if I haven't convinced you, then let me tell you that Tuscany is only a short train ride from Nice.'

Freya sighed. 'I want to argue with you, but actually, I think you're right. I do need to go over there. I'm not bothered about the money, I gave up on my dream of opening a perfumery years ago, but you're right, it's not fair that Uncle Toby's affairs are still outstanding. I know he and my parents didn't get on, but I adored him. He was such fun, a free spirit, and I always had a fantastic time when I went over to his farmhouse for the summer holidays while my parents were away working in some far-flung war zone. If they had any idea about all the crazy parties he took me to they'd be horrified!'

'So will you go?'

'I'll think about it.'

'Promise?'

'Promise. Now, enough about me and my woes, have you heard from Josh?'

Tilly experienced an uncomfortable swoop in her chest.

'I've tried to call him every single day since I arrived in Italy, but I get his voicemail every time. I left messages for him to call me back, but when it got to Saturday morning I'd had enough; he's clearly screening his calls. When I saw a post on his Instagram account—'

'Oh, Tilly, I thought you weren't going to go there!'

'It was just a quick peek,' she said defensively. 'Anyway, he was in a bar in Singapore partying the night away, so I called him and told his voicemail that I had no intention of waiting until we could talk about what happened with Melissa face-to-face, our relationship is over and I asked him not to bother responding to the previous messages I'd left because I was blocking his number from my phone.'

'Do you think that was a good idea?'

'What's there to say, Frey? The bottom line is that I can't trust him anymore. Anyway, if I'm honest, our relationship has been over for some time; we've been leading separate lives – me in Devon, Josh in London – since I left the airline. We don't have anything in common now, and I should have realised that, and so I have to take my share of responsibility. You have to admit, I haven't been the best girlfriend these last two years, have I?'

'There's a good reason for that, Tilly,' said Freya, softly.

'I know, but I should have—'

'Tilly! There's no point dwelling on the past, none of us can change that.'

A pang of remorse swooped through Tilly's heart when she heard the pain in Freya's voice, and she regretted the direction their conversation had turned. She wasn't the only one dealing with a relationship break-up, and at least her break-up with Josh hadn't been played out in full view of her family and friends.

'Sorry, Frey, I didn't mean to—'

'It's fine. So, tell me, are there any handsome Italian guys in San Vincente?'

Although Tilly would have liked nothing more than to regale Freya with every detail of her evening with Matteo, especially their visit to the rose garden, which she knew Freya would have loved, she decided that she couldn't deal with the barrage of well-meaning questions, not to mention the friendly teasing, that would follow, so she went with something else.

'Well, there's Eduardo.'

'Who's Eduardo?'

She smiled when she heard the interest in Freya's voice and knew she had made the right decision. She could write a book on the many questionable gardening exploits she'd witnessed since arriving at the villa, so there was no risk of her friend asking about anyone else on the horizon.

'He's Liv and Enzo's pool maintenance guy.'

'With rippling abs and toned thighs?'

Tilly laughed. 'Not really. He's also supposed to be helping to look after the garden, but so far he's ripped up a bunch of Liv's favourite plants and flowers, dropped a tin of red paint on the swimming pool terrace, which took *hours* to clean up, and he could have killed someone with his less-than-perfect carpentry skills. However, he does arrive for work dressed from head-to-toe in Armani and wearing a pair of Gucci loafers, which he covers with plastic carrier bags so they don't get dirty.'

Freya giggled. 'Sounds right up your street!'

'Unfortunately, he's already got an admirer.'

'Really? She's a brave woman.'

'It's Jess, the girl who's been helping Liv out at the teashop this summer. She's smitten; it's just as well she's heading to med school in September, if they do get together, she'll need her medical training if she's to survive!'

'I'm so glad you decided to go to Tuscany, Tilly. You sound so much happier than when you left, and you've only been there a couple of weeks. The famous Italian *dolce vita* is certainly working its magic on you.'

'And the Cote d'Azur lifestyle can do the same for you. I'll call you next week to make sure you've booked the flights,' said Tilly, hoping she sounded the right mix of firm and supportive.

'Okay, okay.' Freya laughed. 'Speak soon.'

As soon as the connection was cut, Tilly's phone burst into life again and she couldn't help but smile when she saw the caller ID.

'Hey, Liv.'

'*Ciao*, darling, how's *Bella Italia*?'

'Everything's fine. Actually, it's more than fine; those photographs we uploaded last week have increased footfall, and I hope you don't mind but Jess, Carlotta and I are trialling something new. Remember the *Gardens of Tuscany* tour we had in last week for afternoon tea before they headed off to the Boboli Gardens? Well, we decided to make it a themed afternoon tea, with flower-shaped sandwiches and scones.'

'That's an amazing idea,' said Olivia. 'So everything is okay?'

Tilly decided to spare her sister the worry of the flood and the weird soap problem, so she changed the subject before Olivia realised that she was avoiding her question. Olivia was super-astute when it came to spotting little white lies, but that was harder to do over the phone.

'How's things over there?'

'Oh, Tilly, I'm having an absolute ball! Boston is such a wonderful place with a whole host of opportunities that aren't available in Italy. Remember I told you that Enzo was helping Giovanni to finish off his summerhouse?'

'Yes.'

'Well, Giovanni and Daniella's neighbour saw what a fantastic job they were doing, and guess what? He just happens to be the senior partner in one of the most prominent architecture practices in Massachusetts. When he found out Enzo was also an architect and had trained in Florence, they spent the whole day comparing notes, which culminated in Harry inviting him to visit a project he's overseeing in Springfield where they're experimenting with a number of cutting-edge techniques to reduce the energy and water that's used in its construction. I've not seen him so animated about the use of dry mortar and fly ash for a long time.'

'Wow, that's fantastic. And what about you? How are you doing?'

'That's what I'm ringing about,' said Olivia, her excitement bubbling over. 'Okay, so, remember last time we spoke I told you that I was learning a few old Italian recipes from Enzo's mum?'

'Yes?'

'Well, Daniella had a few friends over for supper on Saturday night and I was responsible for the dessert course. I made tiramisù, and a torta Caprese, and a torta Barozzi, but I also added a few of the recipes from Mum's repertoire that were staples at the café and they went down so well that Jodie – that's Daniella's friend who owns a pâtisserie and café in an upmarket suburb of Boston – has asked me to supply her store with a few of Mum's chocolate chequerboard cakes! Oh, Tills, I'm just so excited! I spent all day yesterday practising; Daniella's kitchen looks like it's about to host an edible chess tournament!'

'That's fantastic, Liv, I'm so happy for you.'

'Enzo's mum is helping me, and she says she's thrilled to be doing something useful. Did you get my email suggesting you make Mum's orange blossom tart for the San Vincente food competition?

That's what I was planning to enter before I came over to Boston.'

'Yes, I did, thanks, and I agree with you.'

'You do?'

'Yes, it's the perfect choice. In fact, you probably won't believe this, but Gabriella and I have already done a culinary dress rehearsal and it went really well; she's even promised to make a batch of orange blossom gelato to go with it.'

'What recipe did you use?'

Tilly paused before saying, 'I used Mum's recipe.'

'Really?'

The shock in her sister's voice made Tilly smile.

'Yes, I stumbled across her old hand-illustrated recipe book in the drawer under the console, and, of course, I found all the ingredients I needed at the teashop. But, Liv, even though the tarts were edible, there's no way Jess, Carlotta and I can make anything even approaching the level of excellence that Rocco Bianchi produces in his state-of-the-art kitchen, or should I say *laboratory*. The guy's a professionally trained chef!'

'I know, I know, and I'm not expecting the teashop to take the gold rosette, or even the silver, or the bronze – well, maybe the bronze. All I really want is an acknowledgement that the food we serve at *Té e Torta* is at least worthy of recognition. I've even blended a special orange blossom tea for the occasion, which I think will enhance the experience; so it looks like we'll be presenting a trio of orange blossom deliciousness!'

'Well, in that case, we'll give it our best shot,' said Tilly, relieved that the pressure was off, but still determined to do another practice session to make sure she produced the very best orange blossom tart she was capable of, if only for her own peace of mind. 'I can't wait to see you at the end of next week, Liv. Jess and I will be at the airport to meet you! Would you believe she wants to bring balloons and confetti?'

'Erm… about that.'

Tilly's stomach performed an uncomfortable somersault. 'What do you mean?'

'Enzo would really like to stay until the end of the month. It's just an extra week. Is that okay with you? If you need to get back to Devon, that's fine; I can fly home without him, but if you don't… well, it'd be great if I could stay with him, bake a few more of Mum's cakes for Jodie, maybe take a trip over to see the Niagara Falls. Remember Mum and Dad went there for their silver wedding anniversary?'

Tilly thought of the photograph on Olivia's console in the hallway that her sister had displayed so proudly but which she'd hidden in the drawer, and a spasm of guilt shot through her chest. She loved her sister, she wanted her to be happy, to enjoy her trip to see her husband's family, and to enjoy lots of new experiences, just as *she* was. Freya had told her there was no news yet from Dexter, so she had nothing to rush back to Devon for. How could she refuse?

# Tilly's Tuscan Teashop

'I do remember, Liv,' she said softly. 'And of course it's okay with me. I've got loads of ideas for more themed afternoon teas to try out on your unsuspecting customers. Okay, I think I might have a swim in your gorgeous pool before I head over to the teashop to welcome the Cotswolds Book Club.'

'Thanks again for everything you're doing, Tills. Love you.'

'To the moon and back, Liv.'

After her conversation with her sister, Tilly headed back into the villa to see if she could find a swimming costume amongst Olivia's summer wardrobe. She had just slotted her phone back into her pocket when, to her surprise, it started to buzz again and she assumed it was her sister who had forgotten to tell us something. She answered it quickly without checking the caller ID and was surprised when she heard the panicking voice of Jess.

'Tilly, can you come over to the teashop?'

'Sure, but I thought—'

'Please, just come now.'

And the line went dead.

# Chapter Fifteen

Tilly collected her satchel, hopped onto her Vespa, and headed to San Vincente, her brain bouncing from one dreadful scenario to another. By the time she had arrived at the piazza, she was so wound up that she wondered whether she had time to stop at *Ristorante Rocco* for a quick infusion of caffeine to calm her nerves, but was shocked to see a queue snaking across the front of the restaurant. However, when she followed the direction of the people who were standing in line, her jaw dropped; they weren't waiting for a table so they could sample Rocco's snail gnocchi, they were waiting for a table at *Té e Torta*!

She hurried down the narrow, cobbled street and into the teashop where every seat was occupied and Jess and Carlotta were zipping between the tables, serving everyone with a traditional afternoon tea – at eleven thirty in the morning – as quickly as they could. An upbeat buzz of conversation circulated the room, in a number of different languages, and there was a delicious aroma of warm baked scones floating through the air.

Tilly rushed into the kitchen, pulled on her apron, and started to make a batch of fruit scones, which freed up Carlotta to prepare another enormous pile of crustless sandwiches and arrange them artistically on the bottom tier of six more china cake stands.

'What's going on, Carlotta?'

Carlotta paused in her epic sandwich-cutting marathon to push her long dark fringe from her eyes with the back of her hand. Like Eduardo, the fact that she was at work was no excuse not to look like she was about to attend a Puccini opera; Tilly wished she could pull off the contour-hugging satsuma dress with cashmere cardigan with the same pizzazz. And how Carlotta could manage to do an eight-hour shift in a pair of towering gold sandals she had no idea.

'I was about to ask you the same question! Did you talk to someone from the *Gazzettino*?'

'Yes, I chatted to Elisa… Oh.'

'Apparently a full-page feature, along with photographs, appeared in their Sunday lifestyle magazine and… well, you can see what the result was.'

'Oh my God!'

After slotting three trays of scones into the oven, Tilly turned her attention to slicing a strawberry cheesecake into bite-sized pieces and placing them on the top tier of the cake stands alongside two lavender-flavoured macarons, two miniature cupcakes with a swirl of lemon buttercream and a sprinkle of popping candy, and two tiny Victoria sponge cakes oozing with jam and cream, and took the finished product out to the hungry guests.

'Wow, where have all these people come from?' asked Gabriella, appearing at the door between the rear patio and the kitchen, for once minus her faithful friend, Sandro.

'Did you see the piece in the *Gazzettino*?' asked Tilly, handing Jess yet another completed tower of afternoon tea goodies to take into the teashop.

'Yes, I did. What a fabulous advertising coup! I'm thrilled for you, Tilly. Elisa must have really enjoyed her visit here, but permit me to give you a word of warning. You might want to steer clear of Rocco for the next few days.'

'Rocco? Why?'

'I popped over there for a chat with Stefania earlier – she's going through a few things at the moment – and Rocco was in the middle of bawling her out in the kitchen, threatening to fire her and the rest of his long-suffering staff. When I asked her what was going on, she said he'd also seen the article and was livid because he's been trying to get the editor to do a similar piece on his restaurant for the last six months! He was throwing pots and pans around like a mini tornado, but that was nothing compared to when he saw the queue outside his restaurant and realised that it wasn't for his mango ravioli with mascarpone and espresso caviar, but for the "stodgy fodder" at the teashop!' Gabriella paused, and then smirked. 'You might want to find somewhere else to have your sneaky morning coffee, Tilly, or you *could* switch to tea? Need any help? My cousin Elena is holding the fort at the gelateria this morning, so I'm all yours.'

'Oh, Gabriella, you're a life-saver,' said Jess, as she dashed through the kitchen to collect another of the finished cake stands, that day's ribbons – on brand in powder blue with white polka dots – whipping at her cheeks as she spun round on her toes like a ballerina to return to the teashop.

\*\*\*

For the next two hours, the four of them worked non-stop in choreographed efficiency; with Carlotta on sandwich duty, Tilly baking what felt like a never-ending supply of scones and mini-cupcakes – not only for their current customers but also for the Cotswold Book Club member who were booked in at three o'clock that afternoon – and Gabriella preparing the bite-sized meringues and summer fruit tarts as well as joining Jess on waitressing duties in the teashop and taking turns on the washing up.

'Now that we've cleared the queue, I think we need to put the *Chiuso* sign on the door,' said Tilly, after delivering another teapot of the Lady Grey tea to a table of women who had travelled all the way from Pisa to sample their wares. 'We've got to start preparing the book club ladies' afternoon tea. I've made the scones – do you think three dozen will be enough?'

Jess laughed. 'That's three each; I think it'll be enough. And those sandwiches are absolutely amazing, Carlotta! I adore those little book flags; the idea is inspired!'

Tilly looked at the silver tray where Carlotta had set out a battalion of crust-less sandwiches with a variety of fillings, each one cut into the shape of a book. But that wasn't all she had done; she had also made tiny cocktail-stick flags displaying the titles and authors of well-known books; English and Italian.

'*Grazie mille*,' said Carlotta, her cheeks colouring with delight.

\*\*\*

Thirty minutes later, the teashop had finally emptied – after Jess had all-but forcibly evicted the last stragglers who had wanted an in-depth discussion about the origins of the lapsang souchong tea they had, to their surprise, enjoyed so much. They cleared the tables, quickly dressing them in the tablecloths printed with a profusion of books and bookmarks that Tilly had found on a specialist website, arranged the sandwiches, scones – with tiny pots of cream and jam – and the mini cupcakes with the rice paper toppers on the tiered china stands, then stood back to admire their efforts with all-of ten minutes left to go before the tour group arrived at three o'clock.

'Wow, the teashop looks stunning!' said Jess, taking a few photographs for her Instagram page, then dropping down into a chair with a long sigh of relief, followed by Tilly, Carlotta and Gabriella. 'But I have to admit, I'm absolutely exhausted!'

'Oh, Jess, I've just noticed your manicure!' Tilly laughed when she saw each one of her nails sported a miniature book. 'I love it! I'm ashamed to say that it's been a long time since I treated myself to a manicure, or any kind of pamper session for that matter.'

'Well, you never know when you might bump into the man of your dreams,' mused Jess, her lips suddenly curling into a smile as she honed in on Tilly. 'Oh my God, with everything going on at the teashop this morning I completely forgot to ask you how your date went on Saturday night!'

'What date?' asked Gabriella, sitting up straight in her chair in anticipation of hearing a piece of juicy gossip, her eyes flicking from Tilly to Jess and back again. 'Who did you go on a date with?'

'It wasn't a date,' said Tilly, firmly, trying to ignore the whoosh of heat that had invaded her cheeks. 'Matteo just offered to take me for a coffee… and dinner.'

'Mmm, so it *must* be over with Luciana,' Gabriella mumbled to herself.

'Who's Luciana?' asked Jess.

Gabriella's eyes widened when she realised that she had spoken out loud.

'Oh, no one really,' she said far too quickly for anyone in her audience to believe her. 'Just someone Matteo lived with briefly when he was working in Rome. As far as I know, he hasn't been back there since he left, and I haven't seen Luciana here in San Vincente either. I think if she *had* been up here, then some paparazzo would have snapped her visit.'

'A paparazzo?' said Tilly, confused. 'Why would a paparazzo—'

Fortunately, Gabriella was released from the impending cross-examination – much to her apparent relief – by the timely arrival of the Cotswolds Book Club party, clutching a variety of books, both fiction and non-fiction, paperback and hardback, all set in Tuscany, chattering excitedly about their visit that morning to Cortona to see the villa of *Under the Tuscan Sun* fame.

Tilly had no choice but to pin a welcoming smile on her face and focus on providing the best book-themed afternoon tea in the whole of Tuscany. She saw with delight that the women had not just brought their books with them, as well as their Kindles, but had also dressed for the occasion in tea dresses – one of which was made from fabric printed with books. However, Jess was the only one with a literature-themed manicure, something that caused envy amongst their guests.

'There's a young Italian couple and an elderly English couple asking if we can squeeze them in for a traditional afternoon tea,' said Jess, her ribbons unravelled in the rising heat of the kitchen and dangling around her shoulders like streamers. 'As we still have some sandwiches left from this morning, and a batch of your sultana scones, Tilly, I said they could take the tables we've set up in the courtyard, if that's okay?'

'It's fine. In fact, it's a good idea. I'm all for cutting down on waste,' said Tilly, already reaching for a cake stand and filling it with two afternoon teas. 'Can you make the Earl Grey, Carlotta?'

'Of course.'

'Actually, the Italian couple have asked for the ashwagandha tea.' Jess smirked, collecting a spotty teapot from the shelf. 'Although, if you ask me, they don't need any help in that arena; they can barely tear their eyes from each other. At least the English couple are more enamoured by their art gallery books – they fit right in with the book club contingent.'

\*\*\*

Two hours later, just as Tilly thought she couldn't stand up for a moment longer, the tour party left the teashop for their appointment with a guide who was taking them to see the cobbled streets and alleyways in Florence that Lucy Honeychurch from *A Room with a View* had frequented, leaving just the two couples enjoying their afternoon tea in relative peace.

After saying several heartfelt *grazie milles* to Gabriella who needed to relieve her cousin at the gelateria, Tilly switched on the radio and a soft operatic tune swirled around the teashop as she set about tidying up the crockery and cutlery, then removing the book-themed tablecloths.

# Tilly's Tuscan Teashop

'I think that went really well,' said Jess, bringing a tray piled with teacups and saucers into the kitchen where Carlotta had set up an assembly line to wash, dry and return everything to their designated places on the shelves and in the drawers. 'We'll definitely have to do that—'

'Oh my God! Oh my God! Oh my God!'

The high-pitched scream had come from the direction of the patio. With panic churning, Tilly dropped her tea towel and ran outside, with Jess and Carlotta following in her wake, where she saw that the elderly Englishwoman had jumped up from her seat, her trembling hands pressed to her lips, her face wreathed in distress. She was staring down at her china plate on which sat one of Tilly's fruit scones, sliced in two, ready for a dollop of cream and a topping of Olivia's home-made strawberry jam.

'That's absolutely disgusting!' the woman's husband grimaced.

'What's disgusting?' asked Tilly, rushing to their table.

The woman pointed to her plate and to Tilly's astonishment there was a dead fly that had clearly fallen from the inside of the fruit scone she had baked freshly that afternoon.

'It's a bluebottle,' said Jess, unnecessarily.

Unfortunately, the commotion had burst the young Italian couple's bubble of love and they abandoned their table to join the group. They didn't have to speak enough English to understand what was going, and when their gaze fell on the bluebottle, their eyes filled with revulsion and they all-but sprinted from the teashop after paying.

'I hope you're not expecting us to pay extra for this privilege!' said the woman's husband, clearly recovering from the shock addition to their afternoon tea before his wife. 'Come on, Hannah, I think we should leave these young women to deal with this.'

Tilly, Jess and Carlotta stood motionless as the couple gathered their belongings and headed for the door. Carlotta recovered her faculties first and followed them into the teashop, apologising again and again until they left and she could drop the latch and pull down the pale-blue blind before returning to the courtyard where Tilly and Jess were still standing, mouths agape, staring at the offending insect.

'What the… I don't… Oh, God!' Tilly collapsed into one of the chairs, her heart pounding so hard she thought it would break free from her chest and head for the Tuscan hills. 'I can't believe—'

'Hang on,' said Jess, who had joined Tilly at the table and was prodding the culprit with a knife.

'What are you doing?'

'It's plastic.'

'What is?'

'The bluebottle. Look.'

Jess picked up the fly and handed it to Tilly, who promptly dropped it onto the table before leaning forward to examine it more closely.

# Tilly's Tuscan Teashop

'You're right; it is plastic!' Tilly allowed the breath she had been holding to escape. 'And I can absolutely, categorically, assure you that I did not add that to my last batch of scones! What's going on?'

'I have no idea,' said Jess.

'Sabotage,' said Carlotta.

Both Tilly and Jess turned to Carlotta and said in unison, 'What do you mean?'

'The flood, the soap, now this?'

'But who on earth would do something like this?'

The women exchanged glances.

'Rocco Bianchi?' said Jess.

'I think we would have noticed him if he had popped into the kitchen.'

'Not necessarily; we were all in the teashop serving customers at some point. Anyone could have snuck in through the rear gate over there, through the courtyard and into the kitchen, then left after the deed was done without anyone seeing them.'

'Do you really think this is his style, though? Putting plastic flies in scones?'

'No, not really.' Jess sighed. 'But who else is there?'

Tilly hesitated before she spoke, but she felt she still had to say what had floated across her mind. 'Has Eduardo been to the teashop today?'

Jess looked uncomfortable and Tilly's heart dropped like a stone down a well.

'Actually, he did drop by for a few minutes earlier. We had a brief chat in the courtyard, that's all. Do you really think it could be him though? Maybe he did it as a joke?'

'But it's not funny,' said Tilly, softly. 'What if one of the book club women had been served with that scone? What do you think they would have put in their review? I'm keeping my fingers crossed that the English couple aren't active on social media, or interested in leaving reviews, so I think we should be okay, but do you think you could have a word with Eduardo?'

'Sure.'

Working together, it didn't take long for them to finish the tidying up and, after waving Jess and Carlotta off to party the night away in a bar in Siena, Tilly sank into one of the chairs, her thoughts bouncing from one thing to another like Tigger on a sugar high, more upset than she cared to admit that someone was intent on destroying the reputation of her sister's beloved *Té e Torta*.

In her heart of hearts, she didn't think Eduardo had a malicious bone in his body, but neither did she think Rocco would do something so ridiculously juvenile, which meant there was someone else out there who didn't want the teashop to succeed and that possibility caused her stomach to curdle.

# Chapter Sixteen

By the time Friday arrived, Tilly had been so busy at the teashop that she still hadn't had the opportunity to practice her mum's orange blossom tart recipe again, or have a go at brewing her sister's orange blossom tea, and she was starting to panic. Even Jess had managed to find the time to experiment with her "romance themed" project, the details of which she was keeping close to her chest – apart from a couple of visits to see Gabriella who had promised to make her a complementary gelato.

The San Vincente fiesta was the following day and the village streets were awash with flags and bunting, and a host of wooden stalls had been set up around the piazza for local businesses and artisans to showcase their wares. There was even a makeshift stage in front of the church where, after the presentation of the various rosettes by the mayor, a band would entertain the residents and visitors well into the night.

'Mind if I take these left-over ciabattas home?' asked Jess, removing her apron and tucking a loaf of bread under each arm as she made her way to the door after they'd tidied up following a very successful "Cute Kitten"-themed afternoon tea. 'Waste not, want not.'

'I thought you said you were on a no-carbs diet today?' said Tilly, collecting a cardboard box from the dresser in which she'd stashed everything she would need to make a batch of her mum's orange blossom tarts, along with a brass tin filled with the orange blossom tea that Olivia had blended when she thought she would be the one entering the village's foodie contest.

'No, I said I was on the *carb-cycling* diet.'

'What on earth is the carb-cycling diet?'

'It's where I can only eat carbs while I'm cycling. I've brought my bicycle to work today, so I'll eat one of these on my way home. Is everything ready for the competition tomorrow? Are you sure you don't want me to come over to the villa and help you make the tarts?'

Tilly would have loved Jess's help, but she knew that she was planning to spend an hour or so baking a batch of her "mystery" cakes before meeting a coterie of friends from back home in Cornwall. They were on a backpacking trip around Europe and had stopped off in Florence specially to see Jess, and she didn't want her to miss their get-together, which she knew Jess had been looking forward to for weeks.

'No thanks, I've got everything in hand.' She patted her cardboard box. 'I'm going to spend the night baking up a storm, then enjoying a few glasses of the Chianti Carlotta bought for me from one of the local wineries that I haven't had chance to visit yet. I've got to be up at the crack of dawn tomorrow to deliver the tea and the tarts to the judging booth, so I'm planning on having an early night.'

'Okay, see you later.'

Jess dashed off to collect her bicycle and Tilly couldn't help giggling when she saw her wobbling down the street, munching on the end of her bread stick. She had avoided asking Jess what her fixation with off-the-wall diets was all about for fear of offending her, but the *carb-cycling* diet? Maybe it was time she did have a gentle word with her before things got even more outlandish.

She secured her cardboard box of ingredients to the back of her Vespa and sped back to the villa to make a start on creating the best orange blossom tart she had ever made to do Olivia, and their mum, proud. For the last two years she had avoided engaging in any kind of baking, or cooking even – beyond her staple diet of buttered toast – for fear of resurrecting the grief demons that had plagued her life since her parents' passing. However, her time at the teashop had shown her that, far from increasing the pain, baking actually helped to reduce it. Thinking about her mum hurt, but it also made her feel close to her, too, as though she was still a part of her life.

She skidded to a halt at the front steps of the villa, removed her helmet, shook out her hair and paused to drink in the view. The sun had already disappeared behind the hillside to her right and the sky was awash with a shimmer of dusky pinks, salmons and apricots, the land reflecting a soft golden glow from the day's warmth. The cicadas were out in force, performing their nightly opera, accompanied by the tinkle of cascading water from the Cupid fountain, and there was a faint fragrance of lavender and honeysuckle lingering in the air.

She knew that if she tried to photograph the scene, she wouldn't be able to do it justice, so instead she gathered her cardboard box and carried it into the villa. She poured herself a glass of ice-cold water from the fridge, then headed upstairs to shower away the grime of the day.

\*\*\*

Feeling rejuvenated, she selected one of Olivia's sunflower-coloured spaghetti strapped tops and a pair of denim shorts, tied her hair into a high ponytail, and skipped back down the stairs for an evening filled with culinary fun.

She had just plunged her hands into a bowl full of flour when there was a knock on the front door. She sighed, unsure who could be calling on her at seven o'clock at night. However, she couldn't very well ignore them because her Vespa was parked outside, so she padded down the hallway and pulled open the front door.

'Oh!'

'Well, I have to admit that I've been greeted with *more* enthusiasm.' Matteo grinned, his dark eyes sparkling with amusement. 'It's just that I bumped into Jess in San Vincente and she said you were spending your Friday night "baking into a storm".'

'Baking *up* a storm.' She laughed, loving the way Matteo's sexy Italian accent sounded when he tried out new English phrases. Standing there, on the villa's steps, he looked even more attractive than usual in a pair of buttock-hugging black jeans, a pale pink shirt with the cuffs rolled back to reveal his tanned forearms, and his curls neatly gelled into place. She caught a whiff of his eucalyptus cologne and had to fight the urge to close her eyes, raise her nose in the air, and revel in the delicious aroma.

'Want an extra pair of hands?'

'I'd love that, thank you. Come in, come in.'

Matteo smiled and followed her into the kitchen. 'So, what are we making?'

'I've spoken to Liv and she wants us to enter one of her orange blossom tarts – along with a teapot of her specially blended orange blossom tea to enhance the flavour – into the San Vincente food competition tomorrow,' said Tilly, an idea suddenly popping into her head. 'Hey, why don't *you* make something, too? Your parents owned a restaurant; there must be hundreds of family recipes you could do.'

Tilly saw a Matteo's lips tighten slightly at her suggestion, but he recovered quickly.

'I'm not sure about entering the competition, but I'd love to make one of my *nonna*'s recipes for you to try. She made the best *torta della nonna* in the whole of Tuscany; I think the recipe is similar to your sister's orange blossom tart.'

'*Fantastica!*' Tilly declared, handing Matteo an apron before tying her own around her waist and striding across to the other side of the kitchen. 'This is Liv's store cupboard; it's stocked to the ceiling with everything you could possibly need. So, let's bake!'

\*\*\*

Tilly couldn't help but smile; like her, Matteo wasn't the tidiest of chefs. After making their respective pastries, wrapping it in cling-film, and placing it in the fridge to rest, every surface in the kitchen was covered with a kaleidoscope of spilled ingredients – flour, sugar, butter, eggs – and what seemed like every one of Olivia's culinary utensils and gadgets had been removed from its allocated space and either pressed into use or scrutinised by a fascinated Matteo.

'What's this for?'

'It's an avocado slicer.'

'And this?'

'It's a soda siphon. Enzo loves that.'

'What about this?'

Matteo held up a bright green corkscrew with a spray nozzle on the top.

'It's a citrus juice mister.'

'Why would you need one of those?'

'It's great for salads, and seafood, and for spraying your sliced avocados to keep them fresh for longer.'

When she saw his look of complete incredulity, she selected a lime from the fruit bowl, then reached out to take the mister from him, a zip of delicious electricity shooting through her veins when their fingers touched. She demonstrated a technique that she had learned from Olivia and almost forgotten, laughing when Matteo shook his head in disbelief.

'I have never seen anything so completely crazy!' Matteo said, taking the mister from her to inspect it more closely. 'You know, in Italy we take the preparation and consumption of food very seriously – if you stand still for long enough, someone will feed you – and you will never see an Italian eating "on the hoof". Meals are to be enjoyed, every mouthful appreciated, commented upon, the flavours savoured for as long as possible. Food is one of the good things in life; its creation is an art form that is to be rejoiced just as much as our operas, our paintings, and our architecture. I've been in many kitchens – domestic and commercial – in my life, and I can assure you that I have never seen as many appliances and gadgets as Olivia has amassed here! Is there an appliance that will make our custards for us?'

Tilly smiled. 'No, we'll have to make it the old-fashioned way.'

'Great!'

They worked together in companionable silence, both completely absorbed by their tasks, until they had made their respective fillings and set them aside to cool. Tilly then removed her pastry from the fridge and took her time rolling it out to the requisite thickness before lining six fluted baking tins and sliding them into the oven to bake blind. As Matteo's recipe didn't require his three pastry cases to be baked first, he poured his custard mixture straight into the pastry-lined tins, sprinkled them with a generous handful of pine nuts and placed them on the bench, ready to bake when Tilly's orange blossom tarts were ready.

'Okay, now for the tea.'

She set out a couple of teacups and saucers on the table, then removed one of Olivia's favourite Emma Bridgewater teapots from the shelf above the sink, rinsed it with boiling water from the kettle, sprinkled in a few spoonfuls of loose orange blossom tea, and set it aside. It was important to make the tea fresh when her tarts were ready so they could taste-test them together, and she was disappointed that she didn't have a scoop of Gabriella's promised orange blossom gelato to go with it.

Matteo smirked. 'Tea? Really?'

'Not my idea.' Tilly laughed. 'This is Liv's competition entry, not mine.'

'What would *you* enter, then?'

'Probably my mum's coffee and walnut cake,' she replied without thinking, experiencing a sharp stab of pain for her unintentional slip-up.

'Sounds like your mum was a great cook.'

Tilly swallowed down hard on the emotions that were stirring in her chest, determined to credit her mum with the recipe she had just created.

'She was an *amazing* cook. She owned a café in Cornwall – it was called the Orange Blossom Café – and Olivia and I used to spend our weekends and holidays there, helping in the kitchen and serving the customers; it was a fun time. Over the years, Mum recorded her favourite recipes in a special notebook; it was her dream to publish a cookery book one day, but, sadly, that didn't happen.'

She saw that Matteo was about to press her for more information, but she couldn't face explaining what had happened. She was so desperate to change the subject that she said the first thing that came into her head.

'Gabriella says you lived with someone when you were in Rome,' she blurted, heat whooshing into her cheeks as soon as the words had left her lips. She was mortified at her bluntness, especially when she saw the shock in Matteo's eyes. 'Gosh, I'm so sorry, I didn't mean to—'

Matteo held up his hand to stop Tilly from digging her hole deeper. 'It's okay, Gabriella is right, I *did* live with someone. In fact, we were engaged, but it's over, and it's been over for a while. When I came back to Tuscany at the end of last year, Luciana stayed on in Rome.'

To hide her embarrassment, Tilly made a fuss over removing her orange blossom tarts from the oven and replacing them with Matteo's *torta della nonnas*, then dropped into a seat at the kitchen table. She knew she shouldn't pry any further, but she was curious, and discretion had never been one of her best qualities.

'Why didn't Luciana come home with you?'

Matteo joined her at the table, concentrating hard on the teapot that stood between them, and it was a while before he spoke.

'Lots of reasons; mainly because she's an actress and most of her work is in Rome, not in a tiny village nestled in the Tuscan hills, but also because I came back here because I lost my job at the production company I used to work for, which meant I had no income, and no money for anything other than a tiny studio above a gelateria, which is a huge change in lifestyle from the luxuriously appointed duplex apartment we rented round the corner from the Trevi fountain.'

Matteo paused to fiddle with the handle of the teacup in front of him.

'However, what really sealed the deal was that I had to hand back my Porsche; that was the last straw for Luciana. She wouldn't be seen dead in a rusty old Fiat Cinquecento. In fact, I don't actually think she's ever *sat* in such a tiny vehicle, never mind driven one, and she certainly would never ride a Vespa!'

'She doesn't know what she's missing,' said Tilly, hoping to lighten the mood, but Matteo wasn't listening. His thoughts had scooted back to a place he hadn't visited for a while.

'Luciana was horrified when I suggested we should come back to Tuscany. It was as though I'd asked her to relocate to the Arctic Circle or something, instead of my hometown just a few hundred kilometres up the road. It became clear very quickly that our relationship was over, and I realised that she viewed me differently because I no longer had the title of "film director" and was just plain old Matteo Ferretti without the funds to maintain the lavish lifestyle that she had grown accustomed to.'

'Why did you lose your job?'

Matteo's cheeks coloured and he hesitated before saying, 'I'm not proud of what happened, but I had a "heated exchange" with one of the owners of the production company and… well, he fired me.'

Tilly didn't know what to say. Matteo didn't seem like the sort of person who lost his temper over nothing, and she wondered what had happened to instigate the "heated exchange". Once again, she got the feeling that there was something Matteo wasn't telling her, something that was smouldering deep in the dark crevices of his soul, something more terrible than losing his job and his fiancée.

'I'm sorry about you and Luciana.'

'It's all good; fate spoke and told us it wasn't to be. She's seeing a wealthy producer now and her career has *really* taken off and the opportunities are rolling in. I'm happy for her. It's what she's always wanted.'

Matteo rose from the table to take his *torta della nonnas* from the oven and place them on the cooling rack next to Tilly's tarts, then filled the sink with water, added a generous dash of Olivia's Fairy Liquid, and made a start on the washing up. Tilly smiled, grabbed a tea towel and joined him at the sink, drying the myriad of pots, pans and utensils they had used in their epic culinary marathon.

As she stood there next to Matteo, she felt that invisible pull she had experienced before; comfortable in his presence, as though she had known him forever, and suddenly she wanted to share her own relationship woes with him.

'The fire at my beach hut studio wasn't the only reason I came over here to Tuscany,' she said quickly before she changed her mind. 'That same day, I saw a photograph of my boyfriend dancing in the Balinese waves with another woman – someone he works with – and it was obvious from the way they looked at each other that there was something going on. When I asked Josh about it, he didn't deny it. How could he? It was there on Instagram for all the world to see. I'd been trying to talk to him since I got here, but every time I called him, I got his voicemail. It's embarrassing how many messages I left for him to call me back, and... well, in the end, I had no choice but to leave him a final message telling him it was over between us.'

She paused to catch her breath after saying those words out loud to someone other than Josh.

'I'm sorry, Tilly.'

# Tilly's Tuscan Teashop

'To be honest, our relationship had been over for a while. We've lived separate lives for two years; Josh in London, me in Devon, and I either didn't realise what was happening, or I didn't want to face having the conversation that needed to be had. It's for the best.'

To Tilly's surprise, a weight seemed to lift from her shoulders, and the hard nugget of guilt she had felt about her part in their break-up softened. Relationships were a two-way street; Josh wasn't blameless – he could have come down to Devon more often, just as she could have travelled to their apartment in Pimlico more often.

'Okay, now for the best bit of the evening – the tasting. Yours first!'

'Hang on,' said Matteo, drying his hands on Tilly's tea towel, his cute dimples making her heart sing. 'Italians say that love makes the world go round, but I think the ride is made all the sweeter with a sprinkle of powdered sugar!'

Matteo dowsed one of his *tortas* with a generous dusting of icing sugar, then cut it into slices, selected one, and held it out for Tilly to taste. She stepped forward and took a bite, catching the crumbs in her palm, relishing the flavours of warm buttery pastry and soft, delicate custard that crashing through her taste buds.

'Absolutely delicious. You definitely know how to bake.'

'High praise from a woman who hates desserts.' He grinned. 'I'm honoured.'

'Now it's your turn, but I need to make the orange blossom tea first so you can have the full experience.'

She boiled the kettle, filled the teapot with boiling water and placed it carefully on the table, then added the orange blossom tart with the burnt edges – she was saving the best ones for the competition the following day – slid into one of the chairs and pointed to the seat opposite her. Matteo joined her, watching as she cut into her tart, scooped up a segment with a fork and held it out to him to try.

For the briefest of moments, he held her gaze, and time seemed to stand still. A whip of attraction flashed through her veins and her heartbeat quickened as she slowly raised herself from her seat and leaned forward across the table, closer and closer until she was inches away from him, and as he parted his lips to take the sugary morsel into his mouth… Tilly knocked over the teapot, its lid rolled off, and sent a cascade of boiling hot water across the table and tumbling into Matteo's lap.

'*Dio Mio!*'

Matteo leapt backwards clutching at the front of his jeans, jumping around in an effort to cool down the temperature of the water. Horrified, Tilly reacted automatically. She shot to the workbench, grabbed Olivia's soda siphon, and sprayed the affected area with a torrent of pressurised water until Matteo raised his arms in surrender.

'Oh my God, I'm so sorry, Matteo!'

She watched his expression switch from incredulity to mischief, his eyes sparkling with laughter as he strode towards her, removed the soda siphon from her hands, placed it on the table and pulled her into his arms. After pausing for the briefest of moments, he leaned forward and kissed her, slowly, gently at first, his lips a mere whisper on her own, then with rising passion, his fingers combing through her hair, his thumb caressing the spot at the nape of her neck, sending ripples of pleasure through her entire body.

She kissed him back, every single one of her senses alert to the feel of his muscular body pressed against hers, the sound of their quickening breath, the fragrance of his cologne mingled with the warm, buttery aroma of their desserts. She had never felt more alive, more *in the moment*, and when they finally drew apart and she met his gaze, her heart soared skywards.

Their kiss had been the most natural way to end what had been a perfect evening, and she knew that she would have no trouble drifting down sleep's superhighway that night, eager to arrive at a place where she could replay their passionate embrace in her dreams, over and over again.

# Chapter Seventeen

The day of the San Vincente fiesta arrived with a cloudless sky. Tilly stepped out onto the balcony and inhaled a long, slow breath as she appreciated the panorama spread out in front of her in glorious technicolour; the birds seemed to chirp louder, the sun shine brighter, the lavender smell sharper. Even the tangled vegetation that passed for the villa's garden held a certain charm today.

She would have loved to linger, to photograph the rising sun, to record how the changing light affected the hue of the poppies or the sunflowers that danced to an inaudible tune in the field next door, but time was of the essence, so she took a quick shower, and descended the stairs with a smile on her face and a song in her heart, determined to do everything she could to make her sister proud.

As she walked down the hallway, her eye snagged on the empty space on the console that had previously been home to the photograph of her parents smiling into the camera at Niagara Falls. She paused, her heart quickening; wasn't this her first opportunity to make her sister proud?

She opened the drawer, removed the photograph, and stared at the image.

Instead of the swingeing pain she had expected, she experienced a surge of gratitude for being gifted with such wonderful parents – even if it had been for too short a time. Words Olivia had spoken on many an occasion over the last two years came floating back to her. She'd said that "grief is the price we pay for unconditional love" and, standing there, looking into their mother's soft, hazel eyes, she finally understood that avoiding her pain didn't make it go away. In fact, the opposite was true; it made it worse.

By filling every waking moment with work, work and more work, she had slowed down the process of going through the recognised stages of grief, and she knew now that to move forward she had to start embracing the other aspects of her life, connect with other people, listen to their stories, empathise with their struggles, sympathise with their losses, which in turn would make her own easier to bear.

She wiped away the tears that had gathered along her lower lashes and carefully placed the photograph in its rightful place on the console, then made her way to the kitchen, removed her orange blossom tarts from the refrigerator and placed them into her cardboard box, along with a packet of Olivia's orange blossom tea. She was about to head outside to her Vespa when her gaze fell on Matteo's *torta della nonna* and she hesitated.

Should she?

What harm would it do?

Matteo lived in San Vincente; he was entitled to enter the competition.

Before she could think too deeply about it, she added one of his *tortas* to her box, strapped it securely to the back of her Vespa, and sped off to the village, her heart skipping a beat when she arrived in the piazza, which at nine o'clock in the morning was already a hive of activity. She made her way to the church that was hosting the food competition, filled out the paperwork required to enter her and Matteo's offerings – in triplicate – sent up a missive to the God of Culinary Miracles that the judges would at least feel like *tasting* her entry, then, with a sigh of relief that she had fulfilled her promise to her sister, she headed towards the door.

'*Buongiorno*, Tilly.'

'*Buongiorno*, Gabriella.'

'I'm so relieved I ran into you. I have your orange blossom gelato!'

Tilly watched as Gabriella placed two plastic boxes containing her precious gelato into a specially designated freezer at the end of the row of wooden tables where the judges would sit to sample the food and make their decision, and waited while her friend filled out the forms, peering and squinting and asking questions until the supervisor rolled her eyes in exasperation and filled the details in for her so she could move on and help the next person in line.

'What flavour have you entered this year?'

'I thought I would make something a bit quirky this year, so I've gone for avocado and pancetta, which I've given instructions must be drizzled with my cousin's extra-virgin olive oil.'

'Sounds delicious,' said Tilly, thinking it sounded anything but.

'Thanks, Tilly, that's very kind of you. We all know who's going to win, of course, but I love taking part. I've been doing it for twenty years; it's become a bit of a tradition, and this year is the first time I've tried something completely different, motivated by you.'

'Really?'

'Yes, what you've done at the teashop is inspiring,' said Gabriella, linking her arm through Tilly's as they headed towards the exit. 'Okay, shall we go and check out the food stalls?'

'Absolutely!'

Back in the piazza, Tilly had more time to survey the scene. Everywhere she looked, there was a cornucopia of culinary delights to explore. She estimated that there were probably over thirty stalls selling home-made and artisan produce, every one of them dressed in matching red-and-white cloths and flying the Italian flag or decorated with bunting, with hand-drawn signs informing the visitor what delicacy was on offer.

# Tilly's Tuscan Teashop

She paused at a stall selling figs, amazed at the variety of ways the fruit could be enjoyed. There was fig jam, fig chutney, fig cakes and tortas, fig-speckled cheeses, gooey fig syrups, and rich, brown fig liqueurs; there were even slices of fig-topped pizza. Remembering what Jess had said about the special properties the fig was reputed to have, she couldn't help but smile as she purchased a jar of fig jam for her friend, hoping she would use it when she finally managed to persuade Eduardo to join her for tea.

She moved on to the adjacent stall to taste the most delicious homemade focaccia, soft and chewy, sprinkled with flakes of sea salt and rosemary, and drizzled with locally produced olive oil – pure heaven!

Next, Gabriella insisted they stop at a stall selling all kinds of mushrooms – porcini, oyster, chanterelle, and some that looked like they'd previously been home to a family of fairies.

'Do you think I should make mushroom gelato?' asked Gabriella, picking up a particularly handsome specimen the vendor told them was called a hedgehog mushroom.

'You could give it a go,' said Tilly, privately doubting its appeal.

After squeezing practically every mushroom on the stall, Gabriella eventually purchased a bagful of the porcini mushrooms and they continued their meandering until the clock on the church tower struck noon and she stopped in her tracks, surprised that she had lost all sense of time.

'I wonder where Jess is. She said she'd meet me here at eleven and it's midday.'

To her surprise, Gabriella grinned.

'What?'

'She hasn't told you?'

'Told me what?'

'She's at the teashop.'

'But it's closed for the fiesta.'

'Which is why she's there. She's spent the whole morning preparing an extra-special afternoon tea.'

'What for?'

'Your question should be "who for?".

'Okay, who for?'

'For Eduardo.'

Tilly laughed. 'Oh, that's great news!'

'It's a "Cupid's Delight" afternoon tea.'

'Oh God!'

'She's made cherub-shaped sandwiches, passionfruit scones, and cupcakes with edible rose petals. She's even brewing an extra-strong version of her new "love potion" tea that she says guarantees the drinker will immediately fall in love with the person who serves it to them. I might ask her to save me a packet – who knows, I could do with it! My love life isn't exactly thrumming with passion and excitement at the moment. The last date I had was three months ago and I don't think the guy had all his own teeth; I only realised afterwards that his profile photo was from a movie website.'

Tilly laughed, and an idea burst into her head.

'Why don't we close the teashop one afternoon and do a "speed-dating" afternoon tea?'

'Will there be wine?'

'There can be.'

'Then count me in, and my cousin Elena will probably want to come, too. Oh, and her best friend Angelina has just split up with her boyfriend, so that's three customers already! I could make some gelato with love hearts and… oh.'

'Gabriella? What's wrong?'

Tilly saw that Gabriella's face was wreathed in concern, her gaze focused on something just over Tilly's right shoulder. She turned round to see Stefania, partially hidden behind a rust-blistered blue Ape selling jars of local honey and a selection of honey-based products. She was clearly distressed, and they both rushed over to see what was going on.

'Stefania, are you okay?'

A torrent of high-speed Italian ensued, which Tilly had no chance of understanding, apart from the words "Rocco" and "Ristorante" and she didn't need to be Einstein to hazard a guess at what had happened. Gabriella leaned forward to give Stefania a hug, then nodded and smiled, and they walked back with her to the restaurant.

'Rocco's excelled himself this morning,' Gabriella explained, when Stefania had disappeared into the bear pit that was Rocco Bianchi's kitchen. 'Stefania says he's been up all night perfecting his competition entry so he's exhausted, which means his temper is even more volatile than usual. He's stressed, too, of course, so all-in-all it's an incendiary situation. This competition is a big thing for him. If he loses, it will damage his reputation as a culinary genius, which is a serious matter.'

'He's not going to lose, though, is he?' said Tilly. 'What I don't understand is why he's got any customers left at all. His food might be amazing, but he's so rude to everyone, not just his staff but his diners, too, and I've never seen him crack a smile.'

'Oh, his customers love it! In fact, a lot of them don't come for the food at all, they come for the drama. It's like having a front row seat at a nightly soap opera. Better than the television because it's live and anything can happen. Would you believe he once threw an artichoke at a guest – gave him a black eye – but instead of being angry, or upset, or indignant, the guy was an instant star on Instagram!'

Tilly shook her head. 'But, as we've just witnessed, not everyone can deal with his behaviour so easily.'

'I know, I know, I—' Gabriella stopped, her lips twisting into a broad smile with a soupcon of mischief. 'Okay, I'll catch you later for the judging; it's two p.m. sharp. Don't be late! After all, I'm sure you will want to listen to Rocco's acceptance speech. I'll translate for you, but I'll warn you now, he tends to go on a bit. Why don't you go grab yourself a coffee from Luigi's stall over there? *Ciao*!'

Before Tilly could argue, Gabriella was making a beeline for a stall selling balsamic vinegar and embracing the owner as though she had known her forever. So, she decided to do as instructed and treat herself to a rich dark espresso, maybe even a double, to steady her nerves.

'Hi, Tilly, I thought I'd find you at the coffee stall.' Matteo laughed, leaning forward to deposit the regulation kisses on her cheeks, a gesture that made her heart beat faster, especially as she remembered the long, lingering kiss they'd enjoyed the previous evening. 'Where's Jess? I thought she'd be here with you?'

Tilly told him about the assignation and he grinned, the cute dimples appearing in his cheeks as his eyes twinkled. 'Eduardo is a lucky guy. It's about time those two got together. Come, I want you to try one of Florence's most delicious specialties.'

Matteo pointed to a food van that had been parked outside the village's flower shop with a modest queue outside. She read the sign – *Panino di Lampredotto* – but was none the wiser as to what the chef with the crinkly eyes and salt-and-pepper hair was cooking in a wide pan on the gas ring.

'What's *lampredotto*?'

'Why don't you try it first and tell me what you think?'

She watched as the handsome chef sliced open a panini, dipped it in the cooking juices, then stuffed it to bursting with thin strips of beige-coloured meat and hand it over to her with a nod of encouragement. She still wasn't sure what it was, but that day was all about trying new food experiences, and everything she had tasted so far with Gabriella had been delicious.

She took a tentative bite of the sandwich and discovered it had a strange texture and an even stranger taste. She didn't recognise the meat, perhaps it was beef, but she wasn't certain; she didn't *hate* it, but she didn't like it either. She glanced at Matteo who had already polished his panini off and when she saw the smirk on his face, she knew she'd eaten something exotic. She placed her sandwich on the table next to her, reached into her satchel for her bottle of water and took a long gulp.

'I didn't know you like tripe,' said Gabriella, appearing at her side with an overladen shopping bag. 'Did you have it with the *salsa verde* or the hot sauce?'

Tilly gaped and her stomach growled in objection.

'You're joking, right?' But she could see from Gabriella's face she wasn't. 'Oh my God! Tripe? I've just eaten *tripe*? Gross!'

She turned towards Matteo, but before she could say anything, there was an ear-splittingly loud announcement over the tannoy that ended with an even louder screech-back, not unlike fingernails being dragged down a chalkboard.

'What did she say?' she asked Gabriella, not trusting herself to speak to Matteo.

'That it's time for the judging. Come on.'

Not knowing whether her stomach was churning from her unusual choice of lunch or from anxiety over the competition, Tilly followed Gabriella and Matteo into the church with what seemed like the rest of the village, grateful that Gabriella knew the best place to stand so they could see the proceedings.

'Oh my God, Tilly!' Matteo gasped, grabbing hold of her hand. 'You entered nonna's *torta*?'

Tilly turned towards Matteo, expecting to see him grin at what she had done, but instead she saw a mixture of emotions flicker across his face – shock, embarrassment, and genuine unease. She saw his gaze scour the room, lingering for a few seconds on Rocco – who was leaning nonchalantly against the wall at the back of the church, his arms folded across his chest, smiling as though the judging was a foregone conclusion – and his eyes sparked with loathing.

'Matteo, are you okay?'

'Yes, yes, it's just… Gabriella, do you know who the judges are?'

'The woman wearing the pink and white Versace dress is Mariella Pedrotti, and the guy in the basketweave Armani jacket is Claudio Accardi – they're both from a prestigious cookery school in Bologna. Together, they've got over forty-five years of culinary experience behind them, and Mariella has published over a dozen cookery books, so they're well-qualified.'

'Who's that?' asked Tilly, pointing to a woman who had just picked up a microphone.

'That's the mayor, Dominica D'Emilio.'

Tilly took in Dominica's exquisitely cut black-and-gold dress, sky-scrapper heels and blonde hair that was so beautifully coiffed she could have been about to step onto the stage at La Scala and not the local church hall. Then she glanced down at her own – or more accurately, Olivia's – pale-blue belted tea dress and decided that whilst she was in Italy, she really should start to pay more attention to her choice of outfit. Everyone there took their appearance seriously, and even though she had graduated from her black jeans and tee shirt to a more colourful wardrobe palette, she would by no means win any awards for her attire.

'This is it! This is it!' Gabriella whispered, clapping her hands with excitement. 'They're about to announce the winner of the bronze rosette!'

Mariella Pedrotti accepted the microphone from the mayor, said a few words in Italian, then picked up the huge bronze rosette and a smart shiny bronze plaque, and, after a sufficiently dramatic pause, announced a familiar name to the waiting crowd. For a moment there was silence, then a high-pitched squeal of delight issued forth from the person standing next to Tilly.

'Oh my God, oh my God, oh my God!'

Gabriella's eyes widened, and her hands shot to her mouth in disbelief. Seconds later, she rushed forward to claim her rosette and plaque, and pose for the official photograph, her joy clear for all to see. After saying a few words of thanks, she made her way back to Tilly and Matteo, stopping regularly to accept congratulatory hugs and cheek kisses from her many friends in the packed audience.

'Congratulations, Gabriella,' said Tilly, flinging her arms around her friend.

'*Grazie mille*, Tilly, *grazie mille*.'

# Tilly's Tuscan Teashop

Now it was the turn of Claudio Accardi to announce the winner of the silver rosette and plaque. To Tilly's amusement, he had to all-but wrench the microphone from his colleague – who had been in the middle of regaling the audience with an anecdote about her time training in the kitchen of a luxury hotel in Rome – before he said a few words in speedy Italian.

'What did he say?' asked Tilly.

'That they couldn't decide between two entries so it's a joint second place.'

'Ah, okay.'

Then next thing she heard was Matteo's name followed by the words *Té e Torta*.

Tilly's jaw dropped and her heart crashed against her ribcage, causing her breath to stall in her throat. She met Matteo's equally flabbergasted gaze, but her brain had disconnected from its modem and she was completely unable to formulate a sentence.

The next thing she knew, Matteo had grabbed her waist, lifted her from the floor and spun her round and round whilst everybody around them clapped. She felt as though she was in a dream as he set her down, took her hand in his, and guided her to the judges' table where together they accepted the silver rosette and plaque, with Matteo saying a few words of thanks on their behalf while Tilly just gabbled a string of *grazie milles* before hurrying back to Gabriella.

'I can't believe it,' she muttered. 'I—'

However, she couldn't continue because the proceedings were still going on and the room had quietened as the gathering waited for the announcement of the winner – even though everyone in the room knew who it would be. Mariella reached for the gold rosette and plaque – which was twice the size of the other two, complete with an ornate gilt frame – and beamed at the audience.

'*E il vincitore è… Rocco Bianchi! Congratulazioni!*'

A wave of applause reverberated through the church as Rocco – in his pristine white chef's jacket, his hair newly bouffant-ed for the occasion – strode forward to accept his award, before launching into a long and involved speech about how he'd conceived the dish he'd entered into the competition.

Tilly couldn't fail to see the glint of triumph he had sent in their direction as he smiled for the winner's official photograph that would appear in the *Gazzettino*, but she didn't care. She had never expected to win, and was thrilled with joint second place, alongside Matteo, not for herself, but for Olivia – and for the recognition of British culinary deliciousness – and she excused herself so she could call her sister to tell her the good news.

Unfortunately her call went to voicemail, so she left a message and was about to return to the church when a tsunami of people exited the huge, oak front door, everyone talking at the same time, at the top of their voices, before dispersing to continue their perusal of the many stalls showcasing the best food their little corner of Tuscany had to offer.

No sooner had she been joined by Gabriella, Matteo and a very excited Carlotta, who had arrived with her sister, Adriana, than the band struck up their first tune and the rest of the afternoon was taken up with sampling copious glasses of Chianti, followed by lots of uninhibited dancing that left Tilly breathless and desperately in need of a glass or two of plain old tap water with a slice of lemon and plenty of ice.

'So, have you enjoyed your first San Vincente fiesta?' asked Matteo as they left the piazza – now alight with lanterns and necklaces of sparkling fairy lights – and sauntered down the narrow, cobbled street that led to the teashop.

'It's been *the best day* I've had in a very long time.'

Matteo paused outside the teashop and drew Tilly into his arms, his gaze holding hers for what seemed like an eternity. Then, as the stars twinkled in the sky overhead, he kissed her a second time, his lips a mere graze against hers.

Tilly hooked her arms around his neck, about to return his kiss, when a waft of music floated into the air. She stood on her tiptoes to look over Matteo's shoulder where she saw the flicker of a candle in the window of the teashop. She met Matteo's eyes, then linked her arm through his and, like a pair of amateur sleuths on a midnight stake-out, they crept forward, with slow, exaggerated steps, and peered through the glass.

When her eyes adjusted to the low light, Tilly's heart soared. There, sitting at a table scattered with empty cups, saucers, teapots and cake stands were Jess and Eduardo – kissing.

The image was the cherry on the top of a truly exceptional day.

# Chapter Eighteen

When Tilly woke up the next morning, her bones ached and her head felt fuzzy from the red wine she'd drank, but the feeling of accomplishment washed away the tiredness and replaced it with exhilaration. Humming a jaunty tune from the previous night, she hopped in the shower, selected a pair of Olivia's cream linen palazzo trousers, added a bright red tee-shirt and went to make herself a revitalising coffee, grateful that the teashop was closed that day to give everyone time to rest and recover from what had been a very busy week.

She took her mug of Blue Mountain out to the front steps to watch the sun spread golden shafts of light over the vine-covered hillside below San Vincente, and had just stepped through the front door when, to her surprise, Eduardo came flying past her, his head turned over his shoulder as he tried to outrun whatever was chasing him. As she watched in mute astonishment, he vaulted over the wall of the Cupid fountain, dislodging the statue's arrow in the process, and landed clumsily in the pond. He immediately pushed himself up and spun round to look in the direction he had come from, his face wreathed in alarm, before noticing Tilly.

'Eduardo, what's going on?'

'*Libellula! Libellula!*'

'What's…'

A second later, Tilly saw a magnificent blue dragonfly sail over the top of the fountain towards the honeysuckle that grew in abundance around the fence between the front and rear of the villa and realised what Eduardo was running away from.

'Can you see it anywhere? Do you think it's gone?'

'Eduardo, dragonflies can't hurt you.'

'*Sì, sì*, they bite! They sting!'

She tried to think back to all the times she had spent with her father at his veterinary practice, and out on his rounds, and never in all the years he'd been tending to the animals of Devonshire, and their worried owners, had he been called out to deal with a severe case of a dragonfly sting.

'*No*, I don't think they do.'

Eduardo ignored her and, having satisfied himself that the coast was clear, he dragged himself out of the pond, his white Dolce & Gabbana shirt clinging to his muscular torso like an Italian version of Mr Darcy. Unfortunately, his Gucci loafers were ruined, and so were the neatly pressed designer trousers he always wore to work in the villa's garden, but his hair was still perfectly styled – even a rampage of wildebeest wouldn't have persuaded him to get that wet. He reached down to collect the fallen arrow, then scaled the fountain's wall and tried to replace it, severing the bottom half of Cupid's marble bow, which tumbled into the water with a splash.

'Eduardo!'

Tilly knew how much the statue meant to both Olivia and Enzo; it was a symbol of their union and their love for one another, and they loved it. She hoped it could be repaired before they returned at the end of the month, by someone a little more competent than Eduardo, who, when he met her gaze, had the grace to look contrite, his brown eyes like a puppy's who had just been chastised for a misdemeanour he didn't quite understand.

'I promise I'll mend it; just please don't tell my father.' Eduardo grimaced. 'He's still furious with me about Giuseppe's barn incident.'

She knew she shouldn't ask, but she couldn't help it. 'What barn incident?'

'It wasn't my fault. My brother told me to cut out a rotten beam in the roof with a chainsaw, only he pointed to the wrong beam – he denies it, but I'm sure he did – and the moment I cut through it, the whole place collapsed. We only just managed to get out in time, and it's taken us all weeks to rebuild it. It looks amazing, though; much better than it would have done if we'd just removed the beam and left! Giuseppe was delighted. A new barn for half the price; he's thinking of renting it out as an Airbnb.'

Eduardo dropped down onto the villa's steps and smiled at Tilly, willing her to be on his side, and her heart went out to him. She sat next to him and placed her hand on his shoulder, his shirt still damp from his tumble into the fountain. She was itching to ask for the details of his "Cupid's Delight" date with Jess the previous evening, but then he'd know that she and Matteo had seen them, or worse, might think they'd been spying on them, so she chose to steer the conversation in a different direction.

'Eduardo, you have to talk to your father. You have to tell him that you're not cut out for this kind of work… before something serious happens, before someone gets hurt.' Or worse, she thought.

'I can't, I just can't. He'll be so disappointed. I saw what Matteo's leaving did to his family and I don't want to do that to my parents.'

'We can't always be what our parents want us to be, Eduardo; we have to walk our own path, if we don't, we'll end up living with regret that can morph into resentment and eat away at our wellbeing, our chance of future happiness. Matteo did what he had to do to follow his dream.'

'Yes, and look what happened to him.'

'What do you mean?'

'Well, he's not in Rome anymore, is he? He's not "following his dream", he's back in Tuscany, working as a waiter in his friend's restaurant and his family have moved away to Sicily. How is that a good outcome? Don't tell me he doesn't have regrets.'

Tilly stared at Eduardo. She didn't know why Matteo's family had sold their restaurant, a restaurant that had been in their family for generations, and moved to Sicily, especially when Matteo had just returned home to Tuscany, but she was sure they had their reasons. However, they weren't talking about Matteo, they were talking about Eduardo, so she tried again.

'Imagine that you're sixty, or seventy, or eighty, and you're sitting on the terrace in the sunshine enjoying a glass of Chianti, and you're looking back on your life, and you've never pursued your ambition to become an actor. How do you think you'll feel?'

Now it was Eduardo's turn to stare at her. He opened his mouth to respond, then closed it again and she could almost see the cogs of enlightenment turning in his brain.

'I wouldn't feel good about it.'

'All I'm saying is there's another option…'

To Tilly's disappointment, their heart-to-heart was interrupted by the sound of tyres crunching on gravel and she saw a sparkling white 4X4 vehicle advancing down the driveway towards them before skidding to a stop in front of them. She heard Eduardo groan, and when she saw the logo on the side of the vehicle advertising building and maintenance services, she realised it was his father.

'*Buongiorno*,' said the man, the cadence of his voice more a melodic aria than a simple greeting. He was an older version of Eduardo, with the same broad shoulders and tanned skin of someone who earned his living in the open air, his palm outstretched to introduce himself. 'Roberto Armotti, at your service.'

'*Buongiorno*,' said Tilly, grimacing at the strength of his handshake. 'I'm Natalie Nicholson, Olivia Molinari's sister. Can I offer you a coffee?'

'No, thank you. I—'

She saw Roberto's eyes shoot to Eduardo – whose clothes were, of course, still soaking wet – then dart across to the pool of water on the gravel surrounding the pond and fountain, then back to Eduardo, his forehead creased, his lips tightening at the corners.

'What happened this time?'

Instead of waiting for an answer, Roberto strode over to where Cupid's arrow lay on the ground, picked it up, then surveyed the damage to the bottom half of the statue's bow and came to his own, accurate, conclusion. He said something in Italian to Eduardo, which caused his son to rise from his seat on the villa's front step, give Tilly an apologetic smile, and disappear into the overgrown garden in his father's wake.

Moments later, Tilly couldn't avoid overhearing a very heated discussion taking place, with both sides expressing their point of view vigorously in loud, scattergun Italian. Since arriving in Italy, she'd become accustomed to listening to conversations that sounded, to her, like arguments but which were, in fact, just regular chats between friends. However, she knew that wasn't the case this morning; this was a full-blown row between father and son, and she cringed when she heard the words "*attore*" and "*scuola di teatro*" and her heart flooded with guilt.

Why hadn't she minded her own business?

She briefly wondered whether she should follow them, try to support Eduardo with arguing his case, but she knew that wasn't a good idea, and would probably make things worse. Filled with regret, she made her way back to the villa, and just as she stepped into the kitchen, she heard the still-irate voices increase in volume, followed by the sharp slam of a car door, the aggressive rev of a powerful engine, and the scattering of pebbles propelled in the vehicle's wake.

Feeling miserable about the part she had played in the altercation, Tilly replenished her coffee and took it into the lounge – a room she had rarely frequented since coming to the villa – which was light, cool and airy, decorated in the pale pinks and greens her sister loved, and furnished with two huge, overstuffed sofas. The air smelled of lavender and wax furniture polish and had a calm, relaxed ambiance, the perfect place to hide away from the heat of the day and replenish her energy levels before launching into her final week at the teashop.

She put her mug on a coaster on the white-painted coffee table and went to peruse the bookshelves next to the wood-burner, every available space filled with either the classics or recent bestsellers, in both English and Italian.

She was about to select the first book in a popular murder mystery series and spend the next few hours losing herself in the story, when she spotted the large, carved wooden box that had played such a prominent part of her childhood. Growing up, she, along with Olivia, had loved sifting through its contents – a cornucopia of keepsakes and trinkets their mother and grandmother had collected over the years – and listening to the fascinating and inspiring stories behind them.

Before she could change her mind, she removed the box from the shelf, settled down on the sofa, curled her feet under her bottom, and opened the lid, the memories rushing at her. However, to her surprise, and disappointment, the box didn't contain the bus tickets and cinema stubs from first dates, dried and pressed flowers from bridal bouquets, or the hand-embroidered greetings cards she had been expecting, but a bundle of postcards tied up in a blue ribbon.

She took them out and hesitated, fingering the ribbon for a few seconds.

Taking a sip of her coffee to bolster her courage, she unravelled the bow and removed the first of the postcards – one featuring a gorgeous photograph of the Pitons in St Lucia at sunset on the front. She remembered her parents visiting the island eight or nine years ago when she and her sister had both left home and their endless quest to tick off bucket list items had started. Her mum had obviously bought the postcard to keep her memory of their trip to the Caribbean paradise alive, but as Tilly sorted through the bundle, she realised that there were over forty postcards from various locations around the world; all places her parents had visited.

With her heart in her mouth, she turned over a postcard showcasing the Eiffel Tower and saw there was a recipe on the back, scribbled in her mother's familiar handwriting, for a cherry clafoutis, along with one of her hand-drawn illustrations of what the finished product should look like.

Pushing down on her rising emotions, she then selected a postcard with the iconic Raffles hotel on the front and saw a recipe for a "Singapore Sling" muffin, and then one with the main square in Bruges and a recipe for chocolate waffles, and Central Park in New York with a recipe for a pineapple-topped cheesecake, and so on, until all the postcards were scattered across her lap, the sofa, and the coffee table; a visual record of her mum's love of travelling, but also her life-long passion for baking and sampling dishes from different countries and cultures.

Tilly wiped away her tears with the back of her hand and inhaled a long, slow breath as images of her mum and dad rushed at her, one after another, after another, followed by a wave of almost unbearable loss. However, she knew that every one of the images represented the joy her parents had experienced during their expeditions and adventures, when they were determined to squeeze the most out of their lives with each other, grateful for having the opportunity to do so.

She gathered the postcards, retied the ribbon, and was about to replace them in the box when she paused, remembering what she had said to Eduardo about

# Daisy James

following his dreams. It had been her mum's dream to publish a cookery book – a book filled with the recipes she'd used at her Orange Blossom Café – and Tilly realised with a thud of distress that the postcards she'd spent the last hour perusing were the early preparations of her mum's pursuit of that dream, which would not now come to fruition, and that made her sad.

As she sat there, contemplating not only her mum's life, but her own, she was even more determined than ever to add to her portfolio of photographs for the exhibition at Jonti's gallery at the end of August. It was never too early, or too late, to start pursuing your dreams – big or small, at home or abroad – just like Olivia had, and that thought made her feel a little better about what she'd said to Eduardo, although she was still mortified and wondered if she would see him again at the villa before she left.

Oh, God, what if her interference affected his fledgling relationship with Jess?

Suddenly, she really needed to hear her sister's voice; to tell her what had happened, and get her advice on what she should do to make things right. She also wanted to give Olivia a blow-by-blow account of the competition win, and to chat about where she wanted to display the silver plaque, before moving on to tell her she had found the memories box and, for the first time in over two years, maybe have a conversation with her sister about her parents that wasn't totally one-sided; she was ready, in fact, she was *keen*, to talk to Olivia about the postcards she had found and what her sister knew about them.

She pulled her phone from her pocket and settled into the comfortable embrace of the sofa. However, when she checked her watch and saw it was just after eleven o'clock and worked out that meant it was only five a.m. in Boston, she changed her mind. Her sister had never been an early riser, and she didn't want to disturb her beauty sleep, so she decided to wait a couple of hours. She didn't have anything planned that day, so she would take a leisurely dip in the pool, then stretch out on one of the sun loungers and make a start on the novel she'd found, and call Olivia after lunch.

She had just dropped her phone onto the coffee table when it buzzed into life, and she smiled when she saw the caller ID – she was about to get her gossip-quota after all!.

# Chapter Nineteen

'Hi, Freya.'

'Oh, Tilly, thank God I've caught you!'

'Why? What's wrong?'

Freya wasn't given to overreacting, so the panic in her voice told Tilly that something serious had happened.

'Are you sitting down?'

'Yes, I'm sitting down, but—'

'Josh is here! In Blossomwood Bay!'

Tilly stomach lurched as the words hit her with the force of a runaway express train.

'He arrived yesterday, came round to see me last night, asking where you were.'

'But he knows where I am. I told him I was at Olivia's.'

'He thought you'd be back by now.'

'And he didn't think to check. Typical Josh!'

'He says he wants to talk to you and you're avoiding his calls.'

'What? That's not true! If anyone's avoiding calls, it's Josh. I've left over a dozen voicemails, culminating in the one where I told him our relationship was over, and he's still not had the decency to call me back. Where's he staying?'

There was a brief pause and Tilly's heart crashed against her ribcage.

'He's staying at the flat, isn't he?'

'Yes, he is. I'm sorry, Tilly.'

'Well, it belongs to both of us, so I suppose he's entitled to stay there. It just feels like… well, a bit like an invasion of privacy.' She sighed. 'We need to sort that out… we need to sort a lot of things out… the sooner the better. However, if I know Josh, he won't have the time, or the inclination, to hang around in Devon until I get back. I'll arrange to meet him in London the day I fly back and before I catch the train home.'

'So it's definitely over between the two of you?'

'Yes, it is.'

To her surprise, there was no sharp pang of emotion, just a soft whoosh of sadness, and, if she was honest, of relief that she could now say it out loud, tell friends and anyone else who asked that she and Josh were no longer an item, something she suspected *he* had come to terms with a long time before she had.

'I'm sorry, Tilly,' said Freya, softly.

'It's fine, it really is; it's for the best.'

'But not the way it happened.'

'True, but if I hadn't seen that photograph of him with Melissa, we could have limped on for months, which isn't good for either of us.'

'When are you coming back?'

'Olivia is due home at the weekend, so I'll be back in the UK at the beginning of next week to make a start on collating the photographs for my exhibition at the end of August. Oh, Frey, I can't wait to show you my new material, and it's not just landscapes, either. I'm looking forward to hearing what you think of the photos I've taken at the teashop.'

'How are things going there?'

For the next hour, Tilly regaled Freya with every detail about the themed afternoon teas she and Jess had introduced and how proud she was of the silver plaque and rosette she had won – alongside Matteo – for her mum's orange blossom tart recipe, before moving on to tell her about Jess and her "Cupid's Delight" date with Eduardo.

'Can you bring me a packet of that tea back with you? I could do with a little help in that department. In fact, bring two packets; Holly will definitely want to try it out, too. Oh, maybe Beckie could put it on the menu at the bistro? Once word gets round, there'll definitely be an influx of curious visitors – especially those that are single.'

'There's no guarantee it'll work.' Tilly laughed. 'By the way, I don't suppose there's any news about Dexter?'

'Sort of.'

'What does that mean?'

'Well, as I've got nothing to do at the moment – apart from the occasional aromatherapy appointment at someone's home – I went to offer my services to Beckie and her Aunt Kath at the Boathouse Bistro. Now that they've completed the deep-clean, they've been given the go-ahead to open to the public again, which is great news. I think I told you that Poppy's there, too, making her amazing artisan chocolates, but she's also diversifying into hand-crafted chocolate desserts, which Beckie is delighted about. However, despite the fact that it's the school holidays now, the bistro's definitely not as busy as it used to be.'

'Really? Why?'

'Probably because the boardwalk looks like a post-apocalyptic movie set. My heart cracks every time I walk past it, and no matter where you're staying in Blossomwood Bay, there's always just that faint aroma of charred wood. Some people like it – they say it reminds them of their childhood camping expeditions – but most people don't.'

'I'm sorry, Freya.'

'Anyway, Beckie told me yesterday that she's spoken to Dexter's business manager, Andrew Collins, and he's managed to speak to the owner of a ranch on the trail – they call them "trail angels" – who confirmed that he'd allowed someone of Dexter's description to camp in his backyard four nights ago.'

'That's great news.'

'Maybe.'

'What do you mean?'

'Andrew went on to call three other popular stop-offs along the trail *after* the ranch, but none of them had seen Dexter, which means one of two things; either he's pitched his tent in the wilderness or…'

'Or what?'

'He's gone off-piste. Knowing Dexter, that's the option I think is most likely.'

'Oh God!'

'It's not Dexter's fault.' Freya sighed. 'I suppose he's just following his dream – or one of them, at least. He's worked so hard for the last thirty years, gigging all over the world, he really does deserve some "me time".'

Tilly laughed as she thought of the laidback rockstar – whom she'd never seen without his band's tour tee-shirt, red bandana, well-worn leather jacket and obligatory guitar – stopping off to avail himself of the services provided by a luxury spa in the middle of the Californian countryside, partaking in every session of yoga, meditation, and mindfulness, with a few massages and facials on the side.

'I suppose so.'

'So it could take a while to find him.' Freya paused and inhaled a deep breath. 'Tilly, you know I love you, so don't take this the wrong way, but… do you have to come back to Devon?'

'What do you mean?'

'Well, you could stay on in Tuscany. Spend some time reconnecting with your sister when she gets back from Boston, working together at the teashop, taking more of those gorgeous photographs you talked about. You don't need to be here to prepare for the exhibition at Jonti's; you could easily fly back for the show at the end of August.'

'I can't stay in Tuscany, Frey. My life is in Devon; it's my home.'

She thought of her minimalist, monochrome studio in the eaves of a Victorian terrace house, and then looked out of the window at the rolling Tuscan countryside, still bathed in golden sunshine, and realised with a sharp jolt of self-insight that she had never really made the apartment she and Josh had initially bought as a bolthole, into a "home". It was merely a place to lay her head before she jumped back onto the daily treadmill of her life after leaving London; shower, coffee, work, dinner, sleep, repeat.

She glanced around at her sister's living room, dressed in pretty soft furnishings and filled with personal items, all of which meant something to either her or Enzo. Framed photographs of their wedding day and their honeymoon in Venice, plants which, to her shame, were looking decidedly droopy and in need of water, and a collection of ornaments, some of which Tilly recognised had belonged to their parents. She thought of the kitchen, stuffed to the ceiling with shiny silver appliances and every culinary utensil imaginable, as well as enough food in the store cupboard to see them through an apocalypse.

Villa Avanti was a *home*.

'I'll see you next week, Freya.'

'And you'll call Josh?'

'Yes, but I doubt he'll answer. I'll leave him another voicemail.'

After saying goodbye to Freya, Tilly sat for a long while toying with her phone, thinking about their conversation. Until that moment, she hadn't considered the possibility of staying on in Tuscany when Olivia got back from Boston. Before the fire had destroyed her beach hut studio, she had loved what she created there, and she was determined to rebuild – and to continue to shoot for her dream of an exhibition at a West End gallery – as well as to be there to help her friends do the same. But Freya's suggestion had ignited a spark in her brain, telling her there was another option, and that she should at least consider it.

What if she did stay on?

However, before she started to stroll down that particular path of potential possibilities, there was something she had to do. When her mum was alive, she had always told her and Olivia that when anything unpleasant needed to be done, it was best to do it straight away, otherwise it would fester and start to grow horns. So, she selected Josh's number, unsure whether she actually did want to speak to him after he'd made his unnecessary trip to Devon, especially when his time off was so precious.

She thought of all the fun times they'd had together over the years; the twenty-four hours they'd spent in Miami once, partying the whole time, even ending up sleeping on the beach, the long weekend they'd spent in Tokyo, most of it in a karaoke bar belting out rock ballads at the top of their voices, the week after New Year they'd spent holed up in Toronto because of an unexpected snowstorm, drinking hot chocolate and gorging on bear claws.

To her surprise, she didn't feel as despondent about the end of their relationship as she thought she would. She had loved Josh, and she knew he had loved her, but times and people change, for all sorts of reasons, and she hoped that when they finally got to talk, they could do so calmly, without animosity or recriminations, and remain friends as they drew a line under that part of their lives.

Tilly tapped on Josh's number and a couple of seconds later, as she had expected, she was greeted by his voicemail. She left a message about meeting up in London the following week, gave him her flight details, and then padded into the kitchen to make another coffee and some buttered toast, which she took outside to the pool terrace. She had just settled down with her Kindle when her phone burst into life.

'Hi, Tilly, are you busy?'

Tilly laughed, her spirits soaring at the sound of Matteo's sexy Italian accent.

'Does reading count?'

'Is it an Italian cookery book?' he teased.

'No, it's a murder mystery set in the drizzly streets of London.'

'Then allow me to fill your Sunday with Tuscan sunshine instead.'

'What do you have in mind?'

## Tilly's Tuscan Teashop

'A trip I know you'll love. Grab your camera. I'll be there in five minutes.'

With a smile on her face, Tilly skipped back into the villa, switched her sister's sparkly flip-flops for a pair of more practical Vans, slotted her phone into her satchel and was waiting on the villa's front steps when Matteo bounced down the driveway in his tiny Fiat 500, music streaming from the open windows.

# Chapter Twenty

'Hi Tilly, hop in!'

Tilly dropped into the passenger seat and before she had even reached for her seatbelt, Matteo had spun once around the fountain and was flying back down the tree-lined driveway, gravel flying in their wake like confetti at a wedding.

'So, are you going to tell me where we're going?'

'No, I'm not, it's a surprise. Why don't you sit back, relax, and enjoy the journey?'

Tilly rolled her eyes. There was no chance of that! Even though it was a Sunday morning, the roads were busy with traffic, and every single vehicle, from the tiniest three-wheeled Ape to the sleekest sports car, made it their mission to jostle for a more favourable position, a quest accompanied by vigorous hand

# Daisy James

gestures, lots of vociferous horn-tooting, and the frequent use of invectives.

As they descended the hill into Florence, Matteo was forced to swerve sharply to his right to avoid an oncoming Maserati Bora intent on overtaking a slow-moving tourist coach, despite the fact that it would take him into the path of an oncoming vehicle. Tilly closed her eyes and gripped onto the side of her seat, hoping that wherever Matteo was taking them it was close by.

Fortunately, ten minutes later, they had left the mayhem of the city behind them and joined the autostrade heading westwards, and she decided to do as Matteo suggested, leaning on the headrest and staring at the bucolic countryside that flashed past her window. The scenery must have been both mesmerising and hypnotising because the next thing she knew, Matteo was tapping her on the shoulder.

'Wake up, we're here!'

Tilly peeled open her eyelids, mortified that she had fallen asleep and hoping that she hadn't been drooling, or worse, snoring. She pushed herself upright and looked out of the windscreen, delighted to see they had pulled into a parking space at the edge of a handsome piazza framed by a magnificent stone colonnade that had clearly been designed with the sole purpose of creating awe in the onlooker.

'Where exactly is *here*?'

'Welcome to Pisa! Come on, let's grab a coffee before we explore!'

244

# Tilly's Tuscan Teashop

Matteo pointed to a tiny pavement café where they took a seat amongst the other tourists enjoying a coffee and the ambiance, and he ordered two expressos for them. Tilly removed her phone to take a photograph, then paused.

No matter which way she looked, there was something upon which to feast her eyes. There were the architectural jewels, like the tiny Benedictine church, the handsome palazzo that had been re-purposed as a museum, as well as the many Tuscan buildings with warm yellow or dusky pink facades, dark green shutters and wrought-iron balconies. The middle of the piazza had been taken over by artists perched in front of their easels, creating artwork that was both vibrant and eye-catching, alongside a myriad of stalls selling colourful plastic souvenirs.

The place was bustling with people, every single one of them the embodiment of Italian chic, dressed in tasteful linen suits and beautifully cut designer dresses, their footwear and accessories carefully chosen to enhance their already immaculate image as they strolling along the pavements as though followed by their own personal spotlight. Tilly suddenly felt unkempt in their presence so she pushed herself up in her chair and straightened her shoulders in a futile attempt to join their ranks.

'Why do Italians always look so glamorous?'

Matteo – himself effortlessly stylish in a pair of black dress trousers, a pale blue linen shirt that was open at the neck to reveal a tantalising glimpse of dark chest hair, and the hand-stitched loafers he always wore –

swallowed a mouthful of his coffee and took a moment to consider her question.

'We believe in making *every* aspect of our lives as beautiful as it can be; from how we dress to what we eat and how we drink our coffee, from the form of exercise we choose to participate in to what kind of car we drive. It's called *la bella figura*. It's about looking on the bright side of life, confident that if we do, then it shall be so.'

Tilly sipped her espresso, savouring the rich, bitter taste that she loved so much as she considered what Matteo had said, and something inside her shifted. If you lived life crouched beneath the protective mantle of misery, allowing grief to rule your every waking moment, then it wasn't surprising that sadness and gloom were your constant companions. On the other hand, if you surrounded yourself with beauty, and sunshine, and great coffee, and delicious pasta, then there was surely a better than average chance that your life would also be filled with those things, things that would raise your spirits no matter what issues you were dealing with.

She needed to get herself a *bella figura*!

'Okay, are you ready to visit the *Piazza dei Miracoli*?'

Tilly drained her coffee. 'Absolutely!'

Matteo slid his hand into hers and guided her through the narrow streets of Pisa. They were just one of many couples who had chosen to spend their day in the city strolling along the river, exploring the hidden courtyards and secret nooks and crannies, all of whom at some point ended up in the same place. A few minutes later, they rounded a corner and Tilly came to a standstill, her jaw loose as she stared at the spectacular sight in front of her.

'Wow! I mean… just wow!'

She had seen the Leaning Tower of Pisa in photographs many times, but nothing could have prepared her for the trio of buildings laid out in front of her. First there was the Baptistery of San Giovanni, with its ornate façade topped by an attractive red dome, then there was the Cathedral of Santa Maria Assunta, a masterpiece of Romanesque architecture built from grey and white marble and bristling with columns and arches, and finally, the building everyone in the piazza that day had come to see, there was the famous Campanile that leaned so precariously to the right that it looked like it would tumble to the ground at any minute. To complete the image of aesthetic perfection, the piazza was clothed in the greenest of lawns and watched over by a brilliant, cloudless blue sky. It was just stunning!

'I've got tickets for us to climb the tower, and there's just enough time for us to take a walk around the perimeter of the baptistery first. Come on.'

Matteo pulled her across the grass and headed towards the first building, which was understandably dwarfed by its neighbours. Nevertheless, visitors were still strolling around its exterior, pausing to inspect the many carvings and sculptures, taking photograph after photograph, and Tilly was happy to join them. However, after they had circumnavigated the structure five times and she realised that Matteo intended to go round again, she suggested they moved on to visit the cathedral.

'Sorry.' He laughed. 'It's supposed to bring good luck. It's a tradition for high school students to come here exactly one hundred days before the beginning of their exams to walk round the baptistery as many times as they can; the number of times you walk round is supposed to relate to the mark you'll get on your paper. Sadly, I'm here to report that it doesn't work! Come on, there's one more photograph you have to get before we join the queue for the tower, and I know the perfect place to stand.'

Tilly could see that a whole host of other visitors and tour groups had thought the same thing, and it was a while before Matteo managed to manoeuvre her into the right position for the iconic photograph of her standing on a low wall, her hands outstretched to her right, as an optical illusion made it look like she was holding up the famous Leaning Tower of Pisa.

'Perfecto!'

Matteo turned her phone screen round so Tilly could see the picture he'd taken, then slung his arm around her shoulders, and they joined the line for entry into the tower. As she climbed the stone steps, each one worn down by centuries of people doing exactly the same, she experienced a strange sensation. She *knew* she was walking upwards, from one storey to the next, but at certain points in the spiral staircase, she *felt* as though she was walking *downwards*; it was very disconcerting and she was glad to reach the top.

But the climb had been worth it.

Tilly gasped for the second time that day. Spread out in front of her was not only the *Piazza dei Miracoli*, still milling with hundreds of what seemed like Lilliputian people enjoying their Sunday afternoon visit to one of the most celebrated monuments in Italy, but also the town of Pisa beyond; a tapestry of terracotta-tiled roofs, church spires and lollipop-esque poplars, surrounded by the gently undulating Tuscan hills.

It was a photographer's dream, but it also gave her yet another perspective on life.

The reason the sparkling white tower she was standing at the top of was so famous was not because of its architectural beauty – although that was a part of it – or its faultless engineering, but because of its centuries-old *imperfections*. Imperfection could be glorious, could be awe-inspiring, could be iconic, and even the most beautiful things needed a little help along the way to shine. Would a Campanile in Pisa have welcomed so many visitors from all over the world if the tower had always been perfectly straight? She doubted it.

'Shall we go get an *aperitivo*?' Matteo asked.

Tilly smiled. 'I'd love that.'

***

For the next twenty minutes, they meandered through the streets of Pisa, chatting about the history of the city, marvelling at the abundance of flowers and foliage on even the smallest of balconies, pausing at market stalls selling a wide variety of produce, including fruit and vegetables from every colour of the rainbow.

'Everything you see here is fresh. These carrots, for instance, have probably been pulled from the soil this morning; these lemons, oranges and peaches, collected from trees within a few kilometres of the city. No air miles, no jet lag! And what do you think of these tomatoes?' Matteo spoke to the woman behind the stall and she handed Tilly a plump, deeply ridged tomato to try. 'What do you think?'

Tilly took a bite and the rich, sweet, tangy taste crashed through her tastebuds, unlike anything she had eaten back home where tomatoes had an almost watery taste and texture – this was how a tomato *should* taste. 'It's absolutely delicious.'

'We grow over three hundred different varieties of tomatoes in Italy; that one is the *costoluto fiorentino*, which is perfect for making rich pasta sauces and soups, this one is the *pomodoro di Pachino*, which we use in salads and pizza toppings, and this one is known as the "king of tomatoes", the *San Marzano*, because of its almost seedless flesh and slightly bittersweet flavour and how perfectly it pairs with mozzarella.'

Matteo was clearly on a roll as he strode towards the next food stall, which was owned by an elderly man with an impressive silver moustache and soft brown eyes, dressed in a white canvas jacket and straw Trilby. Tilly smiled; bread was something she was an expert in.

# Tilly's Tuscan Teashop

'This is *pane Toscano*; it's traditional Tuscan bread that's crispy on the outside, soft on the inside and is made without salt or any additives or preservatives, which means it turns hard fairly quickly and makes it perfect for soups and other dishes. In Tuscany we don't believe in waste, everything gets used. Oh, and this is *schiacciata*; it's a flatbread and quite salty and oily and goes really well with prosciutto and *salame Toscano*, and these are *coccoli*, which we eat as a starter with soft cheese.'

Tilly surveyed the beautifully laid out stall with long sticks of ciabatta studded with black olives, squares of soft focaccia sprinkled with salt and rosemary, and flour-topped Pagnotta, as well as sweet bread such as *buccellato di Lucca*, flavoured with aniseed, the little round *brioche col tuppo,* and cornetto, the Italian version of the croissant. There wasn't a sliced white encased in plastic in sight, and it was clear that every single loaf had been crafted by hand, with care and attention to detail.

'Come on, it's *aperitivo* time!'

Moments later, she was sitting opposite Matteo outside a surprisingly quiet pavement café in a tiny cobbled piazza slightly off the tourist trail, sipping an Aperol Spritz and munching on a plate of panini cut into squares and topped with mushrooms, or prosciutto and rocket, or slices of mozzarella and the fresh tomatoes she had tasted earlier with torn up basil leaves, along with bowls of vegetables dressed with extra-virgin olive oil and lemon juice, garlic and sea salt.

Her tastebuds were having a field day after a diet of buttered toast!

But that wasn't the only change that had happened since she'd arrived in Tuscany. Previously, when she was out for a drink with friends, whenever there was a pause in conversation, everyone, including her, would automatically reach for their phones to check their emails or update their social media accounts. She recalled one occasion when a friend of Freya's had picked up the wrong handbag before dashing for her taxi, inadvertently leaving her phone at home, and she managed only thirty minutes at the restaurant before having to excuse herself and head back to get it.

Things were different here. Instead of scrolling mindlessly through inconsequential notifications, people simply sat back, relaxed and took in the world around them, and she found herself doing the same. She exhaled a sigh, tipped her head skywards, and to her surprise, saw that big fat bulbous clouds had gathered, and realised that the humidity had soared.

'I think it might—'

However, her intended observation was moot because she was interrupted by an ominous rumble of thunder, followed by a sudden deluge of rain that pounded the pavements and piazza with a vengeance, sending people scattering for cover. Matteo reached out his hand and she took it, expecting him to guide her into the safety of the café where they could shelter until the downpour stopped. Instead, to her astonishment, he pulled her in the other direction – out into the middle of the piazza – and within minutes her hair was plastered to her face and she was soaked to the skin.

'Oh my God, Matteo! What are you…'

As the rain continued to fall, Matteo lifted her hand high into the air and spun her round and round and round, before drawing her into his arms, holding her gaze for a second, and dropping a tantalisingly brief kiss onto her lips. He then sent her twirling into another pirouette, this time joining in himself, his shirt clinging to his torso as he guided her around the perimeter of the square. All she could do was laugh and embrace the moment; her first dance in the rain with a man who made her heart sing.

Following a performance finale in which he lifted her from her feet and swirled her around in several dizziness-inducing circles, there was a smattering of applause from the café's remaining customers who were sheltering underneath the canopy. They both took a theatrical bow, then Matteo laced his fingers through hers and they dashed along the puddle-strewn streets to where they had left the car.

Breathless, Tilly dropped into the passenger seat.

'Oh my God, I'm soaking!'

Matteo leaned towards her and tucked a tendril of wet hair behind her ear, his warm breath caressing her cheek as his dark eyes delved into hers, the unexpected connection she had felt between them from the moment they'd met stronger than ever. A second later, his lips were on hers, his fingers combing through her hair as he pulled her closer so he could kiss her more deeply.

When the rain finally stopped, Matteo navigated the narrow streets of Pisa – where vehicles of all kinds had been parked at haphazard angles on both sides of the road – then, when they reached the motorway, he turned the radio to full volume and they headed back to San Vincente, singing every song at the top of their voices in a competition to see who could be the loudest.

# Chapter Twenty One

When Tilly made her usual mug of Blue Mountain coffee the next morning, she had never been more relieved that they had decided to keep the teashop closed for an additional day after the San Vincente fiesta. They had one more tour group to cater for before Olivia came back from Boston – two dozen members of a hiking club who were doing the popular Renaissance Ring, a trekking path around Florence that took in monasteries, castles, churches and ancient walled villages – but they had plenty of time to prepare for that the following day.

She'd had a fabulous day out with Matteo in Pisa, but today all she wanted to do was relax by the pool and soak up the Tuscan sunshine before she had to head home to Devon. Even though it was the end of July, there was no guarantee the meteorological gods had read the memo that it was summer and biting winds and lashing rain was *not* the order of the day.

After surprising herself by doing ten laps of the pool without stopping, she stretched out on one of the sun loungers, smiling at the water droplets glistening on her skin like diamonds, and enjoying the feel of the soft breeze laced with the delicate scent of honeysuckle and chlorine. She had just closed her eyes to take a mid-morning snooze, when her phone burst into life.

'Hey Jess, how did you—'

'Tilly, I'm sorry, I know we're supposed to be having the day off, but can you come over to the teashop, like now, straightaway?'

Tilly could hear the anxiety in Jess's voice and she immediately had visions of another queue snaking around the piazza sending Rocco into a tailspin of fury, until she realised that couldn't be the case because she'd personally made sure that the "*Chiuso*" sign was hanging on the door.

'But the teashop is shut today.'

'Yes, which is a godsend; it means we can spend the rest of the day baking, baking, baking.'

'But why would we want to do that?'

'Because Gabriella has just had a tip-off.'

'What kind of tip-off?'

'Oh my God, Tilly, you'll never believe it, but Victor Vitali is coming to San Vincente!'

Tilly's mind went blank. 'Who's—'

'He's Italy's most famous food critic! Someone saw him at a hotel in Florence last night and he told

256

them he was visiting a few places in the surrounding area to sample the local food on offer, and one of the villages he's stopping off at is San Vincente! Say what you like about Rocco, but he *is* a fabulous chef and it would be inconceivable for Victor Vitali not to visit his restaurant to try his prosciutto crème brûlée.'

Jess inhaled a quick breath and continued before Tilly could get a word in edgeways.

'Gabriella says that when Victor was in Bologna last month, he visited five hillside villages and he went to *every single one* of their food establishments, which means when he's in San Vincente tomorrow, there a high possibility that he'll not only visit *Ristorante Rocco*, but *Gelateria Gabriella* and *Té e Torta*, too, which means we have to make the most spectacular afternoon tea we've ever made or Olivia will never forgive us!'

'Jess—'

'And if that doesn't persuade you to give up the rest of your day, I promise to spill all the details of my date with Eduardo on Saturday night. Don't worry, he only broke one plate, and he absolutely loved the "Cupid's Delight" afternoon tea I made for him. Hey, maybe we should make one of those for Victor!'

'God, no way!' Tilly spluttered, immediately abandoning her sun lounger and heading to the villa to get changed, terrified that Jess would start preparing an aphrodisiac-infused afternoon tea for Italy's finest food critic. 'I'm on my way.'

\*\*\*

Like the rest of the drivers on Tuscany's roads, Tilly covered the short distance to her destination in record time, double-parked her Vespa, and dashed to the teashop, which was already a hive of activity. Carlotta was there, too, making a batch of miniature Victoria sponge cakes that would adorn the top tier of the cake stand, along with tiny lemon meringue pies, carrot cakes with cream cheese frosting, and of course, the mini orange blossom tarts.

'We could do with some more help,' said Jess, wiping her brow with the back of her hand after she had buttered three loaves of bread and made five different kinds of sandwich filling. 'I've tried to call Eduardo, in fact I've tried to call him a few times since Saturday night, but for some reason he's not picking up.'

Carlotta laughed. 'Maybe he's lost his phone!'

'Maybe. Was he at the villa yesterday, or this morning, Tilly?'

Tilly's stomach dropped like a stone down a well.

'Actually, he was and… well, I think he might have had a bit of a disagreement with his father.'

Jess paused in the middle of stuffing buttercream into a piping bag to meet Tilly's gaze. 'A disagreement? What kind of disagreement? What was it about?'

'I'm not sure; it was in Italian.'

'I hope he's okay. I'll just try him again.'

Jess disappeared to the patio at the back of the teashop to make her call in private. Tilly felt awful, especially if the argument she'd overheard *did* have anything to do with her urging Eduardo to tell his father about his ambitions to go to drama school, and when Jess returned and shook her head, anxiety written across her face, Tilly reached out to give her a hug.

'He'll be okay; he's probably just busy with work.'

Jess nodded, smiled, and resumed her piping. 'Do you think Matteo can come and help?'

'I'm sure he can. I'll give him a call.'

Tilly was delighted when Matteo answered her call on the first ring and promised to come over to the teashop as soon as he'd finished helping Gabriella and Elena make another batch of her bright blue Puffo gelato. She had no idea what flavour that was and suspected Gabriella might have decided to take a leaf out of Rocco's book when it came to serving off-the-wall concoctions.

'Does Rocco know about Victor Vitali's visit?' she asked Jess, smiling when she saw her friend still sported the manicure from her date on Saturday night – a procession of love hearts, Cupids, and Celtic love knots in a rainbow of colours.

'I'm sure he does. He has his own spies out there in the culinary field. Believe me when I say that he'll be holed up in his kitchen like a mad professor creating the very epitome of culinary alchemy; lobster tortellini sprinkled with powdered eel, bull's eye steak with beetroot juice foam, followed by pesto panne cotta with parmesan air.'

'Okay, enough about Rocco,' said Tilly, plunging her hands into a bowl of flour as she made a start on preparing a batch of fruit scones for the second tier on the cake stand. 'Come on, you promised to tell me and Carlotta all the juicy details about your date.'

Jess beamed. 'Oh my God, it was the most perfect date ever. Everything went according to plan – the heart-shaped sandwiches, the passionfruit scones, the cupcakes with edible rose petals – but do you know what I think swung it?'

'What?'

'My love potion.'

'The ashwagandha tea?'

Tilly saw Jess smirk. 'No, I made my own.'

'You made a love potion? What did you put in it?'

Jess tapped her nose, her eyes shining with mischief.

'Jess, you can't keep that to yourself!' Tilly laughed.

'Why? Do you want some for Matteo?'

'No, of course not, I—'

But she was interrupted by the jingle of the doorbell, and when they saw Matteo standing there in the doorway, all three women burst into laughter.

'What's going on?' said Matteo, running his fingers through his curls and checking his pale-yellow linen shirt for errant splodges of gelato, which made them laugh even more.

'Sorry, Matteo. How was your morning with Gabriella?'

'Interesting, to say the least. She really *really* should make an appointment to see her optician, and the sooner the better. If it wasn't for her cousin, she would have had me tasting broccoli and basil gelato and I *hate* broccoli. She's very excited about Victor Vitali coming to the gelateria, though, and in his honour, she's made three brand-new flavours of gelato, even though it's not a given that he'll pay everyone a visit. So, how are *you* planning to wow our country's most famous food critic?'

'We're doing one of our traditional afternoon teas,' said Tilly, proudly, before going on to list everything that would be on the tiered cake stand. 'Bringing a little bit of *The Great British Bake Off* phenomenon to the culinary paradise of Tuscany.'

'Do you mind if I make a suggestion?'

Tilly met Matteo's eyes, puzzled.

'Of course not.'

'Why don't we do a second afternoon tea, one with a twist?'

'What do you have in mind?' said Jess, pausing as she sliced up a cucumber with a massive carving knife.

'A fusion of English and Italian favourites! So, your *English* cucumber sandwiches alongside my *Tuscan* pecorino sandwiches, you make your delicious, melt-in-the-mouth sultana scones, and I'll make a batch of my margherita-pizza-inspired scones, and you create those gorgeous English cakes and desserts for the top tier, and I'll create chocolate-chip cannoli, lemon custard *pasticciotto*, and pistachio-coated *bombolone*, and maybe even a batch of Chianti-infused cupcakes!'

'And the tea?' asked Tilly, enjoying seeing Matteo's passion for all things cookery-related making a come-back; perhaps his re-kindled dream of owning his own restaurant was closer than he thought.

'Ashwagandha!' Jess declared, her eyes sparkling.

'What's that?' said Matteo, his forehead crinkling.

Tilly exchanged a glance with Jess and Carlotta and giggled. 'Nothing.'

'Well, what do you think?'

'I think it's a fabulous idea!'

'Let's get to work then!'

Tilly switched on the radio and the four of them spent the rest of the day in baking heaven, working in contented synchronicity to create both the traditional staples of a British afternoon tea as well as a selection of Italian-inspired alternatives, and experimenting with a myriad of fresh ingredients that had been sourced locally in unusual combinations.

By the time they had declared themselves completely satisfied with what they had produced, and then scrubbed the kitchen and the teashop until it sparkled, the sun had disappeared from the sky and they were so exhausted that every one of them turned down Gabriella's cousin's offer of dinner at her house in favour of an early night so that they would be bright-eyed and bushy-tailed for the next morning.

# Chapter Twenty Two

Tilly woke before the dawn chorus, her stomach churning and her nerves jangling as she thought about what lay ahead that day. She was much more anxious about Victor Vitali's visit than she had been about the San Vincente fiesta contest – a good review from him would really help *Té e Torta* to thrive – but why couldn't he have come to Tuscany the following week when Olivia was home?

She'd spoken briefly to her sister, when she got back to the villa the previous evening, to tell her about the celebrated food critic's visit, and to her surprise, Olivia's reaction had been decidedly lukewarm, with none of the excitement Tilly had expected. She couldn't help feeling disappointed, until it became clear that Olivia was distracted about the impending arrival of a daytime TV presenter at her new friend Jodie's pâtisserie who had expressed an interest in sampling Olivia's chocolate chequerboard cake, along with other British-based cakes.

After a quick shower, Tilly spent a few extra minutes on her appearance, selecting a pretty aquamarine blouse with puff sleeves and a pair of white Capri trousers from Olivia's wardrobe, then tying up her hair into a neat ponytail. She even added an extra slick of lipstick and a squirt of perfume before snatching up her satchel and heading off to the teashop.

As soon as she pulled into the piazza, she saw Stefania and one of her colleagues scrubbing the outdoor seating area and polishing the silver cutlery at *Ristorante Rocco*; there were even brand-new logo-ed parasols sitting proudly over the tables, and the restaurant looked like the high-end establishment it clearly was. She glanced over at *Gelateria Gabriella* where Gabriella was busy washing the windows of her beloved ice cream shop until they sparkled in the early morning sunshine, and even she had attached a new garland of bunting featuring the Italian flag to the eaves.

Tilly groaned. Since finding out about the food critic's visit, she, Jess and Carlotta had spent all their time focusing on the food and she hadn't even considered dressing the teashop for the auspicious occasion. However, there was nothing she could do about that now. She waved to Gabriella, holding up crossed fingers, then hurried down the shady cobbled street, smiling when she saw both Jess and

# Tilly's Tuscan Teashop

Carlotta's bicycles were already parked outside the teashop. She inhaled a breath and pushed open the door, determined to enjoy whatever the day had in store; they had worked so hard, and she knew that everything they had made – including Matteo's Italian confectionery – was the best they could produce.

'Hi, I— Oh.'

To her surprise there was no one there. She strode into the kitchen, which was also empty. She paused, baffled, then heard the lilting cadence of Carlotta's voice from the patio at the rear of the teashop and, smiling, she made her way outside, where she came to an abrupt standstill, her hand flying to her lips.

'Oh my God! What happened?'

She took in the detritus that was strewn all over the patio – used cartons, cardboard cups, wrapping paper, bottles, bread crusts, various peelings and vegetable matter – all the rubbish from the previous day's baking marathon tossed in every direction and Jess and Carlotta standing in the middle of the flotsam and jetsam, their faces pale, shock written across their expressions, tears lingering along their lashes.

'We're not sure,' said Jess, leaning on the brush she had been using to sweep up the mess. 'Carlotta thinks it might have been an animal of some sort who decided to have a picnic with our leftovers.'

However, Tilly could tell Jess didn't believe that explanation. After all, how could an animal lift the lid off their rubbish bin?

Her stomach lurched at the implication, and a spasm of nausea reared up into her chest. If this was another visit for their cowardly saboteur, this time bent on spoiling the food critic's visit to the teashop, then she was even more certain it was Rocco, or someone acting on his instruction.

Who else could it be?

She wrestled with an urge to storm over to his restaurant and bawl him out in the same way he bawled out his staff, but she managed to reel in her uncharacteristic spurt of anger, putting it to better use by helping Jess and Carlotta to clear up the mess. She grabbed a brush of her own and began to sweep, stopping to smile when she noticed Jess's pretty manicure featuring all the items they intended to serve to Victor Vitali that day. She didn't want her friend's effort to be spoiled.

'Why don't you and Carlotta go back inside and make a start on getting the afternoon tea ready? I'll finish up here.'

'Are you sure?'

'Absolutely.'

She saw the relief on Jess's face as she rushed back inside with a distracted Carlotta following in her wake, and knew she had made the right decision. She filled several black refuse bags with the rubbish, stuffed it back into the bin, then filled a bucket with soapy water – adding a dash of lavender oil to the water to take away the residual smell of day-old waste that pervaded the air – and mopped the terracotta tiles.

***

# Tilly's Tuscan Teashop

An hour later, the patio had been returned to the calm, relaxing space where they had started to seat the overflow of customers from the teashop, and Tilly was able to heave a sigh and sit down for a moment to catch her breath. She took out her phone to check her messages, puzzled that there had been no sign of Matteo who had promised her that he would be at the teashop bright and early to put the finishing touches to his Chianti cupcakes. They had no idea what time Victor Vitali would arrive – or whether he would come at all – but she assumed he would probably go for lunch at *Ristorante Rocco* before he came to either *Té e Torta* or *Gelateria Gabriella*.

Tilly hid the mop and bucket in the cloakroom, then went into the kitchen where the radio was playing soft, soothing tunes, and she was relieved to see Jess and Carlotta were back to their cheery selves.

'Any sign of Matteo?' she asked as nonchalantly as possible.

'Not yet,' said Jess, eyeing Tilly carefully.

'Strange. I think I'll give him a call, just to make sure everything's okay,' said Tilly, selecting his number so she didn't have to meet Jess's gaze. 'Oh, it's his voicemail.'

She left a quick message and then smiled as Jess popped a handful of ice cubes into her mouth and started to crunch on them, pulling a face that spelled discomfort and a soupcon of disgust.

'So what's today's diet, then?'

'The ice cube diet; I'm supposed to eat a litre a day.'

Tilly paused, saw that Carlotta had left the kitchen to check on the tablecloths in the teashop, and decided it was time to say something, in the kindest possible way.

'Can I ask you something, Jess?'

'Sure.'

'Why are you always on a diet? I know it's none of my business, and I don't mean to offend you, but…'

Jess stared at her for a beat and to Tilly's surprise, burst out laughing. 'Oh my God, Tilly, you didn't think… I'm so sorry, I should have explained earlier – it's just research.'

'Research? What do you mean?'

'Mum and Dad think I'm having a gap year before starting Med school in September, but… well, I don't want to be a doctor. I want to be a dietitian. I haven't told them yet, I'm waiting for the right time, but when I *do* tell them, I want to be able to demonstrate to them how much I know about the subject and how passionate I am about everything involved in dietetics. Oh, and I want to train here in Italy, in Florence, so I can keep working at *Té e Torta*, and spend more time with Eduardo. I hope I can persuade my parents that when we do something we're truly passionate about, we will not only be good at it, we'll *excel* at it. If I follow the path they want me to take, I would be miserable, and how would that help my future patients? We have to follow our own dreams, Tilly, wherever they take us, otherwise what's the point?'

Tilly recognised Jess's question. It was the same one she'd asked of Eduardo.

'Have you spoken to Eduardo yet?'

Jess's face dropped. 'No, I haven't. I don't understand it, when he left the teashop on Saturday night everything was fine, better than fine. He told me... Oh, hang on a minute, maybe this is him calling now.'

The hope written across Jess's expression told Tilly how much her friend cared for Eduardo. It wasn't just a holiday romance, but something more, something much deeper.

'It's a text from Gabriella... Oh my God, she says Victor Vivaldi has just left Rocco's and he's on his way here... now!'

'But surely he'll go to Gabriella's first?' said Tilly, panic overtaking her as she ran her fingers through her tangled hair. 'I look like I've been dragged through a haystack backwards. I'd better go and freshen up or he'll think he's come for afternoon tea at a barnyard!'

Jess smiled, surprisingly unflustered.

'It's the food he's coming for, Tilly, and look what we've created!'

Jess pointed to the trio of cake stands on the wooden dresser. They looked like they were about to take centre-stage in a photoshoot for a glossy culinary magazine; a medley of sandwiches, scones and confectionery from both England and Italy, so pretty on the polka dot china, alongside a collection of Olivia's precious teapots. The teashop was at its sparkling best, with no sign of the chaos that had met Tilly when she'd walked through the door that morning.

'You're right, Jess. Everything does look amazing, and I don't want to let the side down.'

Tilly dashed into the cloakroom, forgetting that she had stored the mop and bucket there and receiving a sharp thwack between her eyes when she inadvertently stepped on the pole. She rubbed her forehead to disperse the pain, then re-fixed her ponytail, checked her makeup, and rushed back to the teashop just in time to see a tall, dark and extremely attractive man walk through the door, oozing confidence and charisma.

Tilly didn't know what she had been expecting Italy's famous food critic to look like, but she hadn't been expecting him to be so handsome. With hair the colour of rich espresso – with a generous smattering of grey around the temples that gave him a rather distinguished air – like all Italians, he had selected an outfit that best suited his *bella figura*; in his case a beautifully cut designer suit that espoused the holy trinity of sartorial perfection: quality, fabric and fit. He also smelled amazing, like he'd spent the last hour testing high-end cologne instead of eating lunch at *Ristorante Rocco*.

'*Buongiorno, mi chiamo Victor Vitali.*'

She had expected him to have an entourage, a posse on hand to meet his every demand, but clearly he preferred to work alone, with only his leather-bound notebook and a very expensive gold fountain pen for company. It felt like they were being visited by a real-life celebrity, which did nothing to calm her rampaging nerves, so that when Victor strode forward to shake her hand, to her embarrassment she found herself temporarily unable to string a sentence together. Fortunately, Jess wasn't so awestruck and reached out to take his proffered palm, asking him to take a seat and saying they would serve him with an afternoon tea they had created especially for him.

Tilly watched him choose the table by the window, then followed Carlotta into the kitchen, her heartbeat finally calming from gallop to trot as she warmed the teapots, then prepared one pot of English Breakfast tea, one pot of Earl Grey tea, and one pot of her sister's favourite orange blossom tea, while Jess carried the cake stands from the dresser to his table and explained what everything was.

'*Grazie.*'

All three women stood in reverential silence as Victor poured himself a cup of the orange blossom tea and took his first sip, rolling it around his mouth as though tasting a fine Chianti.

To Tilly's disappointment, he didn't say anything, simply nodded and jotted something in his notebook. He then reached for one of Jess's cucumber sandwiches, took just a single bite, made another note, and moved onto to Matteo's Tuscan pecorino version, repeating the process until he had tried every one of their savoury offerings, before turning his attention to the second tier of the cake stands.

After a brief pause, he selected one of Tilly's scones, dropping it onto his plate with a cringe-inducing thud, then paused again, clearly unsure what to do with it. Jess came to the rescue again, indicating the tiny pots of clotted cream and Olivia's homemade strawberry jam, explaining in Italian about the choice of jam or cream first, giving Victor a smile of encouragement, but not receiving one back. Tilly's heart contracted painfully when he pushed his plate to one side, this time unable to conceal his reaction as he made a start on tasting the miniature cakes on the top tier, choosing one of Matteo's pistachio-coated *bombolone* first, nodding his head with interest before reaching for one of Tilly's orange blossom tarts.

And then it happened.

Carlotta screamed and sprang onto one of the teashop's chairs, her eyes wide with terror, her hands pressed to her face.

'*Topo!*'

Tilly looked across to where Carlotta was now pointing, but she couldn't see anything so she shot a glance at Jess for a translation and immediately wishing she hadn't.

'Mouse, she said *mouse.*'

The next few minutes proceeded as though in slow motion. Tilly saw Victor's jaw slacken in astonishment, then he jumped from his seat, grabbed his notebook and whipped out his phone, clearly horrified by the chain of events.

'*Mi dispiace,*' Jess apologised quickly, her cheeks burning as she made a valiant attempt to calm the situation.

However, it was no use, Victor was already shouting into his phone, asking for his car to be brought from the piazza to the teashop, then he strode to the door and wrenched it open, a stream of high-speed Italian being sent in Jess's direction which Tilly didn't need translating. As she saw the sleek limousine with blacked-out windows draw up in the street outside, along with a small contingent of onlookers hoping for a glimpse of the renowned food critic, a distressing thought burst into her head and, throwing caution to the wind, she raced after Victor.

'Please, don't leave, not until you've…'

Victor held up his palm to silence Tilly, cleared his throat, and to her surprise spoke to her in perfect English, his voice level, his expression neutral. 'I'm afraid that after twenty years of visiting every kind of catering establishment the length and breadth of Italy, I make it a rule not to eat in establishment that play host to… unwelcome visitors.'

Tilly opened her mouth to respond, but her thoughts were whizzing around her head so fast she couldn't arrange them into a coherent order, which gave Victor the chance to continue with his appraisal.

'To be honest, my experience here was just as I had been led to believe; your food is bland and uninspiring – apart from the pecorino sandwich, perhaps, and the pistachio *bombolone*, which were delicious – but the rest was stodgy and dull; my review of *Té e Torta* will not be a positive one.'

Victor turned away from her to open the rear door of the limousine.

'Please,' said Tilly, her voice a higher octave than usual. 'What I'm trying to say is, please don't leave until you've visited my friend's gelateria. Gabriella makes the most amazing gelato in the whole of Tuscany and she's been working so hard to create new flavours in anticipation of your visit. I'd never forgive myself if I was the reason you didn't visit her shop to sample it. It's not Gabriella's fault that our afternoon teas are not to your taste. Please, just ten minutes of your time.'

She saw Victor hesitate, and to her relief, he checked his watch, sighed, then walked back down the street in the direction of the *Gelateria Gabriella*. With her heart pounding hard, Tilly returned to the teashop where Carlotta was in floods of tears and Jess was trying to calm her down. She joined them, sliding her hand around Carlotta's shoulders.

'I saw it! I did, I saw it! I'm so sorry.'

'It's okay,' said Tilly, softly. 'It's fine. No one will know what happened.'

Jess's phone buzzed and when she glanced at the screen she baulked.

'Oh God!'

'What?'

Jess turned her phone towards Tilly; a photograph of rampaging cartoon mice with the words "culinary comedy" and "mouse mayhem" flashing across the image in neon-bright letters, had appeared on her Instagram feed, and then, a few seconds later, there was a comment from the *Ristorante Rocco* account declaring the teashop to be a health-hazard and calling for it to be closed down immediately.

# Chapter Twenty Three

Tilly decided that there was no point in waiting for the inevitable. She locked the teashop's door, turned the sign to *Chiuso*, and, in mutually agreed silence, she joined Jess and Carlotta as they began the depressing task of clearing away the cake stands and crockery from the table where Victor Vivaldi had sat only minutes before, surrounded by their projected hope and excitement, only for it to evaporate in an instant.

After washing up and storing everything in its allocated space, they then set about cleaning the teashop and kitchen from top to bottom with copious amounts of bleach and disinfectant, and despite forensic-like scrutiny of every inch of the place, there was no sign of any mouse or indeed any evidence that they had ever been graced with a visit from the murine community at any time in the past.

The more time that passed, the more Carlotta doubted the sighting, and by the time they had finished scrubbing, scouring, mopping, wiping, sweeping, and polishing everything in sight, she was convinced she had made a mistake, that her eyes had been deceiving her. Although she didn't blame Carlotta for what had happened, when Tilly thought of what her "phantom" mouse sighting had cost them, she experienced a sudden surge of light-headedness and reached out to grasp the countertop.

'Tilly? Are you okay?' said Jess, her voice filled with concern.

'Just a little dizzy. I think it's all the cleaning products.'

'Why don't you go outside and get some fresh air?'

'Good idea. I think I'll just pop over to Gabriella's to see how she got on with her visit.'

She removed her apron, grabbed her satchel, and all-but jogged to the gelateria, which to her surprise also had a *Chiuso* sign hanging in the window. She knocked on the door and she was even more alarmed when it was answered by Gabriella's cousin who was looking pale and distracted.

'Elena, is everything okay?'

'Not really.'

'What do you mean?'

'He's ill.'

'Who's ill?'

'Victor Vitali.'

Tilly experienced an upsurge of panic and a multitude of scenarios flashed through her mind. 'Oh my God!'

'I knew this would happen.'

'You did?'

'I've told Gabriella a hundred times that she needs to get her eyes tested, but does she listen to me? Does she go to the opticians? No, she refuses! She is stubborn, pig-headed and vain.'

'What happened?'

Elena rolled her eyes. 'She served Victor with one of her new gelatos. He loved it, so she suggested he tried the coconut and lemongrass flavour, and he loved that, too. He said it was one of the best gelatos he'd tasted, so then she gave him a scoop of the pistachio and almond – apparently pistachio is his favourite flavour – except it wasn't pistachio and almond, was it?'

'What was it?'

'Wasabi. I thought the poor guy was going to vomit right there in front of me. He only just managed to reach the bathroom in time.'

'Oh God!'

Tilly dropped into one of the upholstered rattan chairs just as Gabriella came into the shop.

'How's Victor?' asked Elena.

Tilly's jaw dropped. 'Is he still here?'

'Yes.' Gabriella smiled tensely. 'He's actually quite ill.'

'Because of the wasabi gelato?'

Gabriella looked embarrassed. 'No, he thinks it's food poisoning.'

'Food poisoning? No way!' Tilly gasped, her breathing tight, her chest feeling as though it was being crushed by a pair of super-sized pinchers. 'I'm so sorry, Gabriella.'

'He's recuperating in the living room so that he's within easy reach of the bathroom. I think it's safe to say that San Vincente isn't going to become the food capital of Tuscany anytime soon.'

'Maybe we can persuade him to just publish a review *Ristorante Rocco*?' Elena suggested.

'Actually, his visit here has already hit social media, I'm afraid.' Tilly squirmed in her seat before telling them about the mouse incident. 'I've decided to shut the teashop before the authorities force us to do so.'

Tears gathered along her lashes as the implications for Olivia's business finally started to sink in, and an image of Rocco Bianchi, his arms folded over his chef's jacket, gloating that he had finally got what he wanted, floated across her mind's eye. Then something else sprang into her head and she turned to Gabriella.

'I don't suppose you know where Matteo is? I was expecting him to be at the teashop this morning to put the finishing touches to his Italian bakes, but there's no sign of him. He's not answering his phone either. I'm worried about him.'

She saw Gabriella exchange an awkward look with her cousin.

'Gabriella?'

'He's had to go somewhere.'

'Where?'

Again there was an uncomfortable pause.

'I… He's meeting someone.'

Suddenly Tilly understood what was going on. Obviously the person he was meeting was Luciana. Maybe she was here to talk about a reconciliation. She knew that he owed her no explanation, but she couldn't ignore the feeling of desolation the thought caused.

'Oh, okay, that's fine, absolutely fine. Right, I'd better get back to the teashop. Please send Victor my apologies and my best regards for a speedy recovery.'

She knew her words had sounded trite, but she had to get away. She all-but sprinted from the gelateria and back down the cobbled street to the teashop, turning her ankle in the process.

'Ouch!'

She pushed open the door, the jolly jingle of the brass bell holding no pleasure for once, her spirits sinking even further when she was met by a white-faced and clearly distraught Jess.

'Jess, what's wrong?'

'He's gone.'

'Who's gone?'

'Eduardo.'

'What do you mean?'

'His father has sent him to help his uncle in his landscaping business in Turin,' said Jess, expelling a huge, heat-rending sob. 'Apparently, he told him he was a risk to their company's reputation, and it was time for him to focus on what was important instead of pie-in-the-sky dreams that would never happen.'

'Oh Jess, I'm so sorry.'

'I love him, Tilly,' she whispered.

Tilly put her arm around Jess's slender shoulders, her mood sinking to new depths until another thought joined the turmoil, and she chastised herself for her unforgiveable oversight. Amidst all the drama, she'd forgotten to ring Olivia and tell her what had happened when Victor had come to call!

As Jess's tears continued to flow, guilt swirled through Tilly veins. Not only had she been instrumental in destroying her sister's business, it seemed she had now had a hand in ruining Jess's chance at happiness by causing Eduardo to be banished from Tuscany. On the pretext of making a pot of strong tea – the universal prescription for all traumatic events in Devon – she left Jess in Carlotta's safe hands and went outside to the patio to call Olivia.

'Hey Tilly, how did it go today? I can't wait to hear all the details. What did Victor Vivaldi think of our orange blossom tarts? I bet he loved them, didn't he?'

The cheerfulness in her sister's voice, which now held a slight American inflection, made Tilly feel even worse, and for a moment she didn't know what to say. But she knew she had to tell her before she read about the nightmare on social media.

'I'm sorry, Liv, it didn't go well.'

'What do you mean?'

She told her sister about the rubbish incident, then about the "phantom mouse" event, assuring her over and over that as far as she and Jess were concerned it had been a figment of Carlotta's imagination, but one which had had terrible consequences. She also told her about Victor's subsequent visit to the gelateria where he'd eaten Gabriella's special gelato and had unfortunately been taken ill and was now holed up there with a self-diagnosed bout of food poisoning, saying it was something he had eaten that day.

'I'm sorry, Liv, but I've had to close the teashop and cancel the Renaissance Ring Hikers' booking, which they sounded really disappointed about. Apparently, their afternoon tea here was to be one of the highlights of their trip.'

'It's the sensible decision and I would have done the same thing. Don't worry, these things happen in hospitality establishments.'

Even in her traumatised state, Olivia's reaction to what could only be described as a catastrophe caused Tilly's suspicion radar to twang.

'Liv? What's going on? I thought you would be devastated.'

'Actually, it's just made my decision easier.'

'Decision? What decision?'

'I didn't know how I was going to tell you this…'

'Tell me what?'

'I've decided to sell the teashop.'

Tilly gasped, not sure if she'd heard correctly. 'You've what?'

'Remember I told you about the TV presenter who was visiting Jodie's pâtisserie?'

'Yes.'

'Oh, Tilly, you'll never believe it, but the visit was a *huge* success; Kirsty loves my Great British Bake Off-style of baking, and she's asked both me and Jodie if we want to take part in a pilot for a new TV baking show that features bakers from different parts of the world who compete with each other to produce a dessert in a particular category, which is then judged by Kirsty and a panel of celebrities. I'm just *soo* excited! A prime-time TV show, Tilly! It's a dream come true.'

'Does that mean you're staying on in Boston?'

'Yes, it does; for a while, anyway. Enzo is loving what he's doing with Harry, and his mum and his sister are enjoying having the family together again, and with the teashop closing, it's made things so much easier. I think we'll stay here for at least another three months, but if the pilot show is a success, we could stay longer. So, if you can change your flight, you can go back to Devon sooner if you want to. Is there any news on Dexter?'

'No, nothing yet.'

'Hey, why don't you come over to Boston? You'll love it here, Tills. It's buzzing with opportunities, and we can spend some quality time together; you can take photographs of the fabulous New England landscape, which will add another dimension to your portfolio, and you can help me plan what recipes I'm going to showcase – there'll definitely be one from Mum's notebook.'

'I'm really not—'

# Tilly's Tuscan Teashop

'We'll probably rent out the villa until we know what's happening; Enzo and I are ready for some space of our own over here, and I've seen this cute little apartment overlooking the harbour, which has a spare room that'll be perfect for you. I'm devastated that the teashop has ended in such a way, but please don't waste your time worrying about Rocco and his cronies; he's got what he's always wanted – to show off his culinary acumen to someone who can jettison his career into the culinary stratosphere.'

'But what about—'

'I'll call Jess and Carlotta now and talk to them about severance pay, and I'll give them each a bonus when the shop is sold, which hopefully won't take too long. Jess was only going to be with us until the end of next month anyway, before she heads off to university, so it's actually all worked out in the end. Okay, must dash, Enzo and Giovanni are in charge of the barbeque and you know what that means! Speak soon. Love you, Tills.'

'To the moon and back, Liv,' Tilly replied, with a little less enthusiasm than usual.

# Chapter Twenty Four

As Tilly lingered outside on the patio, she heard Jess's phone buzz and her heart cracked that her friend was about to get yet another dose of bad news in the space of just a few hours, all because of her. A cauldron of emotions swept through her chest, whipping the breath from her lungs, and robbing her mind of clear thought.

After everything that had happened that day, she felt dizzy and disorientated and suddenly she was desperate to be somewhere else, anywhere but at the teashop. She dashed through the back gate, located her Vespa, and drove like an Italian rally driver back to the villa where she slumped down onto the front steps, her head in her hands as she waited for her heartrate to slow and her breathing to return to normal.

It was late afternoon and the sun was heading towards the horizon, sending shaft of golden light over everything in its path. The air was still warm, with a hint of jasmine from the flowers clinging to the pergola next to the swimming pool, along with the faint tang of chlorine. All around her, the birds, animals and insects continued to pursue their daily tasks, accompanied by the monotonous symphony of the cicadas, oblivious to the turmoil in their midst.

Tilly sighed. She had come to Tuscany to help her sister, to step up because it was her turn, and yet all she had managed to do was make matters worse. If *Té e Torta* had been struggling to attract customers before she'd arrived, it was nothing compared to the situation it found itself in now. Olivia had trusted her, and she had repaid that trust by singlehandedly forcing her business to close its doors, destroying her sister's reputation in the process. She had let her down, after everything she had done for her.

She thought about Jess and her stomach curdled with guilt.

Jess loved the teashop almost as much as Olivia did; it meant more to her than simply a way to earn a living so she could stay on in San Vincente. She had worked so hard to make it a success, jumping on board with every one of Tilly's ideas for their themed afternoon teas, even starting to blend her own teas – although that had been for personal use! She had also confided in Tilly that she intended to stay on in Tuscany, to attend university in Florence and fulfil her dream of qualifying as a dietician. Would she do that now that she had no means of supporting herself?

Tilly's Tuscan Teashop

And what about Eduardo?

If she hadn't interfered, would he still be bumbling along in his father's property and maintenance business, pulling up much-loved plants, knocking down buildings, and running away from members of the insect fraternity? She suspected he would, which meant there was a higher-than-average chance that Jess would have had another chance to test out the efficacy of her own recipe "love potion" and maybe, just maybe, form a relationship with the man she had told Tilly she loved.

How could she forgive herself for destroying their chance at a happy-ever-after?

She thought of Carlotta. How would she feel when she received the news from Olivia that the teashop wouldn't be reopening and she had lost her job? Would she find another one? Would she have to work at *Ristorante Rocco*?!

And she shouldn't forget that there was a man lying on the sofa in Gabriella's living room, in pain, recovering from a bout of food poisoning caused by something she had served him at *Té e Torta*. She briefly wondered what had caused his sickness. The cucumber sandwiches? The Chianti cupcakes? The pizza scones? Had the cream been off? The bread mouldy? She didn't know, but it was something else to add to the burgeoning burden of her guilt.

Tilly expelled another long and ragged sigh. She hadn't felt this desolate since learning about her parents' accident, and all she wanted to do was rush up the stairs, pack her suitcase, and head to the airport to catch the first flight back to the UK where she could do no more

289

damage. She would resume her dull-but-safe existence, living life crouched under the excitement radar so as not to attract the attention of the "bad news" monsters. She had spent a mere three weeks living outside of her comfort zone and look what had happened!

But she would miss Tuscany.

Here, she woke every morning with a smile on her face and a spring in her step instead of her feet encased in concrete. She loved the villa, the terrace, the swimming pool, even the tangled garden held a certain charm, and wasn't the wildness better for the local wildlife?

She lifted her gaze to feast her eyes of the ever-changing scenery in front of her, the sky still a clear cerulean blue without a cloud to spoil its infinite perfection. The village perched on the hillside was so picturesque with its church tower, its higgledy-piggledy terracotta roofs and the emerald-green cypress trees pointing inexorably skywards, the rich vibrancy of the fields, resplendent with red poppies, yellow sunflowers, and swathes of ripening vines; it was a true photographer's paradise.

She loved the sound of the Italian accent, and the fact that snatches of music could be heard wherever she went. She loved that when she rode her Vespa to the village, she was humming a jaunty tune. She loved the taste of the rich, dark Italian coffee, the aromas of freshly baked bread, of dusty sun-drenched soil, and the fact that if you stood still for any length of time someone would feed you. Food was such an important part of the Italian *dolce vita*, and she had enjoyed sampling everything it had to offer; there would be no more buttered toast for her.

But most of all she loved the people.

She loved that they worked to live and not the other way round. She loved that they took the time to have a proper conversation instead of rushing away after a swift *buongiorno*. She loved that they had welcomed her into their lives with open arms and made her feel at home. She loved that everyone seemed to know each other, or a sister, cousin, aunt or grandmother, and that they actually cared about their wellbeing.

The time she had spent in San Vincente had been the happiest she'd had for years. While she still thought of her parents on a daily basis, it was less frequently, and mostly with joy and gratitude of recalled memories brought about by the little things dotted around the place Olivia called home.

In Devon, she had been careful to have nothing in her flat that would remind her of her loss, but Olivia took a different view, and Tilly had to accept that her sister was right. Seeing the beautifully framed photographs of her parents, her mother's treasured recipe notebook and postcards, and favourite ornaments from her childhood displayed on Villa Avanti's shelves, had forced her to take the first step in the process of dealing with their loss.

She had a long way to go, but she was learning to live alongside her grief rather than allowing it to consume her. Olivia was further down the road to recovery, forging ahead with her life, determined to enjoy everything that was on offer and leave the past where it should be – in the past. It was time for Tilly to follow in her footsteps instead of always looking in the rear-view mirror.

She should lift up her chin and fix her eyes on the horizon.

Maybe she could stay on in Tuscany?

Maybe she could get a job as a waitress in a café like Matteo had done when his life had swung in a different direction? Again, she wondered what had happened for him to disappear without a call or a text. She knew they had a connection; she'd felt it the very first time she'd met him after causing chaos at the pavement café next door to Antonio's hire shop, and for her at least it had morphed into something more than friendship.

Where was he?

Why hadn't he come to the teashop?

Was he avoiding her? If so, why?

There was only one way to find out.

If she had learned anything from her parents, it was that if you wanted to do something, then the time to do it was now, that minute, that hour, that day. Don't wait because you never know what was round the corner. She jumped up from the step, flung her leg over her Vespa, and headed back to the village to talk to the person who could give her all the answers – Gabriella

# Chapter Twenty Five

Tilly knocked on the door at the side of *Gelateria Gabriella* and waited, her heart racing. She knew Gabriella knew more about what was going on with Matteo than she was saying, but she also knew that her loyalty lay with him. If Matteo had asked Gabriella to keep his confidence, then she would do so. Tilly just hoped that she could persuade her that she was genuinely worried about him and all she wanted to do was talk to him.

'Oh, hi, Tilly,' said Gabriella, who, to Tilly's astonishment, looked like she was heading out to a posh garden party at a Florentine palazzo. She was wearing a gorgeous navy-blue wrap dress – clearly designer – that enhanced her curves to perfection, with a pair of sky-high heels, and had paid extra-special attention to her make-up, not to mention the fact she smelled like a bouquet of summer flowers. 'Come in, come in.'

'Are you on your way out? I don't want to delay you.'

'No, no, it's fine. Come.'

Gabriella led Tilly to a small snug at the rear of the gelato shop and motioned for her to take a seat on one of the upholstered rattan chairs.

'Is Victor still here?'

Tilly was surprised to see her friend's cheeks flush as she reached up to twist her necklace around her fingers in a familiar gesture, and she was even more amazed when she saw the diamond engagement ring that usually dangled from the chain was gone, replaced by a very pretty gold-mounted sapphire that matched her dress.

'Yes, he is. He's still not quite feeling himself, but he *is* on the mend. Now, what can I do for you?'

Tilly had the feeling she was missing something, but she had other things on her mind.

'I'm worried about Matteo. He didn't come to the teashop this morning, which is strange because when he left last night, he was excited about showcasing his desserts to a celebrated food critic, and I've tried to call him several times but he's not answering his phone, nor is he replying to my texts. Do you know where he is?' Again, she noticed the awkwardness in Gabriella's demeanour. 'Please, Gabriella, if you know something you have to tell me. Is it Luciana? Has she come back from Rome?'

'What? No, no, of course not.'

'Then what's going on?'

Gabriella paused, clearly struggling with what to say next. She met Tilly's gaze, then sighed, her shoulders dropping in resignation.

'He's gone to see his brother; there's no wi-fi over there.'

'Oh, okay.' That wasn't what Tilly had been expecting.

'Fabio owns a small farm in the next valley, just off the road to San Gimignano; it's not far. There's been another… another *incident* there this morning – there's been so many – and, of course, Fabio calls Matteo and he drops everything to head straight over.'

Tilly didn't have to be a psychologist to know that Gabriella didn't approve.

'What kind of incident?'

'Oh, nothing serious, nothing that he shouldn't have been able to handle himself, especially when Matteo has things of his own that he wants, *needs*, to do. It happens all the time; crisis after crisis after crisis, trouble follows that guy around like a bad smell. You'd think after a year at the farm he would have learned how to handle a few simple things himself, but people like that never do.'

'What happened?'

'The sheep got out and went on the rampage. Again. It's the third time this month, and the neighbours are threatening to call the police this time.'

Tilly allowed a sigh of relief to escape her mouth. 'Oh, well, as long as Matteo's okay.'

'You care about him, don't you?'

'Yes, I…' Tilly made a decision. 'Do you think you can give me the address?'

Gabriella hesitated for a fraction of a second before going in search of a pen and paper and saying, 'It's actually quite easy to find, you just follow the road out of San Vincente for about five or so kilometres, at which point you'll see a signpost for San Bernardino. Turn right and you'll see the farm on your left.' She wrinkled her nose. 'You can hardly miss it.'

'*Grazie mille*, Gabriella, I know that—'

'Gabriella, do you think I could possibly trouble you for another… Oh, my apologies, I didn't realise you had guests.'

Tilly gaped and Gabriella's cheeks burned.

'Ah, Signorina Nicholson, we meet again.'

To Tilly's surprise, she saw a sparkle of amusement in Victor Vitali's eyes.

'Signor Vitali, I hope you are feeling better,' she replied, her voice tight.

'A little, yes, thank you. I can see you are upset, so permit me to offer my apologies to you. I'm afraid I have a habit of speaking bluntly when it comes to critiquing food. In my profession, it's the only way of conducting one's self, with honesty and integrity and no room for false interpretations. I did not intend to offend you. My comments on your "afternoon tea" were not personal, and I'd like you to know that I've had no part in the posts I have been reading on social media. The words quoted are not mine. Also, it is far from certain that what I consumed at *Té e Torta* was the cause of my illness.'

'Well, that's a relief,' Tilly muttered, even though his visit had been the catalyst for Olivia closing the teashop earlier than would probably have been the case had Victor waxed lyrical about what he had sampled, and would also, no doubt, affect the sale price.

'And if it wasn't for your heartfelt plea to pay a visit to your friend's delightful gelateria, then I would never have had the chance to avail myself of the restorative powers of this rather wonderful tea.' Victor waggled the teacup he was holding aloft, which Tilly recognised had actually come from the teashop. 'When I so rudely interrupted you, I was about to ask if there was any chance of a refill. It does seem to have settled my stomach much more quickly than anything else I've tried in the past. In my line of work, it might not surprise you to learn that I'm no stranger to the occasional bout of food poisoning, and this tea has proved to be the perfect remedy.'

Tilly glanced at Gabriella.

'Tea?'

As far as she knew, Gabriella only served coffee at the gelateria. To her surprise, her friend didn't respond to her question straight away. Instead, she turned her back on Tilly on the pretext of scribbling Matteo's address on the piece of paper she'd found.

'Oh, it's just something Jess brought over that she thought might help,' Gabriella murmured.

'English Breakfast?'

'No, I don't think so.'

'Earl Grey?'

'I'm not sure.'

Tilly saw something unexpected pass between Gabriella and Victor and was astonished when she realised there was a connection, a frisson of electricity that couldn't be denied, and then it hit her like a slap in the face.

Oh God! No!

Jess couldn't have given Gabriella her specially blended "love potion", could she?

*Now* she understood why Gabriella was wearing her best outfit and smelled like a Parisian lady's boudoir. She took the piece of paper her friend held towards her, and raised her eyebrows in silent enquiry, but she could tell from the look in her chocolate-brown eyes that Gabriella was desperate for her not to delve any deeper into the "remedy" she had given to Victor.

'*Grazie*, Gabriella.'

'*Prego*, Tilly. *Ciao.*'

'*Ciao.*'

# Chapter Twenty Six

Tilly really would have liked to have headed straight back to the teashop to get the full story of Victor's miraculous tea "remedy" from Jess, but she had something more important to do first. She mounted her Vespa, tapped the address Gabriella had given her into her phone, and saw with a soupcon of relief that it was indeed a short journey.

Before she could ponder for too long on the advisability of arriving at Fabio's home unannounced, she set off, navigating the winding roads with typical Italian flair. A mere fifteen minutes later, she was relieved when she saw the signpost Gabriella had mentioned, and a few hundred metres further on she came to a halt outside a small farmhouse situated on a slight incline and surrounded by several barns, which could only be described as ramshackle.

However, the view was panoramic; a typical Tuscan scene of gently rolling hills clad in a patchwork of greens, yellows and browns stitched together by a thick thread of trees, shrubs and fences that meandered across the contours of the land like languid snakes resting in the sunshine. In the distance to her right, she could see the famous walled town of San Gimignano with its many stone-built towers rising into the sky like medieval skyscrapers. It was so beautiful that she felt as though she'd stumbled onto the set of a fantasy movie and that any moment now, she would see elves and hobbits dashing off to fight their next battle.

Reluctantly, Tilly dragged her gaze away from the bucolic landscape, parked her Vespa in the shade of an umbrella pine, then paused. She had no idea what kind of reception she would get from Matteo and Fabio, and anxiety gnawed at her chest. So, instead of heading straight for the front door, she decided to delay the inevitable shock her arrival was bound to cause and explore a couple of the tumbled-down outbuildings.

She identified a well-worn dirt path to the left of the farmhouse, bordered by rows of vines that had clearly been abandoned, but had taken only a few steps when her progress was barred by a rickety wooden gate. She stopped to look over the fence and gasped. There were sheep everywhere; in the bushes, in the hedges, inside and outside the empty outbuildings – they had even mounted the rust-blistered farm machinery for a better view of the countryside they had recently conquered – and they were munching on anything and everything in their path. Now she understood why Matteo had rushed over to help his brother, especially if the people who lived in the elegant villa next door were keen gardeners!

She turned round to head back to the farmhouse, and spotted another barn-like building, except this one had been sympathetically renovated, with a new roof, new window frames with handsome pale-green shutters and a sturdy front door that was slightly ajar. She made her way towards it, and was surprised to see that inside it was hygienically clean with white-washed walls and pristine floor tiles, and that it housed a collection of sparkling silver machinery. When she sniffed the air, she realised that she had stumbled upon the place where the sheep's milk was turned into cheese.

And then she made another connection.

This was where the cheese that Matteo brought to the teashop came from.

But if his brother made the cheese, why hadn't he said anything?

She thought of the tightness and uncertainty in Gabriella's voice when she had spoken about Fabio, and her reluctance to hand over the address. Clearly something had happened in the Ferretti family that didn't concern Tilly. She was interfering again, just like she had with Eduardo, and look what had happened – his father had all-but banished him to Turin.

She had to get out of there!

She spun on her heels and scrambled down the track to where she'd left her Vespa, and she had almost made it when she heard her name being called.

'Tilly? Is that you? What are you doing here?'

Her heart skipped a beat when she saw Matteo emerge from the front door of the farmhouse, his curls more unruly than usual, and yet still so handsome in a lilac linen shirt and dark blue jeans. His face, however, screamed confusion, and a twist of apprehension, and guilt flooded Tilly's chest. Why hadn't she just minded her own business?

'Hi, Matteo, I'm sorry, Gabriella gave me the address. When you didn't come over to the teashop this morning, well, I was worried about you. I've tried to call you a few times, sent you a couple of texts, left a message to tell you that Victor Vitali came and he hated everything about our afternoon tea, said it was stodgy and leaden, and it's all over social media, and now he's got food poisoning, and we've had to close the teashop, and Olivia says she's going to sell it, and Jess and Carlotta don't have a job, and Eduardo has been banished to Turin, and everything is my fault!'

The whole speech rushed out in one long, garbled sentence, the words merging into one another, just so she could get everything out in one go. When she'd finished, she had to inhale several quick breaths to calm her rampaging emotions and to stop the tears that were threatening to fall. Matteo was clearly dealing with his own issues, and she hadn't intended to come over to his brother's farm to dump another barrage of problems on him.

'Tilly, I'm so sorry I wasn't there this morning. I figured you, Jess and Carlotta had everything under control. I should have called you before I left – I'd forgotten there's no signal up here – and believe me, I had no idea about what happened to Victor. Is he okay?'

'Yes, I think so. Gabriella's looking after him.'

'You looked stressed out. Come on, I'll get you a glass of lemonade.'

Matteo hooked his arm around her shoulder, the familiar fragrance of his cologne providing some solace to her ragged emotions as he guided her to a shady spot where a set of sun-bleached table and chairs had been arranged to take advantage of the scenery, and left to fetch their drinks. As she waited for him to return, she marvelled again at the view, surely one of the best in the whole of Tuscany, and this time she took out her phone to record the way the late afternoon sunlight fell on the landscape.

'It's beautiful, isn't it?' said Matteo, handing her a glass filled to the rim with ice.

'*Grazie.*' Tilly took a sip of her drink, relishing the zing of real lemon juice, then met Matteo's eyes and saw the glowing ember of repressed frustration she had seen before. 'What's going on, Matteo?'

For a moment she thought he was going to bat away her question, but he changed his mind.

'This farm belongs to my brother, Fabio. It's a long story, one which has caused a great deal of upset and pain, anger and recriminations, as well as financial trauma.'

'What do you mean?'

Matteo averted his gaze, and it was a while before he spoke again.

'Fabio has always been impulsive. When he gets an idea in his head, he just won't let it go. Unfortunately, this time my parents didn't tell me what he'd done. I was in Rome, living my own life, and they didn't want to bother me with yet another of my brother's epic disasters, so they tried to deal with things themselves which, of course, made matters even worse.'

Matteo paused to inhale a breath.

'When I left home to go to university, Fabio stayed on at the family trattoria, but he, too, wanted to do something for himself, to follow his own dreams, just as I was doing. So, when a "friend" mentioned that he knew someone who was selling a very successful business at a knock-down price, and that Fabio could have first refusal, he jumped at the chance. Except he didn't have the cash to buy it, even at a knock-down price, so…'

Tilly could see how difficult it was for Matteo to recount the story, and her heart gave a twist of sympathy. She reached out and laced her fingers through his, offering him her silent support and a smile of encouragement.

'So he asked my parents for a loan. But they didn't have the funds either, so, against their better judgement, they borrowed against the restaurant.

Fabio assured them that he'd been told that the cheese farm was a thriving business that made a good income and their very generous loan would be paid back, with interest, within months, no problem. Except that wasn't true, and our mutual "friend" knew that.'

Matteo's jaw tightened as he tried to keep a grasp on his emotions. Tilly wanted to ask who the friend he was referring to was, but she didn't want to interrupt the flow of Matteo's story, so she stored the question away for a more appropriate moment.

'It took Fabio six months to realise that he'd been conned, that the farm was, in effect, bankrupt, and by that time the previous owner had disappeared with his money and our so-called "friend" refused to say where he was. My parents were mortified about what had happened; gossip circulated, some people came to the trattoria to ask questions and offer moral support, some to gawp at the people who had been taken in by a con-man, but a lot of people avoided the restaurant through embarrassment, and my father in particular couldn't deal with it.

'Unfortunately, the decline in bookings meant that they couldn't keep up with the loan repayments, and rather than face the shame of declaring themselves bankrupt, they sold the trattoria, paid back the bank loan, and went to live in Sicily with my mum's sister. Since then, there's been a rift in the family, with both my parents and Fabio stubbornly sticking to their version of events, neither willing, or able, to talk about what actually happened.'

Daisy James

'I'm sorry, Matteo,' said Tilly softly, but he didn't hear her.

'Fabio was humiliated about being so easily tricked, mortified about what his naivety had done to our parents, and his mental health began to deteriorate. I started to come back to Tuscany every weekend, and as much as I could between filming assignments, but it wasn't enough. I could see him getting more and more depressed, the farm was losing money every day, and I was exhausted from all the travelling, which culminated in me having a heated exchange with the owner of the production company I worked for, and losing my job. As you know, I asked Luciana to come back to Florence with me, and she *did* come with me to visit the farm, once, but that was a disaster.'

Matteo laughed without humour as he glanced around at his surroundings, which were as far away from the glamorous and cosmopolitan streets of Italy's capital city as you could possibly get.

'But I had to come back, I had to be here for my brother. So I left Rome, my friend gave me a job at the café in Florence, and I come over here to the cheese farm most days either before or after my shift to help Fabio care for the sheep and make the cheese. I'm proud of what we've achieved; it's taken a while, but I think we make the best *fresca* and *stagionato pecorino* in the whole of Tuscany, and I'm reliably informed by Gabriella, and by your sister who was kind enough to place an order, that they agree.'

Matteo sighed, his face suffused with regret.

'We've just started to break even, and I think we might have even turned a profit next year. We've added ricotta to the list of cheeses we make and had even been talking about diversifying into offering cheese-making and cheese-tasting classes, maybe even cookery lessons at some point, with a focus on recipes using our cheese, but that's not going to happen now.'

'Why not? I think it's a great idea,' said Tilly, and then something occurred to her and she looked over her shoulder to the open front door of the typical Tuscan farmhouse. 'Where's Fabio?'

'He's gone.'

'What do you mean?'

'He left last night, which is why the sheep were making a break for freedom this morning, only stopping off on their adventure to feast on Old Alberto's prized geraniums. Fabio's given up; he's abandoned the farm and the animals, and gone to stay with friends in Milan, and he made it abundantly clear that he's not coming back, that he never wanted to be a cheese-maker. He told me to sell the place, get what I can for it, and to give the cash to Mum and Dad.'

Matteo ran his fingers through his curls, his hands shaking as he contemplated what lay ahead. It wouldn't be easy to find someone to buy the farm in the condition it was in, even though it did make the "best pecorino in the whole of Tuscany".

'I can't be angry with him, Tilly; he's my brother and I love him. My parents have struggled to forgive Fabio for what he did, but Fabio, too, has found it difficult to understand how they could have left him to fend for himself when he needed them most, purely because they were worried about what people thought of them. Before this happened, we'd been talking about taking a trip to Sicily next month, to start building bridges. Life is short and we have to forgive those who make mistakes, otherwise our anger will continue to fester and eat us up inside.'

Matteo turned towards Tilly and met her eyes.

'You need to talk to your sister, tell her that she shouldn't sell the teashop because of the subjective views of one man who thinks he knows everything there is to know about food and its preparation. Taste is a very personal thing; what one person thinks is delicious, another thinks is disgusting. And how can Victor be so sure it was something he ate at *Té e Torta* that caused his food poisoning? He ate at *Ristorante Rocco*, too.'

'Olivia's decision isn't really about what happened this morning. To be honest, she had already made her decision to sell the teashop *before* I told her about the food poisoning incident.'

'Why?'

'Because she's already pursuing her next adventure – and this one happens to be in Boston. It…' Tilly paused, her emotions swirling. 'It sort-of runs in the family.'

Matteo didn't say anything, he simply held Tilly's hand in his and waited for her to continue, and suddenly she wanted to talk to him about her own parents.

# Tilly's Tuscan Teashop

'My parents were always searching for *their* next great adventure, too. When Dad retired from his veterinary practice, Mum sold her café in Cornwall and they set off on a mission to strike the items from their bucket list. They went everywhere, and they loved every minute doing all the things they had always wanted to do, making wonderful memories, collecting postcards and local recipes, living life to the full. They were happy, until…'

Tilly paused; she hadn't spoken about their accident for almost two years, but now she felt an overwhelming urge to get the words out, to pierce the balloon-like pain in her chest that seemed to increase with every passing day, allowing it to escape so she would finally be free to move on.

'…until they went on a trip to Cappadocia. It had been Mum's dream to fly over the rock formations and cave dwellings at dawn in a hot air balloon, and of course Dad went ahead and organised it for her. They were so excited. They sent me and Liv a selfie of themselves, standing in front of a red, white and blue balloon with glasses of Champagne, smiling into the camera and telling us they would send lots more photographs from the sky… except we didn't hear anything else from them that day.'

Tilly swallowed down hard, determined to ignore the little voice in her ear that told her not to go there.

'At first, we weren't worried, but after forty-eight hours had passed, we grew more and more concerned, and then we got the news that there had been an accident, some kind of a malfunction that the pilot didn't know how to deal with, that the balloon had burst into flames and crashed to the ground, and... that there were no survivors.'

Hot tears trickled down Tilly's cheeks and a sharp whip of pain scorched through her veins as she re-lived those heartbreaking hours after hearing the worst news a person could receive. At the time, she had felt like she was caught up in a nightmare where everything was happening to someone else, and she'd had to keep reminding herself that this time her beloved Mum and Dad were not going to come back home with stories, photographs, and souvenirs, already making plans about where they wanted to go next.

The fact that they had been so full of life had made their absence even harder to bear. It was as though the lights had gone out and she was living in perpetual darkness, frozen in time, acting like an automaton under the gentle direction of Olivia with the staunch support of Enzo and his family who had rallied round to support them both. Josh had been there, too, but only in short bursts, keen to maintain his busy flight schedule, which she now understood was his way of dealing with what had happened.

'I'm so sorry, Tilly.'

Matteo drew her into his arms and held her there until she had no more tears left to shed. When she finally dried her eyes, the sky was a rich rainbow of pinks, oranges and mauves, and a blanket of tranquillity had descended across the valley. Even the cicadas' song was muted.

'Come on, I'll drive you home.'

'What about the Vespa?'

'I meant on the Vespa.'

Matteo returned their glasses to the kitchen, locked the farmhouse door, and strode to where Tilly had left her Vespa snoozing in the shade. He hooked his leg over the seat and gestured for her to join him. She laughed, which felt good after the trauma of the last few hours, and hopped on behind him, curling her arms around his waist, her body moulded onto his.

Within moments, they were on the road back to Florence, the Vespa's engine objecting vociferously to the additional weight as they climbed a steep incline, but when they reached the top, and Tilly saw the landscape spread out before them, bathed in the last rays of that day's light, she experienced a wonderful sense of lightness, of liberation.

As they descended the hill, she raised herself from her seat, closed her eyes, stretched out her arms, and tipped her chin towards the sky, relishing the cool breeze on her cheeks, her hair streaming into their slipstream. She felt like a bird floating in the air, relieved from the burden she had been carrying around with her for far too long.

# Chapter Twenty Seven

The following morning, Tilly woke to another sun-filled day, but while the birds still greeted her with their symphonic melodies, and the bees still visited the lavender on her bedroom windowsill for their daily quota of nectar, she felt different. The fog that had clouded her thoughts for so long had melted away, and she could see her future more clearly, and the beginnings of an idea had formed in her head, triggered by something Matteo had said the previous day. It would be a lot of work, and she needed to talk to Olivia about it, but she knew what she would say.

*Go for it, Tills!*

And that's exactly what she intended to do.

She dashed into the shower, dressed quickly in a sky-blue tee-shirt and white cropped trousers, and adding a pair of white Vans. She then skipped down the stairs, humming a jaunty tune, and skidded to a standstill when she stepped into the kitchen and saw Matteo standing there, proffering a tiny cup of espresso, which she knew would have a spoonful of sugar in it.

'Oh my God, Matteo! You almost gave me a heart attack.'

'Sorry.' He grinned as he watched her knock back the espresso like a native Italian. 'But you did ask me to come over early.'

'I did, I've got plans.'

'What kind of plans?'

'Let's head over to the teashop and I'll tell you.'

'Before we go, I checked with my friend Filippo this morning, and there's a job for you at the café if you want it.' Matteo stepped forward to pull her into his arms, his gaze holding hers for a long moment, sending a pleasant ripple of attraction through her body. 'Please, Tilly, don't leave.'

'I don't intend to.'

'You're going to stay on at *Té e Torta*?'

'No, I have another idea.'

Matteo lowered his lips to hers, a bare whisper of a kiss causing her whole body to tingle with pleasure. She stood onto her tiptoes and kissed him back, hoping to show him in that one simple gesture how much he meant to her, how much she appreciated everything he had done for her since she'd arrived in Tuscany. She felt alive, exhilarated, like she'd been handed a second chance, and she didn't intend to waste a single moment putting her plan into action.

# Tilly's Tuscan Teashop

Breathless, she reluctantly extracted herself from Matteo's embrace and smiled.

'Come on.'

\*\*\*

Their journey to San Vincente passed quickly, but for the first time Tilly relished every twist and turn, every bump and bounce, every waft of summery fragrance, as she drank in the kaleidoscope of colours from the scarlet of the poppies dancing in the morning breeze, to the yellow of the sunflowers' faces turned towards the sky, from the vibrant green of the blossoming vines, to the silvery ruffle of the leaves on the olive trees that bordered the road.

When they arrived at the teashop, she paused in the doorway and took a moment to look at the space with a fresh perspective, the ideas that had been ricocheting around her head throughout the night re-assembling into a sharply focused image.

'You know, I think it really could work.'

'What could?' said Matteo.

'It was something you said yesterday, when we were at the cheese farm. I love what Liv has done here, but if *she* couldn't make it work as a café, then no one can. So, what do you think about being a partner in a business offering cookery classes – a mixture of Italian and English recipes that can be tailored to our customers' requirements? We'll start here at the teashop, and move on to lessons in cheese-making at the farm, like you suggested. Maybe we could turn one of the barns into a workshop, and another into a place where the students can sit down and enjoy what they've created, along with freshly baked bread and a bottle or two of the local Chianti?'

Matteo stared at her, his lips curling into a slow smile.

'That's an amazing idea! So I'll get to run a kind-of restaurant after all?'

'Absolutely, and there's no time to lose! Let's get started!'

She strode over to the dresser and started to remove the teapots, cake stands and china plates so they could clear the teashop of all the furniture – not just the dresser, but the tables and chairs, too – and she could see how much space they had for what she had planned.

'Are we doing this by ourselves?'

'Of course not,' said Tilly when she realised how heavy the solid oak dresser was. She took out her phone and called Jess, experiencing a sharp pang of anxiety when she didn't answer and then remembering that Olivia had spoken to her about the sale of the teashop. However, when she called Carlotta, she picked up on the first ring.

'*Ciao*, Tilly.'

'Hi, Carlotta, are you free? Can you come over to the teashop?'

'I thought it was closed for good.'

Tilly couldn't fail to hear the distress in her voice.

'There's been a change of plan; we're giving it a new lease of life.'

'I'll be there in five minutes.'

'Do you know where Jess is?'

'She's at the Santa Maria Novella station.'

Tilly's heart bounced down to her toes. 'Oh no, is she going home?'

'Home? No, she's meeting Eduardo off the train.'

'Really? He's come back?'

'I'll let her tell you about it herself.'

Tilly sent a text to Jess, telling her that she had some news and asking her to come to the teashop with Eduardo, then she called Gabriella and asked if she could come over, too.

'Is it okay if Victor joins us?'

Tilly hesitated, but this was a fresh start, time to put what had happened in the past behind her. She didn't plan to offer food to the general public, so she hoped that his forthcoming review of the teashop's fayre would have minimal impact, and anyway, it sounded like Gabriella was smitten with her new friend and Tilly was thrilled for her and what the future might hold. She certainly deserved a chance at happiness.

'Of course.'

'*Grazie*, Tilly.'

As soon as she had said goodbye to Gabriella, Carlotta was standing at the door alongside Jess and Eduardo who were clutching each other's hands, beaming from ear-to-ear, with Eduardo sporting an enormous rucksack – the top of which kept knocking the brass bell again, and again, and again. Tilly stepped forward to hug everyone – and to gently steer Eduardo away from the bell – and thanked them for coming, then fixed her eyes on Jess.

'Oh, Jess, I'm so pleased you're here. You, too, Eduardo. What happened?'

'I had some time to think about things on the train up to Turin. By the time I arrived at the station, I'd made a few decisions, the first of which was that I didn't want to work at my uncle's landscaping business. I don't even think *he* wanted me to work there; he knows as well as I do that that I'm not cut out for that kind of work. My heart just isn't in it, and that's why I keep making a mess of things. To be honest, I think he was relieved.'

'Then he called me!' said Jess, looking at Eduardo with adoration.

'Then I called Jess, told her I loved her, she told me she loved me, and I booked a return ticket to Florence, and then...' Eduardo paused, clearly hoping to ratchet up the anticipation for his big announcement. 'I did what I should have done three years ago; I enrolled on an acting course in Florence – I start in September – and Jess starts her university course there, too. I'm not looking forward to having the conversation with my father, but I'm not going home. Jess and I are planning on renting an apartment together, so we'll both be looking for a job as soon as possible. I want to thank you, Tilly, for helping me to see that I wasn't living my best life.'

'I'm just pleased that you're happy.'

'What's going on here?' said Jess, casting a glance around the room.

# Tilly's Tuscan Teashop

'Matteo and I are repurposing the teashop.'

'What do you mean?'

'I need to talk to Liv first, but I was thinking of getting rid of these tables and chairs, and the dresser, and investing in six workstations and a demonstration bench, and starting a new enterprise offering a mix of Italian and English cookery classes. So, would you, and Carlotta, be interested in joining Matteo and I, first of all here at the teashop, and then over at Matteo's cheese farm?'

'Absolutely! I'd love that!' said Carlotta, her eyes sparkling with enthusiasm.

'We'd make sure it fits around your studies,' Tilly added, still waiting for Jess's answer.

'Then it's a yes from me,' said Jess, beaming even wider, before glancing at Eduardo.

Tilly's heart sank. What would it be like working alongside Eduardo in an environment where there were so many potential hazards? Knives, blenders, cheese-wires, meat-grinders, boiling hot water, naked flames, toxic cleaning chemicals? Fortunately, Matteo stepped forward and clapped Eduardo on the back.

'And it would be great if you could help me make a start on renovating a couple of barns over at the farm, after we've secured the perimeter fence.'

'What about Fabio?' asked Eduardo, dropping his rucksack onto a chair and watching in surprise when the chair tipped over and his bag crashed to the floor. 'Will he be there, too?'

'Fabio's gone.'

Daisy James

'Really?' said Eduardo, not as surprised as Tilly thought he would be.

'Yes, he's gone to stay with friends in Milan and won't be coming back any time soon, so I'll be looking for someone to help me run the cheese farm. How are you with sheep?'

'I love them.'

Tilly stared at him. 'I thought you hated animals!'

'Not animals, just insects.'

'Okay…' said Tilly, making a mental note to warn Matteo to hide the chainsaw.

'What do you say, Ed?' asked Matteo.

'Sounds awesome, thanks, Matteo.'

Moments later, the door sprang open and Gabriella stood there with a smiling Victor.

'Thanks for coming, Gabriella,' Tilly said with a smile.

'No problem, how can we help?'

'We're re-inventing this space into a cookery school, so I'd like all the crockery, cutlery and glassware packed away into boxes, the table linen and bunting stored in the dresser, and the tables and chairs moved outside to the patio so we can measure up and decide what the best layout will be. I also want to give the place a really good scrub from top-to-bottom, every inch, every nook and every cranny.' Tilly smiled, picked up the mop and bucket and handed them to Victor, along with a pair of Olivia's yellow Marigolds, delighted when she saw the confused expression in his eyes. 'Let's get started, shall we?'

# Chapter Twenty Eight

Everyone got on with their allocated tasks without complaint, and while Matteo and Eduardo removed the furniture and stacked it up on the patio, Tilly took the opportunity to make a call she had never expected to make.

'Hi, Liv, can I ask you something?'

'Sure, go right ahead.'

Tilly gave her sister the shortened version of what had happened the previous day at the cheese farm, and a brief outline of her idea to offer cookery classes at the teashop, but made it clear that she would only do it if Olivia was on board.

'Oh, Tilly, that's a fabulous idea. I'm so proud of you.' She heard her sister's voice crack with unconcealed emotion. 'This is the start of your adventure, and I couldn't be happier for you.'

'Thanks, Liv, that means a lot. I'll call you about the details later.'

She wasn't completely sure about how the finances would work, but when she eventually managed to speak to Josh, she intended to tell him that he could have their London apartment if she could keep the Blossomwood Bay studio. She would then put it straight on the market, and when it sold, she would hand the money over to Olivia for the teashop so that her sister wouldn't be out of pocket, and as Olivia had said she and Enzo intended to rent out the villa, they would also have a ready-made tenant until they made a decision about their own future in Boston.

'I'm sure it'll be a huge success, Tilly, and there's another bonus.'

'What's that?'

Her sister laughed. 'At least Rocco will be happy there'll be no more competition in the village to lure away his precious restaurant patrons! He can continue designing his deconstructed pizza margarita and his ricotta and frozen pea crème brûlée to his heart's content.'

To Tilly's surprise, an unexpected flare of anger ignited in her chest.

'That man's a complete menace! Someone needs to tell him that his behaviour is totally unacceptable. Why on earth is he scared of a little competition? You'd think he would relish it! In fact, you know what? I'm going to go over to his restaurant *right now* to give him a piece of my mind.'

'No, Tilly, I don't think that's a good idea. It will only—'

'Speak soon, Liv. Love you.'

'Tilly, I really—'

Tilly cut the call, and before she could talk herself out of it, she wrenched open the back gate and stepped into the narrow alleyway beyond.

'Where are you going?' said Matteo, joining her, his forehead creased.

'To see Rocco; I *know* he's responsible for the recent chaos at the teashop – the flood, the soap, the scattered rubbish on the morning Victor came, the *mouse*! – and I'm not going to let him get away with it! In Italy, it seems like every village, town, and city has a wide selection of places offering food that caters for everyone's taste. Why should San Vincente be any different? What Rocco has done is totally out of order! I… What's wrong?' She saw that Matteo was staring at something over her shoulder, his face wreathed in dislike. 'What are you looking at?'

Tilly spun round and her jaw dropped. Standing there, in the middle of the street, was Rocco Bianchi, dressed in his chef's whites. He had clearly been making his way towards the teashop. She glared at him, her hands on her hips, ready to go into battle. She knew Olivia had made her decision to stay on in Boston independently of what had happened at the teashop, but she still blamed him for bringing its closure forward.

'Ah, Tilly, I've come to—'

'Are you happy?'

'Happy?'

She saw Rocco's jaw slacken in surprise; he obviously hadn't been expecting such a heated reception. He flicked a glance at Matteo, who had taken his place at Tilly's side, his hands thrust deep into his pockets, his face still sporting the expression of loathing, his jaw clenched as though trying to keep a tight hold of all the accusatory words that were fighting to escape.

Rocco, on the other hand, was now running his fingers through his sandy hair, causing it to look even more bouffant than usual, and his posture screamed discomfort, and dare she say it, contrition. She saw Matteo point to the jumble of chairs on the patio behind the teashop, then say something in Italian, and they all took a seat and waited for Rocco to explain.

'I've come to say I'm sorry.'

'So it *was* you?'

'Yes, I only realised this morning when—'

'Everything? The mouse as well?'

'Mouse? What mouse?'

'The mouse that—'

To Tilly's annoyance, Matteo held up his hand to stop her in her tracks. She had a whole speech she wanted to deliver, about decency and integrity, and being community-minded, and she didn't think Rocco deserved the opportunity to state his case first, but before she could argue, Rocco was speaking again and it was her turn for her jaw to drop.

'I came here to offer my sincerest apologies for the Victor Vitali food poisoning incident. I'm embarrassed to say that a number of other people who dined at my restaurant yesterday lunchtime have experienced a similar fate which, after a careful investigation, I have narrowed down to the honey-drizzled oyster comfit. I, therefore, have to accept that it is *Ristorante Rocco*, and not *Té e Torta*, or *Gelateria Gabriella*, that is at fault. *Mi dispiace.*'

Tilly could see from Rocco's expression that his apology was genuine, and how much it had cost him to come to the teashop and admit to her, in person, that something he had created had caused one of Italy's most celebrated food critics to suffer a bout of food poisoning. However, she wasn't ready to let him off the hook yet.

'And the other things?'

'I don't—'

'The flood? The soap? The rubbish strewn across this very patio on the morning Victor was due to arrive in San Vincente? The mouse?' She saw Rocco cringe under her glare. 'So it was you!'

'No, it wasn't me, but I do know the person responsible.'

'You do? Who?'

'Stefania.'

'Stefania? Why would she do something like that?'

To her astonishment, Rocco's cheeks coloured. 'I think it's apparent to everyone that I love what I do. I take my profession very seriously indeed, and for me, it is imperative to deliver perfection every time. To that end, I have a tendency to become… irritated, at times, obsessed with every tiny detail, which leads to me losing control of my temper, and I sometimes take this out on my staff. Most of them have grown accustomed to my passionate expression, but I know that others find it difficult to deal with. I had an argument with Stefania a couple of months ago, which culminated in me inferring that if the *ristorante* failed to win this year's golden plaque, there was a chance I would relocate my business from the sleepy backwaters of San Vincente to a more cosmopolitan setting in Firenze where I wouldn't be requiring the services of substandard employees.'

Rocco paused, his eyes softening fractionally.

'It might not surprise you to know that I'm guilty of not being completely up-to-date with the various issues my staff are facing in their personal lives. Stefania, apparently, is unable to return to her family home because of a particularly difficult situation with her mother's second husband. When I found this out, I immediately apologised for my outburst and assured her that her job was safe, but I know now that she took my threat to heart, and matters into her own hands to ensure the teashop closed its doors. What she did was totally unacceptable and I intend to terminate her employment at *Ristorante Rocco* forthwith. Would you like to accompany me back to the restaurant to say a few words to her when I do?'

'Say a few… no, no, I wouldn't,' said Tilly, quickly. She couldn't begin to imagine what Stefania was dealing with, and the anxiety she must have felt about the possibility of having to return to a place where she was less than welcome, or worse. 'There's no harm done, really, because the teashop isn't closing down.'

'It's not?'

'No, so maybe you could give Stefania another chance?'

Rocco held Tilly's eyes for a beat, then looked across at Matteo and said, 'Do you believe in giving people a second chance?'

Tilly saw Matteo hesitate. She knew he disliked Rocco, for whatever reason, and throughout their conversation he had clearly found it difficult to look him in the eye, his hostility towards the celebrated chef barely concealed under a forced guise of politeness. However, as the two men held each other's gaze, she realised Rocco's question had a deeper meaning.

What was going on?

'Matteo?'

And then it hit her with the force of a hurricane and she gasped; the "friend" in his brother's story was the man sitting in front of them, his dark eyes filled with such fiery intensity as he waited for Matteo's response.

'Why should I give you a second chance? You destroyed my family's business!'

'I know—'

'And you caused a deep rift in our family that has still not been repaired.'

'Matteo, I'm sorry. I did try to speak to your father, but understandably he refused to talk to me, beyond making his feelings known about my lack of integrity. Mario lied to me, too, about the viability of the farm, and it wasn't until your brother had signed the papers that I realised what he'd done. I did tell Fabio to get his own lawyer, but, well, you know your brother; he has always been impetuous.'

Matteo opened his mouth to respond, but Tilly placed her hand gently on his arm. It was clear that Rocco had more to say and she felt it was important for Matteo to hear all the facts before saying anything further.

'I had no idea things were so bad, and I was as shocked as everyone else when I found out that your parents had sold their trattoria and left Tuscany for a new start in Sicily. I felt responsible—'

'You *were* responsible!'

'Which is why...' Rocco paused, uncertain whether to continue. 'Which is why I've been sending Fabio a monthly allowance for the last twelve months to keep him from going under until his cheese-making business started to turn a profit.'

'You've been... What?'

'Fabio didn't tell you?'

'No, he didn't,' said Matteo, his shoulders sagging as everything Rocco had said started to sink in, and once again he had to accept that his brother has been less than up-front with him.

'If I am not returning to my *ristorante* to fire a member of my staff, shall we go over to the farm to speak to Fabio, so he can confirm what I have said, and I can, once again, offer my apology to him in person?'

'Actually,' Matteo began, the look on his face telling Tilly that he suspected his brother was probably sipping beer with his friends in Milan by now, already working on his next great business idea. He stood up, paused, then offered Rocco his palm. 'Thank you, but that won't be necessary.'

Tilly watched the two men shake hands, then rose from her own seat.

'Please don't fire Stefania.'

Rocco held her eyes for a beat, nodded, then walked away.

# Chapter Twenty Nine

'Shall we go back inside?' said Tilly. 'I could really do with a drink.'

'Tea?'

'I was thinking of something a little stronger.' Tilly laughed, lacing her fingers through Matteo's and pulling him closer, enjoying the wisp of minty cologne that danced in the air between them. 'Maybe we could go to... Oh my God, what's this idiot doing?'

She sprang to her left, only just managing to get out of the path of a bright red Ferrari, which to her surprise skidded to a stop a few feet away – on the footpath. She rolled her eyes at the audacity of the driver, until he opened the door and she performed an involuntary double-take.

'Josh!'

'Hi, Tilly, or should that be *ciao, bella*?'

'What are you doing here?'

'I came to see you.'

Josh abandoned his hire car and strode towards her, his blonde hair, as always, neatly barbered, his skin sun-kissed. He was clearly channelling his inner Italian in a white linen shirt – sleeves rolled – blue designer jeans, and shiny leather loafers. He leaned forward to drop a kiss on her lips and she was so shocked by his arrival that it took her a few moments to react.

'I…'

She pulled back swiftly and turned round to introduce him to Matteo, but he had disappeared into the teashop, clearly deciding to give them some space. She pointed to the trio of chairs she, Matteo and Rocco had just vacated and sat down, preparing herself for another awkward conversation.

'Why didn't you call to tell me you were coming?'

'I wanted to surprise you. I missed you.'

'You missed me?'

She couldn't believe what he was saying.

'And I've got some great news that I wanted to deliver in person.'

'What kind of news?'

She felt as though she'd entered another dimension, one where the last month had never happened, and she felt as though her head was about to explode. She knew she needed to take control of the situation, but her thoughts were acting like a flock of escaped lemmings.

'Oh, Tilly, you're going to be so excited,' said Josh, leaning back in his chair and hooking his ankle over his thigh. Unlike Tilly, he was completely relaxed in his own skin, not concerned at all about what kind of reception he would get after what had happened and the fact that he'd not returned any of her calls since she'd arrived in Tuscany.

'Josh, I—'

'Please, Tilly, just hear me out. Last week I was on a flight back from JFK and I met a guy who owns a gallery in Manhattan. We got talking and I ended up showing him some of your work, and guess what? He loved it, said it was just what he was looking for, for an exhibition he's planning at the end of October with the gothic edge you do so well; all those dark and moody black-and-white photographs of wild and lonely landscapes, and… he wants you to call him, and send over some more of your stuff!'

Tilly's jaw dropped as she saw Josh's pale blue eyes fill with enthusiasm and not a little pride at pulling off such an awesome coup on her behalf. He sat there, smiling, waiting for her to throw herself into his arms and the effusive praise to start flowing in his direction, and when it didn't, she saw the merest chink of uncertainty appear in his armour of supreme confidence.

'Isn't it your dream to showcase your art to a wider audience? I don't think you can get a much wider audience than at an art gallery on the Upper East Side of New York!'

As her shock began to abate, Tilly's head cleared.

'Actually, my work is different now; it's much more vibrant and colourful and not in the least bit "dark and moody", so it's probably not what he's looking for, to be honest.'

'Oh…'

'Josh, can I—'

'Well, if I'm honest, that wasn't the reaction I was expecting, but never mind, I'm here for another reason, too.' Josh leaned towards her and took her hand into his. 'I owe you an apology, and an explanation, which can only be made in person. I'm sorry about the video you saw of Melissa and me in Bali. It wasn't what it looked like; it was just a bit of fun. You know what it's like when you're on an extended stop-over, we'd all had a few too many drinks, we started dancing on the beach, one thing led to another… but it'll never happen again, I can promise you of that. I've had some time to think, and I've decided we should sell the apartment in Pimlico. I'll move down to Devon – did Freya tell you I was down there? – and we'll use the proceeds of the sale to invest in a new gallery, somewhere more suitable than a rickety old beach hut. And to prove to you how serious I am…'

As Tilly watched on in mute astonishment, Josh began to fish around in his pocket. She heard a sharp intake of breath from the door that led into the teashop and when she looked over her shoulder she saw that Jess, Carlotta and Gabriella had appeared on the threshold, with Matteo and Eduardo standing behind them, their expressions a mixture of shock, curiosity and disbelief. When she turned back to Josh, she too gasped when she saw that he had produced a black velvet box and was about to flip open the lid.

'Oh God! Josh, please, just hang on a minute.'

She saw his habitual confidence stutter again, his lips twitch in confusion. She reached out to curl his fingers closed around the box and push his hand away. She had never been more certain of anything in her life. She was ready to move forward, to take the next step on the rollercoaster journey that was life, but that journey would not be with Josh. She glanced again over her shoulder, and saw that only Jess remained standing there, her face pale, her eyes wary.

'Sorry, Josh. I'm not going back to Devon. In fact, I was going to talk to you about selling the flat there.'

'Sell the Devon flat?'

'You can keep the apartment in Pimlico, or you can sell that, too, if you want. It's over between us, Josh. It's been over for some time and I think you know that. We've grown apart, led separate lives for the last two years and that's not your fault, it's mine. My grief was all-consuming. You wanted to help, I know you did, but I pushed you away time and time again and I understand how that must have made you feel and I'm sorry. I was devastated when I saw you with Melissa – especially when I saw the way you looked at her – but you deserved to enjoy your down-time; heaven knows I was no fun to be around.'

'Tilly…'

'In the end, you did me a favour. If I hadn't come here to help my sister at her teashop, I would still be in Devon, weighed down by the yoke of grief, terrified of doing anything out of my comfort zone for fear of provoking the director of fate into delivering another deadly blow. But if my parents taught me anything, it's that wrapping ourselves in cotton wool and shying away from every possible threat to our wellbeing is not the route to happiness. And while I won't be taking a hot-air balloon ride anytime soon, I do intend to follow their example. It's time for me to start a new chapter; one filled with new ideas, delicious food, amazing coffee, and photographs that reflect every colour of the rainbow. I'm staying in San Vincente, Josh, I love it here.'

A few moments of stunned silence followed as her words sunk in, then Josh rose from his seat, pulled Tilly into his arms and held her there for a few long seconds before drawing back, his eyes softened, a smile on his face.

'I'm disappointed, but I'm happy for you, Tilly. Good luck with whatever you have planned here.' Josh nodded his head in the direction of the teashop. 'I'll call you about the apartment.'

'Thanks, Josh.'

'I suppose this is goodbye, then? Or should I say *ciao*?'

'*Ciao.*'

Tilly watched Josh walk away, slide into the driver's seat of his red Ferrari, and then disappear from the street and her life. A whoosh of relief flooded her veins, along with gratitude that Josh had accepted her decision without any argument or resentment, a sure sign that he knew she was right.

She hoped he would find contentment in the next stage of his life, too, whatever he decided to do.

She smiled, pushed herself up from her seat, and went inside the teashop where she found Jess, Carlotta and the others hanging out in the kitchen, sipping coffee, clearly on tenterhooks as they waited for her to tell them what had happened. However, there was someone missing.

'Where's Matteo?'

She saw Jess exchange a glance with Gabriella.

'Jess?'

'He's at the gelateria; he saw Josh with a jewellery box. Did you—'

'No, I didn't!' Tilly groaned and shook her head. 'Back in a minute.'

She walked into the teashop and paused briefly to look around. Now that the space had been stripped of all the furniture and decorations it had played host to before, she could see its potential much more clearly and she couldn't help but smile when she saw that someone – she suspected it was Eduardo – had sketched out where the six workstations and the demonstration bench could be placed, with thick black marker pen.

She couldn't wait to get started. Now that she was free of the grief that had demanded her constant attention for the last two years, ideas had started to bounce around her head, one after the other after the other; paint colours, gadgets, recipes, a new website, promotional events, cheese-and-wine tasting competitions at the farm. However, the best part of what was in store was that she wouldn't be doing any of those things alone.

She all-but sprinted down the cobbled street to *Gelateria Gabriella* and pushed open the door at the rear of the shop. When she saw Matteo sitting at the kitchen table with a cup and saucer in front of him, she slid into the seat next to him, laced her fingers through his and met his gaze, seeing everything she needed to know in his chocolate-brown eyes.

'Matteo, I—'

'Later,' Matteo whispered, leaning forward to place a soft kiss on her lips that sent a delicious tingling sensation spiralling through her body. He pulled back for a moment, and Tilly smiled, her heart bursting with joy as Matteo drew her into his arms and kissed her properly this time, a long, lingering kiss that she wished could have gone on forever as they both tried to show each other how they felt, the way that mere words could not. When they finally pulled apart, laughing and breathless, Tilly glanced down at the table and instead of the espresso she had been expecting to see, Matteo's teacup held a faintly yellow-hued liquid.

'What are you drinking?'

'I'm not sure; Gabriella told me it was something Jess gave her. Don't tell her this, but I won't be giving up my daily espresso anytime soon! Have you tried it?'

Tilly giggled. 'No, not yet.'

'What's funny?'

'Nothing.'

# Tilly's Tuscan Teashop

'Tilly?'

'It's just a new blend of tea Jess has been working on, which so far has had a surprisingly successful launch.'

She thought of Jess and Eduardo, making plans for a new life together, following their dreams and doing what made them happy, not what others wanted them to do. She thought of the sparkle that had appeared in Gabriella's eyes as she put her past behind her and took a chance on a new relationship after a decade of being alone.

Everyone deserved a second chance and when it presented itself, it should be grasped with both hands. Life was filled with trials and tribulations, and sometimes terrible trauma, but staying in the shadows, hiding from potential pain, fearful of the light, was no way to live. With a little courage, taking a leap into the unknown could bring real happiness, and she couldn't wait to see what the future held for her, and Matteo, in their little corner of Tuscan paradise.

# Chapter Thirty

*Three weeks later*

'Are your eyes closed?'

Tilly smiled at Jess's unnecessary question, but she knew how excited her friend was about that day's big reveal. With Olivia's blessing, and Enzo's advice from an architect's perspective, they had spent the last few weeks stripping back the teashop to its bare bones before getting busy with the paintbrushes, and then assembling the beautiful workstations Tilly and Matteo had designed with white marble countertops, built-in ovens, and sparkling silver sinks with elegant swan-necked taps.

Their new website, created by a very proud Carlotta, had ensured that their new venture had attracted a great deal of interest, and they already had bookings for a pasta-making class from a group of primary school teachers from Bath, a cake-decorating class from the members of a knitting circle in Cheltenham, and their very first cheese-making and wine-tasting venture at the newly refurbished barn at the cheese farm from a group of amateur archaeologists touring the many museums in the area.

Everything was ready to welcome the first of their guests the following day, or so Tilly had thought. When she and Matteo had turned up at the newly-painted front door that afternoon, expecting to toast everyone's hard work with a few bottles of Prosecco, they'd been ambushed by a very animated Jess and told to cover their eyes because there was a surprise awaiting them inside.

'Are you ready?'

'Yes!'

'*Sì!*'

'Okay, you can open your eyes!'

Tilly looked around the room, smiling at all the people who had come to wish them well in their new enterprise. Over by the doorway leading to the kitchen was Carlotta with her best friend Maria, and a bunch of friends from college who had clearly already made a start on the fizz. And there behind the raised demonstration bench were Gabriella and Victor, along with Gabriella's cousin Elena, who had brought numerous platters of antipasti, adhering to the unshakeable Italian tradition that it wasn't a celebration unless it was accompanied by a mountain of food.

To Tilly's right she saw a beaming Eduardo, standing next to his father, Roberto, who had helped them with the plumbing and electrics, and an extremely handsome guy – whom she assumed was Eduardo's brother – who was attracting the not-so-covert interest of Carlotta's posse of friends. The only person missing was Olivia, but Tilly had spoken to her that morning and had promised to interview everyone who came to the party via a live video call.

She was about to step forward to hug Jess, and thank her for what she had done, when her eyes snagged on the silver-framed photographs hanging on the wall to her left and she gasped.

'Wow!'

For a moment she couldn't speak as her emotions swirled unchecked, whipping the breath from her lungs and sending hot tears to her eyes. She stared at the collection of pictures, all of them taken by her – using only her phone – since arriving in Italy, every single one zinging with a kaleidoscope of colour. The many shades of greens of the rolling Tuscan countryside, the various tones of red from the town's zig-zag roofs, the potted geraniums, her trusty Vespa, the vibrant yellows of the sunflower-filled fields and the facades of the village's houses, everything watched over by the infinite cerulean blue of the sky.

She looked over her shoulder and saw a second collection, one that featured the images she had taken with the help of Matteo shortly after arriving in San Vincente; the pretty china cake stands, the polka-dot teapots, the pyramids of scones and cupcakes, the chocolate cheesecakes, and, of course, her orange blossom tart that had won the silver rosette, along with more recent pictures of Matteo's pistachio-dipped cannoli, strawberry tiramisù, and *torta del nonna.*

But it was when she saw what was hanging above the demonstration bench that she couldn't prevent the tears from rolling down her cheeks; there, in pride of place, was the same photograph that stood on the console at Villa Avanti, enlarged and encased in a simple silver frame, of her mum and dad smiling down at her, their happiness clear for all to see, reminding her to follow her dreams, wherever they may take her.

'Do you like it?' asked Matteo, his voice tinged with uncertainty.

'Oh, Matteo, I absolutely love it. *Grazie, grazie mille.*'

Jess handed them both a glass of Prosecco and they toasted the teashop's reinvention, then everyone crowded around the workstation where Gabriella and Carlotta were handing out plates, piling them high with the antipasti as though they hadn't eaten for weeks, asking questions about the origins of the olive oil, the prosciutto, and the juicy figs, and swooning over the savoury cannoli with anchovy mousse, the crostini smothered with mushroom pate and topped with pickled artichokes, and the deep-fried courgette flowers stuffed with the cheese from Matteo's farm.

Tilly wasn't hungry, so she replenished her drink instead, and when she saw Victor standing by himself in the kitchen, leafing through a notebook, she decided to join him.

'Hi, Victor.'

'Oh, Tilly, there you are. Is this yours?'

# Tilly's Tuscan Teashop

She smiled when she realised that he wasn't reading any old notebook.

'No, it belonged to my mother.'

'She was a chef?'

'I suppose she was; she spent most of her life working with and enjoying all kinds of food. Those are just a few of the recipes she collected over the years, and later during her travels around the world – including her famous orange blossom tart, which will feature in every one of our cookery classes. She did all the illustrations herself, as well,' she said, smiling at the note of pride that had crept into her voice when she spoke of her parents, and grateful it was no longer accompanied by the sharp spasm of pain. 'Mum was multi-talented; Dad, too, although in a different field.'

'Would you mind if I showed this to a friend of mine?'

'Of course not. Are they a chef, too?'

'Not exactly,' said Victor, already pulling his phone from his pocket.

As the Prosecco corks continued to pop, the food disappeared, and the room filled with energetic conversations in both English and high-speed Italian, Matteo snaked his arm around Tilly's waist and pulled her close, pausing briefly for a moment, then, with his voice filled with emotion, he said softly, '*Ti amo*, Tilly.'

'I love you, too, Matteo.'

Tilly smiled, gratitude whooshing through her veins.

She had come to Italy out of a sense of guilt and a desire to repay her sister for all the times she had supported her when she had needed it most, and in return she had been gifted with acceptance, friendship, and her own little slice of *la dolce vita* that had calmed her mind and body, infiltrated her soul and healed her. She had exposed the hard nugget of grief she'd carried with her for far too long to the golden light of Tuscany and it had melted, banished to the dark days of the past.

Life was filled with pain and sadness and risk, but it was also filled with hope and love and adventure.

Like her parents, and Olivia and Enzo, she was about to embark on her own adventure with the most wonderful man by her side. Their destination was unknown, and she knew they would encounter a few unexpected twists and turns along the way, but there would also be fun and excitement and joy, too, and she was wise enough now to know that it was on the journey itself where the true magic happens.

**The End**

Did you enjoy reading *Tilly's Tuscan Teashop*? Are you wondering what happened to the other beach hut owners at Blossomwood Bay? If so, perhaps you'd like to follow Freya's journey as she swaps drizzly Devon for the sunny French Riviera in the next book in the series, *Freya's French Farmhouse*.

Or, if you fancy a trip to gorgeous Corfu, why not head over to *The Hummingbird Hotel* and join Abbie and Nikos as they run one of their fun-filled retreats amidst the stunning countryside of the Ropa Valley?

Daisy James

# ACKNOWLEDGMENTS

First and foremost, I'd like to say a huge thank you to my amazing editor, Laura McCallen, whose skillful guidance and eagle eye has made Tilly and Matteo's story all the more vibrant and polished. I'd also like to thank Berni Stevens for the gorgeous cover which I think truly reflects the stunning colours of the Tuscan countryside; every time I look at it, it makes me smile.

I'd also like to say a great big *grazie mille* to my friends Kate and Gino who provided inspiration, as well as a delicious selection of home-made torta, biscotti, and cannoli to ensure my research was authentic.

The romance writing community continues to be a source of inspiration and support for me, and I thank each and every one of them – authors, bloggers, designers, social media gurus – for their kind words and encouragement.

And finally, a massive thank you to all my amazing readers! I have you in my mind and in my heart all the time I'm sitting at my keyboard, immersed in all-things Tuscan, trying to write the best story I can, hoping that I'm doing you proud.

# ABOUT THE AUTHOR

Thank you so much for reading *Tilly's Tuscan Teashop*. I really hope you've enjoyed spending time with Tilly, Matteo, Jess, Gabriella and Eduardo in gorgeous Tuscany. The story was inspired by a wonderful trip my family and I took to Florence a few years ago where we were awestruck by the beauty of the city and its architecture, enjoyed sampling all the amazing food that was on offer, and learned all we could about the famous Italian *dolce vita*.

I've had a fabulous time writing this book, and I especially enjoyed the many hours I spent doing the research into all the spectacular locations mentioned in the story, dreaming that one day we might get to make a return visit to the land of pizza, pasta and pecorino. As always, I would love to hear your comments. Do you love Italy, too? Have you holidayed in Tuscany or another part of the country? Do you have photographs or anecdotes to share? What is your favourite foodie treat? Is it tiramisu, zabaglione, or cannoli? Or maybe, like me, you're rather partial to a slice of Matteo's *torta della nonna* accompanied by a glass of limoncello?

If you have enjoyed your trip to *Tilly's Tuscan Teashop*, I'd really love it if you'd consider leaving a short review – one line is fine! I truly appreciate every single one, as well as every blog post, every retweet, and every Like on my Facebook and Instagram pages. You can also contact me via my brand-new website at www.daisyjames.co.uk where you can also sign up for my newsletter. Your reviews and encouraging comments are why I keep writing (as well as getting to taste-test all the foodie treats that my characters create – only in the interests of authenticity, you understand).

Much love,

Daisy

XXX

# Also by Daisy James

## The Blossomwood Bay series
Tilly's Tuscan Teashop
Freya's French Farmhouse
Holly's Hawaiian Holiday

## The Hummingbird Hotel series
Escape to the Hummingbird Hotel
Summer at the Hummingbird Hotel
Snowflakes at the Hummingbird Hotel
Spring Blooms at the Hummingbird Hotel
Sunny Days at the Hummingbird Hotel
Confetti at the Hummingbird Hotel

## The Cornish Confetti Agency series
The Cornish Confetti Agency
Summertime at the Cornish Confetti Agency
Christmas at the Cornish Confetti Agency
Tropical Skies at the Cornish Confetti Agency
Tuscan Dreams at the Cornish Confetti Agency
A Summer Wedding at the Cornish Confetti
Agency

Daisy James

# Tilly's Tuscan Teashop

Made in the USA
Las Vegas, NV
03 November 2023